SHE CAME BY THE ~~BOOK~~

"Engaging . . . a snapp~~y~~ ...
bard Street."

EMMA VICTOR is . . .

"An interesting and thoroughly likable protagonist."
—*Publishers Weekly*

MARY WINGS is . . .

"One of the most exciting authors to find her niche in lesbian mystery writing." —*Outlines*

More praise for Mary Wings and the Emma Victor mysteries . . .

"Bravo!" —Nancy Pickard

"Wonderful writing." —Sandra Scoppettone

"Wings has a saucy, witty way with dialogue and description." —*Elle*

"An unorthodox, likable protagonist." —*Library Journal*

continued on next page . . .

"Intricate description and grin-getting dialogue . . . strong and appealing lesbian characters."   —Sally Gearheart

"Hip, witty, and fast-paced . . . the cast of characters is outrageous!"   —*Boston Phoenix*

"Riveting . . . written with great skill."
     —Michael Nava, author of *The Hidden Law*

"Immensely readable, tightly plotted."
     —*Bay Area Reporter*

"Well-paced . . . vibrant . . . enjoyable . . . Wings writes straightforward, intelligent prose."
     —*Publishers Weekly*

"The psychological tension she creates kept me up late last night."
     —Barbara Wilson, author of *Trouble in Transylvania*

"Fast-moving style, dry humor, and more than a tinge of social concern . . . well worth a read."   —*Outwrite*

SHE
CAME
TO THE
CASTRO

MARY
WINGS

BERKLEY PRIME CRIME, NEW YORK

SHE CAME TO THE CASTRO

A Berkley Prime Crime Book/published by arrangement with
the author

PRINTING HISTORY
Berkley Prime Crime hardcover edition / April 1997
Berkley Prime Crime mass-market edition / February 1998

The Putnam Berkley World Wide Web site address is
http://www.berkley.com

ISBN: 0-425-16222-2

Berkley Prime Crime Books are published
by The Berkley Publishing Group, a member of Penguin Putnam Inc.,
200 Madison Avenue, New York, NY 10016,

The name BERKLEY PRIME CRIME and the BERKLEY PRIME CRIME
design are trademarks belonging to Berkley Publishing Corporation.

PRINTED IN THE UNITED STATES OF AMERICA

10 9 8 7 6 5 4 3 2 1

ACKNOWLEDGMENTS

Thanks to Tod Booth, house manager of the Castro Theatre, who let me into the theatre's secrets. Friendly concession workers generously shared their psychic experiences and gave CASTRO some unexpected twists.

More thanks to Betsy Callaway for her legal details. Molly Martin, San Francisco electrical inspector, and Sergeant Marlene Ottone of SFPD gave me civil service background.

Jeff Freiert and Linda Allan showed patience and perspicacity with the manuscript. Agnes Bousquet fed me the perfect food: cheese from her *fromagerie*, while I finished the last draft. John and Georgia Geller provided some sanity.

And finally, thanks to Jeffrey Sunshine for his sunshine, when the fog is thickest.

THE SAN FRANCISCO MAYORAL ELECTION CANDIDATES:

Antonio Shay, incumbent mayor - Republican

Margo Villanueva, Supervisor, widow of Joseph
    Villanueva

Calvin Smith, Democratic State Assemblyman,
    mayoral candidate

Dee Dee Hammerman, Margo Villanueva's secretary

THE SAN FRANCISCO LESBIAN AND GAY FILM FESTIVAL

Jason Jeeters Jones, director, *Pale Refugee*

Martel, star of *Pale Refugee*

Kimilar Jones, sister of Jason Jeeters, goat farmer,
    supplier of fleece to Ina Ho for *Outlaws*

Carla Ribera, still photographer for *Outlaws*

Emma Victor, employee of Willie Rossini

Willie Rossini, Criminal Attorney

Sergeant Laura DeLeuse, Emma's house partner

Mona Marie Lee, Electrical Inspector

Rose Baynetta, president of Baynetta Security Systems

Blake Fortier, hacker and employee of Baynetta
    Security System

There is, of course, a gold mine or a buried treasure in every mortgaged homestead. Whether the farmer ever digs for it or not, it is there, haunting her daydreams when the burden of debt is most unbearable.

—FAWN M. BRODIE (1915–1981) U.S. biographer, *No Man Knows My History* (1945)

CONTENTS

THE CASTRO THEATRE

Location:

The Castro Theatre is situated one hundred feet south of 17th Street and occupies one hundred feet of frontage on Castro Street. It is San Francisco's one hundredth historical landmark.

Statement of Significance:

An exceptionally fine example of 1920's theatre design, the Castro represents a major work of one of San Francisco's finest architects, Timothy L. Pflueger (1894-1946). It was the first and grandest major theatre built by San Francisco's oldest movie-business family, the Nassers. While never the largest neighborhood theater in San Francisco, the Castro was unquestionably the most ornate and exciting, a distinction it never lost . . .

Architecture:

The evolution of movie theater design in the 1920's represented a very deliberate effort to mirror architecturally the fantasy realm of the screen. In this service, the architects who specialized in theater tapped every conceivable period style, adapted, of course, to the massive scale required by theater design. In the East the palace of Old World royalty provided the most potent models, but in California, the Spanish Colonial period was by far the most popular for adaption to theaters. So it is with the Castro. . . .

The major element of the exterior is a large mullioned window nearly as high as the building itself. The window is functional at mezzanine level and blind above, but through concealed fixtures it can be illuminated throughout its entire height. This large window is flanked by two smaller windows at mezzanine level. Both are functional and open onto the roof of the marquee. Following a small fire in the early 1930's Pflueger made some minor changes, primarily decorative to the interior, and modernized the vertical sign. The areas around the windows are decorated in shallow relief strongly suggestive of cathedrals in Mexico. The facade is painted a very light buff, save for the two panels which are pale pink. This is the original scheme, the theatre having always been painted in kind.

The first story features an

island-type (freestanding) ticket office. Glazed and unglazed tile finish the entry to the foyer, a simple beamed room which features the concessions stand. The auditorium seating 1450, is laid out with a main floor and a single balcony. The proscenium opening is framed by a pair of columns and a highly decorated lintel, from which the curtains hang. Invisible to the audience a small, almost square, highly ornamented proscenium and the original silent film screen is still extant. The addition of the big screen, done in the 1950's, was done with a minimum of damage to the original screen and its proscenium which remains behind it.

Large murals showing fountains, flowers, and colonnades in exaggerated perspective decorate both sidewalls. The murals are executed in scraffito, a wet plaster process similar to fresco and have retained their color very well. Spotlights on the balcony rail illuminate these murals at all times.

The Castro's ceiling is an extraordinary affair, being cast in plaster to resemble a tent. The swags, ropes, tassels, etc, which would be present in cloth canopy are all recreated in plaster, and the effect is very convincing. The entire surface of the canopy is painted in muted shades, primarily green, orange and copper leaf. From the top of the canopy hangs a large lantern, originally provided with parchment light diffusers, but now adorned with sheet metal reflectors, which does not in any way dilute the effect.

History:

In 1907 the Nasser brothers converted their candy making factory at 18th and Collingwood Streets into a tiny theatre called the Liberty. The Liberty was superseded in 1910 by a 600 seat theatre at 485 Castro, which was itself replaced in 1922 by the 1875 seat monument at 429 Castro Street. The Nassers ran the Castro continuously from its opening on June 22, 1922 until August 4, 1976, when the operation was leased by Mel Novikoff's Theatre Company. The theatre is currently operated by Blumenfelds, another San Francisco movie-business family.

Save for a shift in the screen position, done to accommodate CinemaScope, the Castro has remained essentially unaltered inside and out, a very rare phenomenon in the movie business which likes to spend its money conspicuously. All work has been done with great sympathy, and the Castro represents the finest extant example of a 1920's neighborhood movie house in San Francisco. *—researched and written by Stephen Levine*

SHE CAME TO THE CASTRO

I'm sorry about the gun, Mom.

But everything else has turned out okay. Things have grown out of the soil, grown out of myself, that I never expected. A few divorces, the Big One got away about a year ago. It surprised everyone, even her, so I can't say I was one kind of fool. Star-crossed, double crossed, not a little numb but not driven by revenge either.

My mortgage would make your hair curl. Even without those tortuous permanent waves you saved for, after the schoolbooks were bought. You taught me how to live with empty hands, how to fill them. How to read.

And, Mom, that femme skill you said I could always count on: I can type 165 a minute, but my fingers are busy with other things—the gentle manipulation of disc tumbler locks and growing tomatoes in the fog. Who were you quoting when you said, *"She who ceases to use her hands tastes the breath of death"*?

You will never know this: I have turned into a private detective, seeking out the violence you abhorred. Kindness and patience were your legacy; unfashionable qualities, but a legacy I can use; a legacy not quite learned.

I'm really sorry about the gun. I hope I never use it, never pull the trigger except on the practice range where all the targets are paper torsos. Bullets do terrible things to a human body, to the soul of a city.

So, Mom, I'm sorry about the gun. But it's the only thing I'm really sorry about.

CHAPTER ONE

LET THERE
BE LIGHT I

"What are you, some kind of animal?" the man had snarled at me. Against the steady drone of a commuter flight the words took on an indelible quality. The moving mouth of Dr. Harlan Knapp replayed itself like an endless film loop in my brain as stewards roamed the aisles. I played with a paper doily on a plastic tray, but I only saw the little rows of white teeth glimmering under the twisted lips. He had been wearing a corduroy robe with greasy satin piping. Anger rolled off of him in bilious waves, an ocean of defensive hostility and nervous sweat. Dr. Harlan Knapp was a dentist, used to making other people sweat. "What are you, some kind of animal?" he had said.

"They *can* see better in the dark. Dr. Harlan Knapp, I hereby serve you with this subpoena," I had said. His hands had snatched the summons to appear in court. He narrowed his eyes, reading. The text became a snarl on his face.

"You can tell that fuckin' bitch she's gotta lotta nerve."

"You can tell it to the DA, sir. Or we could agree to settle out of court," I handed him the card. "My name is Emma Victor and I am employed by Wilhemina Rossini," I handed him the card. WILHEMINA ROSSINI, ATTY. AT LAW, it said. "Ms. Rossini represents your former wife."

1

"'Lawyers! Animals!" He spit from between his teeth. The shimmering glob landed on a poinsettia leaf, assuming the bootlike shape of Italy.

"Sir, animals are my friends. Now, we'd like to talk to you, give you a chance to—" Four panels of solid oak slammed in my face. Eye to eye with my own reflection in the brass knocker I listened to the sounds inside. From behind the door a sharp yelp like a kicked dog or baby. "Fuckin' fuckin' animal!" From the further reaches of the house the voice of his second wife, placating, anxious. "What is it, dear?"

The stewardess came and took my tray. I pushed the button on the seat, leaned back, and closed my eyes. I didn't want any coffee. I didn't want a warm, hot towel smelling of chemicals. And no, I wasn't an animal. But I was a hunter. A people hunter, just trying to make my mortgage.

One day I was going to make the big jack. Then I could kick off to Baja, stretch my toes in the sand. I would take a few months off to work on the homestead, mend the fences, plant the next spring's bulbs, and caulk the tiles around the tub.

Meanwhile, I was still stalking through the computer files, finding phone numbers, paying off underlings who have big eyes and ears and sometimes bigger grudges. Jumping on and off commuter airplanes that like to crash when the wings ice up. So far, the big jack had eluded me.

At least I had the San Francisco Lesbian and Gay Film Festival to look forward to. I'd cleared out my schedule to make room for a round of films and festivities at the Castro Theatre. I had already ordered my tickets.

"Can I get you anything?" The stewardess drew me back into the highly varnished world of corporate humanity.

"No. No, thank you."

What are you, some kind of animal?

The words wouldn't wash out of my brain, riding on bad air and leavened as they were with a righteousness that I would never understand. *What are you some kind of animal?* The incantation merged with the hiss of the pressurized air, the binging of the seat belt signs, and the clunky extension of the wheels.

Animals don't run out on their five kids while conducting a second marriage and a dental practice two states away. The DA went after such cases with more vigor now; but sometimes the aggrieved party used a private lawyer first. As far as I was concerned, the DA could have this guy, with pleasure. The tires skidded as they landed on the runway, the unpredictable bumps of earth. My overnight bag was light as I hiked the corridors out to the short term parking lot. The stretch of asphalt seemed endless before I found my personal transportation device, a small, yellow, slightly dented Alfa Romeo convertible.

The twenty-five-year-old convertible was something new for me. Sports cars have a tendency to be invisible in the rearview mirrors of sixteen-wheel rigs, but a special favor for a friend netted me Romeo, or Romea, as payment. One seat still had the original black leather upholstery, except for a bald spot on the driver's side where horse hair stuffing was revealed. Other than that, it was in perfect shape. The passenger seat was a look—alike vinyl, but the dashboard was mirror matched walnut, the grain of the wood extending like some big Rorschach test past various round gages and gadgets. She had a reasonable backseat, for a sports car.

Romea handled hills and curves with ease and hugged the foggy road out by the ocean like a long lost girlfriend. There were times, lately, when I drove her out to Ocean Beach and just let my foot push the pedal against the mat. Close to flying, and no one sharing the air.

The traffic was congested today and Romea was but a yellow bug on the clogged arteries of freeway. Eventually the "Army St." exit appeared and I took two right turns off the cloverleaf and drifted up what was now called Cesar Chavez—or Chavez's Army.

Posters grinned and glittered from every lamppost. The earnest faces of Supervisors and their promises provided a unique narrative through the Mission. *Margo Villanueva for Mayor! Villanueva for a Villanueva!* She was the gust of fresh air in a hot winded horse race.

I drifted by past the projects, the gangs, the tiny girls dressed to kill, and fruit stands with their swaying pinatas. *"Trust!" "Integrity!" "Experience!"* said the politicians, smiling into the anonymous traffic. Politics was, indeed, show business for the unattractive.

San Francisco Lesbian and Gay Film Festival, a bus stop glowed with the blue clouds of the Festival poster. *Let There Be Light.* Tickets on Sale Now. *Villanueva the ONLY choice!* asserted the Alice B. Toklas Democratic Club.

Villanueva was the only elected official—the only heterosexual elected official—to go on the record for lesbian and gay marriage. Who would have ever thought that commitment ceremonies would become the touchstone that would unite the community this time? And now the dreaded Marriage Act defining marriage as a union between one man and one woman, was before Congress. Even if the President didn't sign it, the Defense of Marriage Act would surely pass.

Antonio Shay, Your Mayor! Your Future!

Too bad the past had been so bad under incumbent Antonio Shay.

Nobody really thought Shay would be elected. Even the voters west of Twin Peaks didn't want him in office anymore.

Calvin Smith! Experience Will Bring San Francisco a New Life! Term limits were of course the reason why Calvin Smith, known as "the Emperor" was interested in being mayor of San Francisco. *His* new life as mayor meant he would have to work full time and give up his lucrative law practice.

Finally, Villanueva, the dark horse, had bucked the Democratic party to run for mayor as an independent. Nicknamed "the Madonna of the Neighborhoods," her biggest success had been the creation of Bridgeways, a model drug rehab center. The First Lady flew in for the opening and Villanueva's son was appointed to the federal bench. All politics is local politics.

.

I pulled up to the Victorian duplex I owned with Police Officer Laura Deleuse and plucked all the door hangers off the knob. *Calvin Smith. Experience Brings Results.*

I got out of the car and disarmed the security system with the little round key. I had a million keys now. And lock picks. I carried my car key on a detachable ring so as not to ruin the ignition with all the keys and equipment I had to carry around these days. I still had the original Romea key, a blue and red enameled *R* on a shield. It made me feel like a fucking aristocrat just about every day.

The red lights blinked on and off, welcoming me to a home safe against anyone who couldn't disarm a security system. The expensive system was my neighbor's idea.

Cops. Always worried about their guns. Laura didn't know about mine.

I opened the garage with the remote and guided Romea into her cozy stall. My eyes drifted over the garden equipment, put away and oiled for the winter. A narrow plank door led to a root cellar where tulip bulbs and dahlia tubers started their big sleep of the winter. Bulbs. Existing completely in miniature, holing up with their own food supply. Everyone waiting for spring. Everyone waiting for something. I was waiting for the phone to ring.

The phone was ringing at all moments of the day now. Intimate moments, moments braving harried traffic or trying not to watch drunks barfing on the street. I could be enjoying a peaceful moment in the park, on the way from one subpoena to the next and the phone would ring. A cellular phone and a mortgage had a strangle hold on my life. But tonight I had a date with Mona for the late show, at the Film Festival.

Mona Lee was a city electrical inspector, one of the first to blaze a trail for hard hatted women who crawled in little tiny places. Mona herself was very thin. I was recently divorced and losing weight.

We had drifted socially in and out of the same circles. Mona knew enough about the wiring in San Francisco to keep me up to date on the latest security systems. Conversation was never difficult at the occasional barbecue, volleyball game, or film festival reception. A little champagne and Mona Marie Lee positively bubbled; she was given to wearing cream colors with black.

"Emma, I want you to meet—" Frances would pull me away from Mona Marie's purported biceps and guide my fingers toward the soft flesh of a cash cow. There had been so many people to meet in Frances's life. And I was always the silent partner. The tall, quiet one in the corner, trying to blend in, trying to be gray.

Her commitment had had me on fire; but the reality of the work seemed far from its origins. Originally glued to a test tube, Frances dressed up for a lot of fund-raising, a lot of phonies, and a lot of weekends away. Frances and I were different people at forty than we were at thirty two. "I can't bear thinking of you risking your life, Emma. You seem to invite chaos," Frances had said. Lesbian bed death haunted us, a grim reaper on satin sheets.

Nothing had worked. Not the couples therapy. Not the notes on the refrigerator or the edible bikini.

"I can't make love unless we talk," Frances would say.

But I couldn't talk unless we made love. And so the bikini melted into a big sugary lump of artificial coloring as Frances flew off to be with someone as familiar with working government commissions as I was working a double tumbler lock.

It was a good choice for Frances, I thought. Unfortunately it left me with a hole in my heart and a big San Francisco mortgage to handle.

Someday, maybe someday soon, I would land a heavier assignment; something with a higher class kind of crook; something where if I kept two steps ahead of them I would walk away with something more than an hourly wage and a pat on the back. The big jack. I bent over to pick up the mail.

Lesbian and Gay Film Festival—the cream-colored envelope offered me an invitation to tonight's opening reception. I wondered who did me the favor. Probably Carla

Ribera, the fashion photographer, who owed me a favor or twenty.

Two bills, the mortgage notice, a postcard for Frances which I would have to forward if I didn't keep losing her latest address, two newspapers, and the newsletter of the local *GLAD*, the Gay and Lesbian Anti-defamation League. I scanned the first few paragraphs. The right wing—the far-right wing—was getting closer and closer. Republicans in Congress were crowing in anticipation: the Marriage Act *would* pass. Fascism, indeed, was the future refusing to be born. A buzz from the hip holster and the cell phone was at my ear. "Emma Victor," I said.

"My office, five o'clock," came the familiar growl.

Five o'clock. "What's up?"

Willie heard the reluctance in my voice. "I need you."

"Time and overtime Willie."

"I appreciate that I can count on you."

"I've gophered every subpoena you've served the last nine months. I need to count on *you*, Willie. I need to move on."

"This is something," a pause in the voice of the employer who never paused, "something special." Willie sounded sad and angry at the same time.

I knew it. Saw blades, chisels, and aluminum flashing glimmered on the wall.

The big jack.

"You can count on me," I said.

"You'll want this one, Emma. You'll want this one as much as I do. And there will be cash in it," she sighed.

"Okay. Five o'clock." I clicked the phone off and walked up the front stairs. Things were looking up. Willie Rossini took on enough pro bono cases to keep her conscience clean, but her billable hours were high. She paid me well and let me in on the office health insurance plan.

No lawyer was immune to dirty dealing; dealing was what lawyers did. I just offered Willie the truth; she had heard a lot of unwelcome information in her time. And Willie did what she liked with it, and I rarely knew what that was, or even the outcome of my investigations. That's the way I liked it, and I liked Willie. She knew my boundaries. She paid my daily wages and something over the going rate for subpoena serving. Maybe this was a family matter, something beyond money. Willie had sponsored my application to the sheriff of the County of San Francisco to carry a concealed weapon. The license had been granted just a month ago.

At the top of the stairs I disarmed the upper unit security system, opened the door, and felt a deep softness on my calves. Mink furiously rubbed against my legs, whining; she could have knocked me over. I fed her and checked my face for damage in the mirror. Some cold water made me look more alive. Throwing myself upon the couch I lay there for a moment, the hum of jet engines still alive in my ears, my feet still trying to land on earth. *What are you, some kind of animal?*

The comforts of home are important for the people hunter. My cave was covered in jeweled red carpets, lined with books. More comfortable now that Frances, with her high-tech taste, was gone. I picked up the catalogue of the Lesbian and Gay Film Festival. A blue and white cover showed a lightbulb refracting rainbow prisms across a San Francisco sky, proclaiming the theme of this year's festival. *Let There Be Light.*

Long a member of the Film Festival, I had already made my choices and ordered my tickets. Who would be this year's star director? Which film the dark horse? I thumbed through the pages. Thirty-six features and fourteen hundred shorts from all over the world, and revealing many previously unknown worlds. Once a year a window opened on the rest of the lesbian and gay world; and queer San Francisco jammed into the Castro to see it all.

Outlaw, a light Western musical, was the critics' choice, featuring chain-smoking, spandex-wearing lesbian rock star Stilletta and a chorus line of thousands of ultra-butch ballerinas in costumes designed by Ina Cho.

Mighty Muff, the first lesbian cartoon feature, sponsored

by the lesbian contracting collective Outhouse, had already sold out. *Pale Refugee* was hardly the dark horse; its star director, a former prison inmate, had made the covers of *Vanity Fair* and *Interview. Lilies of the Valley,* a lesbian romance from Serbia, would be set against a background of wildflowers, and probably shot with a Vaseline coated lens. Mink crawled onto my chest and began to purr. My eyes were heavy; I drifted with the throbbing, soft sounds coming from Mink's throat, and the thought of all the films before me.

"The Family Values Coalition is in town tonight on the eve of the Lesbian and Gay Film Festival," the television blatted. Mink was gone; she'd jumped onto the TV remote and turned it on. I stood up and turned the TV off, stretched four ways, took about twenty deep breaths, and cleared my head. The phone rang.

"Emma, who are you voting for Tuesday?" the no nonsense voice of my upstairs neighbor came through the line.

"I don't know yet," I said, just to avoid debate.

"I hope you're voting for Calvin Smith, Emma."

"Like I said, I don't know yet. I saw his speech on the Embarcadero. They say the fog was so thick you could see his promises."

"Calvin Smith can get things done."

"That's why they called him the Ayatollah of Sacramento."

"I think he called himself that, actually. Look, Emma, the city is going to lose six hundred million in federal funds for health care if Calvin isn't elected."

"There's no doubt Shay has botched the neighborhoods."

"I'm telling you, Emma, you've got to vote for Smith."

"I don't *have* to vote for anybody, Laura. After all, Smith is just running because his term is up. He looked much better flouting conflict of interest laws in Sacramento than dealing with the politics of streetlights and dog-do."

"The FBI checked him out. He was completely clean. The investigations never went anywhere."

"He's a machine politician, Laura."

"So what. Homeboy Shay appointed a regular schoolyard bully as a chief and every lieutenant down the line came from St. Mary's High School. Emma, my life is miserable!"

"You're breaking my heart."

"I know you don't want Shay in office. So just vote for Smith, okay?"

"What about Villanueva? She's the only straight politician who's come out against the Marriage Act."

"Don't *even*!" The cigarette moved back and forth and Laura's words rode on a long, smoky disparaging sigh. "She doesn't have a *chance*."

"Integrity? Trust?"

"Campaign slogans, Emma. She's a spoiler."

"We just have different politics, Laura."

"And we both think we're right, Emma. If Shay wins the election because Villanueva splits the vote I just don't know what I'm going to do. Smith *has* to win. Listen, both the unions and the Police Officers' Association are behind him!"

"My kinda guy."

"Just do the smart thing, okay?"

"Anything you say, Officer." We hung up. I stared out over the Mission rooftops. I wouldn't have chosen Laura Deleuse for a housemate in a million years. She had been a friend of Frances's. But Laura was okay in her own way. She was honest and intelligent. Besides, she was out of the house nearly all the time. Her views on privacy made the separation between our two apartments absolute. We only heard each other's footsteps and consulted on the occasional political, horticultural, or structural problems. We didn't talk about the Film Festival or anything remotely social, I realized. And it was just fine with me if it stayed that way.

I checked my office; it was still locked, all security systems in place. I turned the television to the local news. It blatted away the latest murders, the latest political grandstanding.

The First Lady had been in town campaigning against drugs. This was not news. The First Lady in town *taking* drugs, that was news. I opened the *Chronicle* and saw the same stories with a few extra paragraphs of text. A few oddities, a baby hippo at the zoo, and a European consortium buying up Napa Valley vineyards an hour to the north. Phyllis Schlafly announced the formation of an ad hoc political party of mothers to protest abortion. Ladies against women.

But Margo Villanueva had "given away" one of her political aides in a marriage ceremony. Their partnership sealed with a kiss, Margo Villanueva stood behind the two men, happily beaming, and spoke out against the Marriage Act. I reached for an ivory vellum envelope. It held an invitation to a five-hundred-dollar benefit for Margo Villanueva for Mayor. A few Hollywood stars would make an appearance. Maybe even (probably not) the First Lady. But her name was on the support committee. Reach for that wallet!

A special report at ten: Hispanic and Chinese Americans in the Richmond wanted to be able to add on units to keep the extended family together. Villanueva would be on the scene to listen. Later a huge chorus of rehabilitated drug addicts would sing her praises.

The Villanueva invitation floated into the garbage can. A notice from the kitties' vet said they needed their shots. I put the vet notice on my desk and threw the rest in the garbage. I looked at my watch. I would get to Willie's. And I would squeeze some extra bucks out of the deal. And I would have my date with Mona, sitting next to her on a red plush velvet seat at the Castro Theatre. Would I be describing a tango on her palm? Would we talk politics, security systems, heart-throbs? Would she squirm as the celluloid world rolled by, would her hand curl and perspire? Fingers would dip and tuck, and we would roll home happily, happily ever after for a few weeks. I was in another film festival, I decided. Reality was such a drag.

"We know you've been avoiding the dentist!" a sinister face warned me from the cathode ray tube. *"Just call 1-800 Dentist and we'll put you in touch with a dentist right now!"* I switched the box off, stood up, and looked out at the fog pouring into downtown, where all the money was made in San Francisco.

It was 4:45 when I guided Romea into the Sutter St. Garage and five o'clock when Willie's receptionist waved me straight into the inner office. Cluttered with a forest of massive walnut bookshelves and tables, Willie's office always brought me back to a nineteenth century kind of feeling about the Law, starched cuffs and quill pens, before lawyers chased ambulances and advertised on television. The secretary buzzed me into Willie's office.

I walked into the dimmed room and it was a few moments before I found my employer. She had turned her desk lamps off, only the ambient light from the windows illuminated the office. Big pieces of massive oak furniture were a dark forest. Only the oil painting on the wall, an early Impressionist self portrait of Gwen John, was illuminated. Hands on hips, high button blouse, she stared at the viewer intense, daring you to come closer.

Willie herself was hunching in the window, her back to me, Coit Tower and the Bay Bridge provided her backdrop. The attorney's silhouette looked strangely shrunken, beaten. The tiny lights of the faux Italian drug rehabilitation village, Bridgeways, lined the shore. From time to time a cloud of smoke rose above Willie's shadowed figure, a signal I couldn't read.

Big polished chunks of black obsidian trapped the two columns of papers on her desk. Behind her, a few family portraits perched on the leather top. A faded photo of Willie's former husband in uniform was in the shadow of a column of paper, as he had been in the shadow of her career. Small brass frames held a crowd of nieces and nephews, Italian profiles holding strong through the generations.

People in trouble were Willie's business, and she usually dispensed with emoting or moralizing quickly. It was all just work to be done. But something this time around was different, all the physical symptoms underscored a new aspect of my employer.

"Sit down, sit down," she barked suddenly, spinning her chair around to look at me, straightening up, adjusting her trifocals. Her face was lined, draped with flesh, a pleasant apricot with wild, untended eyebrows that could do just about anything she wanted in front of jury. Her hands were a road map of big cases and high blood pressure.

A double strand of black pearls fell over a white knit jersey; the banker's suit today was anthracite-gray. She handed me a piece of paper, watching my face as I focused on the 8½ × 11 piece of standard bond on which was pasted a collage of headlines from tabloids.

The paper came closer, it was cool to the touch. Firmly taped to the center, about the size of a postage stamp, a black-and-white shiny square winked at me. Someone had snipped off the lower right hand corner before they had attached it to the paper with cellophane tape. It had a striped look, like a television, like a video.

Clustered around the photo were headlines from tabloids. Lots and lots of headlines, laid side by side and overlapping carefully. "TANYA'S SECRET AFFAIR" and "NICOLE'S LESBIAN HELL." The headlines, of course, were meant to suggest that the photo might be published. Ah, the sleaze trade. And in wrinkled, cut out letters from a newspaper that were tacked along the bottom with mucilage glue, was a collaged promise to call at 5:30. It was 5:20.

I pulled the shiny contact print up to my face. The lower right-hand corner had been snipped cleanly off, a line that indicated a straight edge, a razor blade.

I pulled the scene closer. In the upper left hand corner a curtain blew open to reveal a partial view of Twin Peaks. And the light revealed more than that. Flowing across a crowded dresser, the whiteness of a thigh glimmered, a long shimmering triangular shape, a figure in recline upon a bed of mussed sheets. And a tiny face that popped out at me and exploded in my brain. Jesus.

I sank back into my chair. At the bottom were typed instructions: *Price of first half of video—*

"They have this on *videotape*?" I asked.

"Gone are the days of still photographs, apparently."

Price of first half of video $35,000. Price of second half of video to be named, I read.

"I want to get him, Emma."

"Yeah?" I was holding my breath. The face in the photo shimmered with the life of fame and familiarity. A face from a dozen speeches, an old political name, a head that now appeared to me on top of a naked body. Politicians weren't supposed to have bodies. Especially not Margo Villanueva, dark horse candidate for mayor of San Francisco.

"We'll never be able to spin this one," Willie sighed.

CHAPTER TWO

SPIN CONTROL

Spin is the weaving of a shroud that conceals a basic truth, a glimmering veil that the public and press can peer at, never guessing at the truth beneath.

"What did the Supervisor say about just coming clean? Going to the press. Does she have a good professional backpedaler?"

"We discussed it for a heartbeat. It would take far too much spin control this late in the game." Willie shook her head. "Brush fire to forest fire just days before the election?" Willie thumbed through a mental Rolodex of spin doctors. "No one could handle it. Certainly not that press secretary Margo has now—what's her name, Dierdre, Debby, no *Dee Dee*. There should be a cutoff point in a woman's life for cuteness. Blue blood from Bethesda. I can't even get an appointment or a return call from Margo. She guards Margo like a hawk. But apparently she *has* brought in some short end cash," Willie mumbled and made up her mind. "No, Emma. We can't let this thing get out; we'll have to play their game, for a while."

"Where was this shot?"

"I don't know."

"Local hotel?"

"Yes, at least I think so."

15

"You don't know?"

"Margo's busy with the election. It's been really hard to get through to her. She stopped by this morning with this. We didn't have a lot of time to talk. Her press secretary was waiting in the car. No one, no one except you and I and Margo know about this, Emma."

"Is it really such a big deal?"

Margo Villanueva, widow of Joseph Villanueva with a hundred thousand grandchildren, hardly seemed morally suspect. And this was San Francisco!

"That's not for you to decide," Willie said.

I folded the blackmail note in half, concealing that body, that ecstatic expression, giving Margo a little belated privacy. The phone rang and Willie nodded to an extra phone on her desk. We each picked up a receiver at the same time and heard a throaty growl, the raspy breathing, that would become familiar to me in the days to come.

"Ten-o'clock. I'll-tell-you-where. Come-alone-or-you-won't-get-the-video. Bring-cash, used-hundred-dollar-bills,-unmarked-and-don't-try anything-or-the-deal-is-off and-the-papers-get-the-trash."

Willie's eyes flickered at me through her trifocals. Her voice was twisted with control as she assented to the plan. "Okay" she said. "How—"

"I-will-call."

Willie recited a phone number, *my* phone number, into the receiver. I just hoped that the call wouldn't come during the opening night film of the *Film Festival.* Willie cradled the receiver gently. "Sounds like rough trade, Emma," she said.

"Rest easy," I said. "I've been throwing money away all my life. Only this time I have a gun."

"Okay, Emma." Willie's lips twitched, tiny lines seemed to grow deeper at the edges of her mouth. "This is the plan. You make the first payment in cash as requested. On the second drop you'll inform me of the time and place of the meeting. You'll have backup on the second payment. It's all getting worked out." She handed me the blackmail note and lit another cigarette.

"Let me guess, the second payment is old newspapers."

"Whatever fills up the bag, Emma." Willie shrugged. "I think they're counting on big bucks for the second half."

"Really? What's this about backup?"

"Someone will be there to take him in."

"What kind of backup?"

"It's delicate."

"You're not going to tell me who's backing me up?"

"Well—"

"You mean you don't want to use Antonio Shay's police department to nab Villanueva's blackmailer?"

"Something like that."

"Or something like the Antonio Shay for Reelection Video Camera Club might be behind the gig?"

"There's a lot of somethings in this business. Right now I just want to get this over with." Willie was looking me over. She was ready to start handing me the heavier business. And I knew that there were clients who had come to Willie with any number of nasty secrets and people in their pasts. There were problematic errands and people with guns. And a lot more money. She sighed. "A risk, Emma. You want the job or not?"

I let a silence fall and took a long look into the shadowy world I was about to enter. A world away from slimy divorce cases. A step into a world of parasites who fed off public figures, fungi who lived fast, rodents who lived to die in a reckless volley of gunfire.

Did I want to step into that world? Did anyone?

No.

I started mentally working percentages and risks. I wanted the money. Several grand and a percentage payoff. I was in good shape, schedule cleared of everything but the Film Festival; my mind was quiet. I made my decision. I would carry a gun and try to get the money back.

And I would try not to become one of them.

"Sure, Willie, I'll do it."

"Good. Make the first delivery. Get me his name if you can. Try to identify him, collect some evidence. Let me know when you're to meet him for the second time."

"And arranging the backup? How do you want me to contact you?"

"I'm going to a judicial reform conference in New Orleans, Emma. I'm leaving tonight, probably well before he makes contact. Leave a message with my answering service when the second payment will be made. Say you'll be making a flower delivery. Specify the exact location. The arrest will be made on the second payment. Make sure you can positively identify him. I'll be in touch with you."

"Salary—"

"What do you think, Emma?"

"Five thousand, twenty-five hundred for each trip."

"Twenty-five hundred? You're looking for a big raise." Coit Tower took Willie's attention away. She stared at it for a moment, as if it might do something it had never done on the horizon of San Francisco. Meanwhile her cigarette burned in the ashtray and trails of blue smoke wafted through the heavy oak furniture. I said nothing, I wasn't going to let Willie's Marlboros psyche me out. "Care to tell me how you arrived at that figure?" she asked.

"Finding him is not going to be easy, if he's smart I will never see his face. I'm going to have to do background and some stalking, chasing, if not breaking and entering, to figure out who this guy is and get your client out of danger. I expect this is rough trade. This is a person with a worked out operation. He's probably armed. Nobody knows who he is, so he doesn't have a lot to lose if someone gets in his way."

The attorney looked at me in a different kind of way, her fingers played with the pearls, fingertips brushing the delicate crepe skin on her neck. "I understand." Willie took a short breath, the pearls rose and fell, her hand hit the desk. "Okay."

"And I want one third of whatever I recover from the thirty-five grand."

"*What?*"

"I'm going to try to get your client's money back."

"Really!" Lips twisted into a tight little grin, right at home under her nose.

"Give me the incentive to get your client's money back,

Willie. I'm sure your client would appreciate it. Two thirds of thirty-five grand looks a lot better than nothing. And I'll go after it, Willie. You know I will."

"Okay, okay, okay," Willie's gnarly fingers stubbed out her cigarette and I rested my case. "Maybe I can get you some more work, if you can handle this," she said quietly. I sensed I was making a deeper inroad into the practice of Willie Rossini. Judicial reform conference, and Willie would be out of town for the whole thing, leaving it all to me. A third of thirty-five grand was twelve K and a small one, keeping the mortgage company at bay for almost a full year, a beach in Mexico stretched before me, white sand, hot sun, and Guadalupe with roses on her cape.

"I'll keep this." I folded the blackmail letter, making sure not to crease the contact photo inside. I put it inside the breast pocket of my shirt. Willie winced as she saw the dangerous image disappear. "Don't worry. I'll be careful. I have a safe at home, remember. Now, the thirty-five thousand and twenty-five hundred for my first drop. By the way, I'll need an extra grand for expenses."

"Emma—"

"Look, our man dropped some big change to get that picture. You've got to let me compete."

"A *grand*?"

"Let's not get cheap on this end, Willie. What do you think their figure for the second drop is going to be? They had their expense money lined up."

Willie walked over to the Gwen John portrait, her eyes level with the tight knot on the artist's fluffy bow underneath the stubborn chin. Willie ran her fingers behind the frame and pushed a button. The painting and small brass lamp which illuminated it swung into the room and revealed a safe. Willie stood in front of the lock, head tilted back, eyes adjusting to the magnification of the lowest of trifocals, I could hear the tumblers falling as she twisted the dial. Her hand dove into the dark hole and she closed the door of the safe, spun the combination dial, and returned Gwen John to her rightful place on the wall. The artist, standing behind Willie, sternness in Impressionist strokes, seemed to be warning me that I'd better put the bills to good use. Willie removed a lot of messy bills, banded and counted.

"Forty thousand?" Willie said simply.

"Not marked?"

"That's right." She counted the money out onto the table. "Four thousand, four thousand five hundred, five thousand . . ." She looked up from time to time to make sure I was with her, the greenbacks reflecting in her glasses.

"There's four thousand there for expenses." Willie's eyes looked watery and tired. For the first time I looked at Willie and actually thought the word *elderly*. I wiped the word out of my mind as I heard Willie's anger. "We've got to get this bastard, Emma. Margo Villanueva is—she's a friend—"

"I know, Willie."

"A lot of politicians are jerks, Emma, but Margo lives for public service, for the people of San Francisco. We need her. She's the real item. And she has a whole political career ahead of her. Some jerk shouldn't be able to ruin her life, everything she's worked for." A large blue vein appeared above one of Willie's eyebrows. "I know you're armed these days, Emma, and I know you've become a really good shot. But be careful. I'm less worried about the money than I am about you."

That was nice, but it still didn't pay the mortgage.

CHAPTER THREE

GLOW
WORM

Blackmail is a form of extortion; it is illegal. Public persons become accustomed to receiving letters of all kinds, impugning their careers. Or showing them buck naked on a bed, should they engage in adulterous gymnastics. Politicians are always doing the right thing and the wrong thing at the same time.

The best rule is to simply ignore the letters or to discover the identity of the author. If you feed a blackmailer he just gets hungrier. He can't give up the tool that is his meal ticket. Why should he? There're always copies. Our man had already copied a videotape, something that would require some technical expertise. Easy to make extra prints. So if you're going to make a payment, it's only in the hope of entrapping the blackmailer. Getting the videotape would be kind of nice too.

Mink waited at the door, demanding attention. I filled her water bowl and stroked her. To each cat her own pleasure spots. Others might net me a quick claw.

I called for Friend, the second cat who lived outside. Friend's food bowl was empty. I filled it with food and returned it to the porch, looking out over the garden. Tomatoes, their big heads hung down, guiltily, hardening on the vine. Twisted forms in the fog. Dahlias, this summer, big as dinner plates, crawling into their tubers just under the dirt.

I locked the back door and went into my workroom, letting Mink follow me inside, a special perk. The room was formerly Frances's office, I had completely renovated the interior into a space which housed all my current investigative needs and a few more I hadn't come up against yet.

A floor safe was sunk into concrete. Over it, bars on the window of bubbled glass. A large workbench was dominated by a heavy vice clamped to its side. A Peg Board to the right held a cordless drill and skill saw and an assortment of hand tools. Twenty-five baby food jars with their lids screwed to a plank offered a precise combination of Philips head and slotted screws and bolts for all possible applications, wood, concrete, and metal. To the left of the workbench I was mounting practice locks. Disc tumblers, mortise and warded tumblers, and various padlocks, the syllabus for a course given by a senior citizen known as Penny the Pick. Her particular night school class was held in her Tenderloin hotel room. She was patient but demanding, and you always paid your tuition on time.

The space was not only well lit, it was extremely well ventilated. A three-speed exhaust fan was vented through the window. The blades ran so silently on their ball bearings they wouldn't even attract the notice of Officer Deleuse on one of her toss and turn nights.

Built-in cupboards held a limited photography setup. A quality enlarger, pans and chemicals and a red light. So far the juiciest photos were kitty portraits taken in the garden and the only locks I'd picked were on the car doors of friends who'd left their keys inside.

A small enamel kiln, just to make the place look like a hobby shop, and a portable acetylene torch. A large assortment of glass cutters, chisels, keyhole saws, slim jims and other such devices were locked out of sight in an automotive cabinet. A computer and a modem were in the farthest corner, away from anything warm or toxic.

I set up a recording machine on the cellular line to record the ten o'clock call. I brought the jar of phosphorescent powder from a shelf onto the workbench. The powder, for theft detection purposes, was available through security mail order services, and the local magic shop. With the proper black light it would make anything glow like a blue moon.

I put the cat outside the office door. No point in having a glowcat at night, I was having enough trouble sleeping lately, and I had a feeling it wasn't going to get any better for a while. When did Willie say she was going to be home from the conference? Did she say?

Wearing white cotton gloves, I pulled the Ziploc bag full of the lavender powder out of the jar. I held my breath, the stuff was pernicious, easily getting into every crack and crevice of your skin and your clothing.

You couldn't wash, blow, or vacuum it off; the glowing trail only wore away after a week or two. Until then, like some strange homeopathic remedy, the glow powder would take on a life of it's own, spreading to attach a big guilty sign to the extortionist and all his accessories; Hansel and Gretal never had it so good.

It was seven o'clock when I brought the stacks of bills out and ran my fingers over the slightly embossed intaglio printed bills. Getting easier to counterfeit every day, the black ink now contains ferrous oxide for the Fed's scanners. Even with a good printer, the stock, produced exclusively for the United States government since 1879 by Crane and Company, would reveal your bills as phonies. These bills all had the red and blue fibers embedded in the cotton and linen paper, which meant no counterfeits had crept in. With a thin sable brush I dusted the center of each hundred-dollar bill with an invisible sprinkling of the phosphorescent powder, trying to keep the stuff within the borders of Benjamin Franklin's face on the center of each bill. I always liked Benjamin Franklin. When his glasses fell on the floor he discovered bifocals, proving that clumsiness is sometimes the mother of invention. With his lavender powdered face he looked like a ponytailed Kabuki actor. Three hundred and fifty Franklins took me the better part of half an hour.

I put the bills in three equal piles and tightened rubber

bands around the top and bottom of each pile. I put the bills in two large ziploc bags. I turned off the light and trained a small penlight on the workbench.

The jar of phosphorescent powder lit up like a lantern. But the Ziploc bags, bills firmly clamped together, didn't glow. The glow powder had been successfully confined to Franklin's face in the center of each bill. Not a glimmer came through. Not even on the edges. Not yet. I put the cash back into the safe, along with the blackmail note, and gave the dial a good twist. Eight o'clock.

I locked the office door and took a shower, washing my hair. Powdered, oiled, blow-dried, soft as a baby, but still a little buff, I pulled on my silk boxer shorts, a pressed white shirt, and black jeans, soft, worn in. I pulled on the treadless black tennies and my green leather coat. The coat was custom made for me by a Eurotrash designer in North Beach. Three quarter length, it was slick and dark as a leaf, and cut in an inverted A shape to hide any number of items, and to camouflage my holster. Two larger pockets on either side of a Goretex lining would hold the two packets of cash. Only a dash of red lipstick would make me visible from a distance.

I was in one of my best physical conditions ever. Friends had remarked on a weight loss. Divorce can make you shed a lot of things; with nerves jangling and heart breaking I built my sit-ups back to one hundred and sixty count; I could run Bernal Hill three times around and not even be winded. My feet took me far from love, far from Frances. And when there wasn't that, there was the shooting range.

I opened the safe and found the simple five-shot police special .38 revolver, handmade shoulder holster, and ammunition. I reached for the weapon. It lay passive, in my hand; unloaded it was a useless lump of metal, a hammer.

I had replaced the wooden grip with molded Packmeyers, rubber grips which fit my palm perfectly. They increased my accuracy another ten percent. I put the revolver down. As much as I hated and respected the gun, I loved the shoulder holster.

The thick leather straps became pliant quickly, they conformed to my shoulders, my posture, my movement now.

The halter was nearly part of me. I slipped the leather over my arms and felt the empty pocket of the holster underneath my armpit. It had a spring closure and I could cross draw the weapon in just under three seconds.

I pulled out a pair of speed strips, designed to quickly reload the gun, and a pair of handcuffs and put them inside the specially designed pocket of my right arm. The cuffs served to counterbalance the weight of the revolver under my arm, but in a pinch they were an excellent way to incapacitate a criminal. I should be so lucky.

I took five of the strange, hollow point bullets out of a little blue box. Hollow point bullets are odd-looking things; a lot of people wouldn't recognize them as ammunition. Little punched-in, concave tips, they looked more like curtain weights. But because they weren't pointed they couldn't penetrate a wall or ricochet, hitting an innocent bystander. That was my second worst fear about carrying the gun. The first one was having to use it in the first place. I loaded the hollow point bullets into the chambers. One. Two. Three. Four. Five little bullets, I hoped I would see them again when the night was over.

Blackmailers are easy, I told myself. Usually they're lazy parasites. Bottom feeders. Not dangerous. A mantra for loading my gun: I am in good shape and blackmailers are cowards and one third of this thirty-five grand is coming back to me.

That's right, Emma. And you're going to live happily ever after and a third party will save this country from crazed right wingers. And you are not an animal. I sat down on my workbench stool, practiced my cross draw, taking dry shots at the dust motes in the corner. Nine-thirty. I picked up the phone and called Rose Baynetta, my friend in the security business. Rose had gone from small-time eavesdropper to small businesswoman. Our ascent in the sneak and creep business had been concomitant; we both learned and helped each other out as we went along. But Rose had established herself in an office with employees and payrolls, management and business lunches. I was still a backstage worker, a footloose prowler with no clients to impress. Rose had worked hard, worried harder, and never took a vacation, a lifestyle which suited her.

The source of much of our acquired skill and equipment had been Rose's father, Fred Baynetta.

While Rose scored microwave alarm know-how and a lot of referrals, her old man turned me on to years' worth of connections. Penny the Pick was on Fred's payroll as an advisor. I had fashioned my own tools, a double-pronged tweezer tension wrench that would pop any number of barrel bolts. Penny was a hard taskmaster, she was hardly impressed when I popped open a disk lock in seven seconds.

"Baynetta Security Services hours are 9 A.M. to 6 P.M."

I waited for the message to end. "Rose, are you there? It's Emma, pick up—"

"Yeah?" the syllable in a sleepy voice.

"How would you feel about doing a profile on Villanueva's organization?"

"Emma! What's up?"

"I need a little basic research."

"Sure. Who do I bill it to?"

"Me."

"Okay. Anything for the cause. Villanueva's got to win. Every Democrat in the country has sold us out on the Marriage Act. Villanueva is the only candidate who won't cave."

"She's running for *mayor,* Rose, not President."

"Yeah. And without her as mayor you can kiss San Francisco Gaylandia good-bye."

"She's got my vote. Get back to me when you've got the info."

"Over and out, boss."

The phone rang again.

"Emma, this is Carla Ribera." The dusky voice of the fashion photographer rose over the background of a stand-and-shout cocktail party. "What's keeping you? I thought I would see you here!"

"Were you responsible for that Film Festival invitation in my mailbox?"

"Yeah, I did all the still shoots for *Outlaw,* don't you know?"

"Yeah, I saw the photos in the catalogue. Very dramatic. Startling, even. Congratulations."

"I'm pretty happy with them myself. Aren't you coming to the reception?"

"Thanks but I just stepped off the plane. Things have been hectic."

"You have your tickets for *Outlaw,* don't you? The fashion alone is going to gut Jean Paul Gaultier. How long have we been waiting for someone to put his brand of fashion misogyny out of business? Ina—Ina Cho has *done* it, Emma. Her Homicidal Lesbian Terrorist line will revolutionize fashion once and for all." I could hear Carla's museum replicated pre-Columbian earrings clattering against the receiver like an Amazon tap dance. "We're going to put them *under* the table in Paris next spring—"

"I'll watch the satellite news."

"Listen, Emma, there's this really great young woman here and I hoped you would be willing to see her. She could really use your help."

"Here comes the favor," I sighed, moving the receiver away from my mouth. Carla was not exactly a wrong number, but she had been known to misdial. The last case I'd tangled with featured Carla in a minor role, one that nearly had me in prison for accessory to murder. "I'm busy right now."

"I think this is a worthy cause."

"Causes don't pay. Carla, are you on a hardwired phone?"

"Emma! *Compadre!*" Chuckle. "You never fail to underestimate me! Of course I'm on a hardwired phone. Besides, they don't provide remote phones and cell phones at the Festival, yet." Carla's voice disappeared for a moment. I heard the popping of corks in the background, a cheer, and some sweet bubbly close to the receiver.

"Carla?" I could hear her sipping.

"Emma, *amiga,* you can make difficult things seem," she paused, "easy."

"'That's what the Homicide Inspector said when I ran into one of your friends in the wrong way."

"Emma, Emma," Carla purred. "And I understood that you had your way."

"That's what the inspector thought too. But he didn't think it was an asset to my reputation. I think he called the charge accessory, aiding and abetting, something like that. He didn't like the idea of me walking around as a free woman. He wanted to lock me up and throw away the key. I need to lay low, Carla. I need to stay out of trouble with the law."

"Which is why, this time, *amiga*, I'm doing you a favor, throwing a very simple little job with a potentially fabulous commission your way. And, you won't believe this, she's a real *farmer*!"

"Uh-oh, I smell a trend."

"A woman of the soil, Emma. Seriously, Emma. You know how big organic produce is? Well, Kim is producing organic fiber. But not just *any* old rayon amalgam or hemp."

"Let me guess."

"We're talkin' organic *cashmere* . . ."

Cashmere. The feel of an old sweater came back through my memory. I remembered the sweater my mother always wore in the morning. An old moth eaten cardigan, a leftover from a twin set, a piece of luxury from her past life. "Okay, okay. You've got me interested."

"And one more thing, Emma," Carla whispered, "she's really beautiful in a rugged sort of way. I just know you guys will hit it off like gangbusters!" Carla handed the phone over to my new best friend.

"Is this Emma Victor?" A drawl across the phone line stretched south of the Mason-Dixon line. "I really, really appreciate this."

"Don't be grateful yet. I don't know what you need and I don't know if I can do anything for you."

"I just need to find a certain indiv-i-jew-al here." A certain Southern formality was still preserved in her speech.

"It's a big town. What's your name?"

"Kimilar Jones."

"'Listen, Kimilar. I'm pretty booked. Couldn't be anything in a hurry—"

"Oh!" Pause. Sounds of cocktail party, corks popping, sounds of Carla, her laugh faint, fainter.

"Are you there?"

"Yes!" Her voice hit a note of panic. "I'm sorry; I happen to be in town for a few days only. The Film Festival paid mah travel expenses. It's pretty hard for me to leave the farm; I don't know when I'll come back. I've got to find my ex. He's in San Francisco someway-ah," The drawl became thicker as her voice hit a higher pitch. "I think it might just be a simple matter of finding out where he is. I have a post office box number. He's received mail there."

"'So why doesn't he answer?" I asked, but I knew the answer to that one. One more slimy divorce case.

"I'll explain when I get there. Please. I promise not to take up much of your time."

"When?"

"Tonight."

"Tonight? Impossible—"

"It would only take me a minute. I have a rental car. What are you doing now? Please, just let me stop by. It means everything—everything I've ever worked for."

That did it. I just hated to see a good woman lose something that she'd *worked* for. That is, if her hands were covered in honest dirt. I could work *her* in between loading my gun and receiving the phone call from the extortionist. Since Frances had left there was not one person who had crossed my threshold. I was out serving subpoenas to pay the mortgage night and day, returning home to crawl into a deep and hopefully unbroken sleep. And now, as luck would have it, another slimy divorce case right in my living room; déjà vu all over again. "Actually," I said, "I'll meet you at the Cafe Flor. It's just down the street from the Castro Theatre."

"Cafe Flor?"

"Corner of 16th and Market."

"That little outdoor place with the patio?"

We agreed to meet. I hung up the phone and a car alarm started whining down the street. I went back into my office. The thirty-five thousand dollars fit nicely in the extra large inside pocket of the coat. The cell phone was clipped firmly to my belt buckle. The Eurotrash cut, ample under the arms, helped hide any unsightly bulges, I thought, checking my figure in the front hall mirror. I drew a nude shade of lipstick across my mouth and blotted ever so carefully. All ready to cruise the Castro, with forty K and loose change, for some business I didn't want.

CRUISING
THE CASTRO

The Castro is more an emotional than a geographic location. As you draw closer you see them: couples clutching in the fog, women in leather jackets, the kisses no longer tentative in public.

Approaching over the steep hill from 24th Street, the angle afforded you the best view of the six square blocks which might be called the heart of the Castro. A florist advertising rainbow bouquets for National Coming Out Day had set his wares upon the sidewalk.

Even from the top of the hill I could see a knot of stretch limos and Muni buses which clotted the sidewalk in front of an architectural sugar tart lit in baby pink and blue. The Castro Theatre was the beloved heart of the neighborhood. Opening night of the Film Festival and I could almost hear the crowds cheering, almost see filmmakers and actors flushed with success, almost feel the anxious politicians jockeying to get up on the stage. Fourteen hundred and fifty votes would be sitting there, waiting for the film to begin.

The thirty-foot vertical sign, comprised of six huge letters which throbbed with pink and blue lights. C-A-S-T-R-O, C-A-S-T-R-O, C-A-S-T-R-O winked at every passersby and a marquee of pink and blue neon zigzags kept the crowd dry from any condensed fog.

Past the bus shelter the crowds were hiking down Market. What would it be like as a theme street? There was already a Tower Records. Further down the hill would be a Warner Brothers' Store and a Hard Rock Cafe with Pottery Barn potentially biting at their heels.

I turned into the two-story garage next to Cafe Flor. The hollow stairway led to Tower Records, where a smiling security guard was chatting up a customer. Opening the French doors I stepped into the hothouse hut that was Cafe Flor. Plants crowded the full-length windows; men were lined up at tables writing in notebooks, chatting together, the place warm with coffee, steam, and laughter.

And the smile of Kimilar Jones. Five foot five and probably fifty-five, the woman who had to be Kimilar Jones waved at me and flashed big teeth in an almost horsey grin. Her weathered, dark face was in contrast to her long, flaxen, hair. Her brown suede jacket, a hand-me-down from Davy Crockett, was nearly as weathered as her face. The whole getup was so authentic I wouldn't have been surprised if she had been carrying a lasso.

She rose from her chair, putting a small, sinewy hand on the little marble table to steady herself on tiny heels. Kimilar Jones wore the tackiest white patent leather country western boots ever made, and I smiled at the sight of the white fringe which sprouted and shimmied from silver medallion studs up and down the woman's delicate hocks. As I came closer to the table I saw a huge purse, bigger than a bread box and smaller than a coffin, at her side.

"Hi, I'm Emma Victor," I said, reaching out a hand, keeping my distance from her as I do with short people, not wanting to make them look up, not wanting to look down.

"Jones," she said, her mouth smiling, big white teeth taking center stage in her face. She extended a hand and pumped mine in a shockingly strong grip. "I didn't think you'd be so tall," she said.

"Nobody did." I motioned her to sit down in her chair. Her eyes were light, light blue, and had a kind of innocence in contrast to the rest of her weather-beaten face. A long, thin nose might have been broken once. Her hands were working hands, scars on knuckles, nails which, despite a recent manicure, were still torn. The little boots squared off under the table as she sat down. A large mouth smiled in a lopsided way; she kept her lips closed, covering a large overbite.

"Thanks for meeting me on such short notice." Kimilar hauled her big purse onto the marble table, crossed her legs, silver-tipped boots flashing. On her lap the high quality leather shone like a mirror, the buckle of solid silver was cast in a knot. "Let me start from the beginning."

"Oh, no, not the beginning," I murmured.

"Yew in that much of a hurry? C'mon, you're a private detective, I gotta tell you my story, right?" Kimilar had me in her pale sights and it wasn't an entirely bad place to be. Her slight build was deceptive; I could see Kimilar's history in the strength of her arms, the calves of her legs, the scars on her hands. Hauling the suitcase handbag onto her lap, she popped the silver knot open and took out a large presentation book.

Under a plastic slipcover an 8 x 10 glossy of a goat had been carefully inserted. It was not just any goat. It was the quintessential goat, the kid of our imagination, something Walt Disney could turn into a drawing with the voice of Doris Day except the goat was black. Kimilar's hands parted the cover and I saw what the Kimilar connection to Carla had been.

A group of waifs looked as cheery as pallbearers dressed in black leather tutus with knitted bodices. Behind them blazed photos of the Wild West, as imagined by set designer Slavid Prockney. "Well, it ain't' exactly my style either," Kimilar apologized. "I thought the idea was to keep you *warm*, but whatever."

"Here," Kimilar's hand dipped into her suitcase. I expected the usual paperwork to emerge. Instead I found myself holding a piece of fleece, a cloud, denser than velvet. "This is the product in its combed state. My sweater here is the woven example." Kimilar gently offered the shoulder of her sweater, I reached out to touch, a fabric, not a person, a piece of magical stuff. Weightless, so soft it barely existed, so deep and thick it exuded warmth, it enveloping my hand in a happy black cloud. I put the fluff ball down on the marble; it disappeared just as quickly back into Kimilar's bag.

"So, you are a fur producer and you have a problem—"

"It's not fur. All the garments you see here are from the cashmere of the type of goat you see on the cover. It's fleece, not fur. The fleece will be woven, it ain't knitted. One of the features of our line is that the colors, especially this here black, are what we been callin' lifelong black. It's a natural material, not dyed. The process is environment-friendly and the black has a quality of infinity."

Infinity. The word tripped off her lips easily. I looked into Kimilar's eyes and I thought I saw something of the great American rural diaspora. From the Alleghenies to the runway in Paris.

"Fleece," Kimilar was saying. "It wears absolutely forever. Of course, the most fun is shearing the sheep. Too labor-intensive now, but in the beginning, why, you just grab them critters and hold on to 'em real tight, take a shears to 'em and just watch the bags fill up. Six bucks a goat. Fifteen goats an hour. That's how I got into it in the first place." Her accent diminished in direct proportion to her business spiel, not unusual for Southerners. I took the book gently from her hands and leafed through the layouts, from farm to fashion. A profit and loss statement didn't look good so far, but the setup costs were considerable. The projections, if you believed them, were fabulous. I put the book down on the coffee table in front of her.

"Very interesting. Looks like quite a business, but I have one too. It's late, Ms. Jones. I'm on a tight schedule."

Kimilar took off her jacket and I stopped thinking about the seven minutes I had allotted her. Thick fur made into a short sleeved sweater so deep and dark it nearly obscured the features of the wearer. Nearly, but not quite.

"This is the problem. A problem with a fast and easy solution, I hope. You see, Emma, I don't have clear title to the goddamn farm. There's somebody else's name on the title." Kimilar's accent was in ascendence and I was getting a depressing feeling. Divorce work. "I gotta get clear title before I develop the business further, before I can borrow money from banks and start signing contracts to supply the fleece." Her hands clenched together. "My fucking goddamn ex don't like to stay in one place for long. He's a rolling stone, that's for sure. Not one to work the land. And he sure as hell ain't gonna work me neither. That farm is mine."

I looked back at the book. Herds of goats perched nonchalantly on cloven hoofs. The steep rocky hillsides were presumably in New Mexico, just like the book said.

"It's just beautiful there, wintertimes." Kimilar's deep voice was velvety, far away. "I got me a big stone fireplace, in a room made outta logs. Big enough not to feel cramped, small enough to heat up real toasty. December, March. Time to slow down, take long walks with the dogs. Make my own candles, have me a good pipe and take me a good book every night. Friends come and visit. Sometimes I go up into the mountains with Blue. There's a sweat lodge there. God's country, for sure."

"But right now the property is held jointly."

"No shit," the tips of her boots moved up and down in an agitated rhythm and the blue eyes went cold.

"When did you last see your—boyfriend?"

"I last saw the jerk—" Kimilar crossed her arms over the fuzzy sweater, as if to contain her temper. "Fifteen years ago we bought the piece of land together, a piece of the most beautiful mountain desert in New Mexico. It's got colors there that you ain't never seen before."

"How'd you meet him?"

"That asshole was actually in college, can you believe it? Said he was going to study agriculture. As far as I could tell, he just studied the vultures, man. He was beautiful, with deep brown eyes. He could charm the rattle off a snake. But once he got what he wanted from me, and he decided he didn't want to be a farmer, he was, like, history, man. I never did see him again."

"Any hobbies, or interests?"

"Besides scammin' and blood suckin'? Racing. He likes racing."

"Horses?"

"Naw. Cars. The man had no feel for animals. Didn't even
like lookin' at them, watch the little babies run and play in
the field. Would never get his hand close, afraid of animals,
can you imagine? Couldn't tell the difference between a
sheep and a goat. But I did and I thought it would settle him
down. I thought I was in love, in love with a farmer. Turns
out I was in love with the farm," she laughed. "Stupid, ain't
it? The way we think we can make people into just who we
want. Put his name on the title and then he splits. Turns out
I was the farmer all along. Now I got to track the shit down
to get my business on the road."

"What kind of improvements have you done to the land?"

"Right away I started addin' the amenities, water, electricity. Awl by my lonesome. Somebody laid a few goats on
me. I wasn't interested in dairy, but these was fur-bearing
goats. You ever see a little baby cashmere kid? Right away
I kinda fell in love with the little creatures. Gets damn lonely
out there, but I took on some help and started siring the
goats myself and selling 'em. Started traveling and gener-
ated a great deal of interest in the goat trade. Once the co-
operative was set up it seemed like a natural to develop the
herd and sell the animals as well. Meanwhile, the fleece is
piling up. So I have fifty samples of material made up. Then
I set off to the biggest fashion show I could find in New
York City. When I saw Ina at the show I just knew we would
get along. The clothes I could do without, but Ina is great
and she's got a really hot name right now."

"Sounds like you got it all worked out."

"Almost. Almost. There's a big call for domestic cashmere. I can raise it, sell it and live the life I want. There are
banks who are interested in financing me and potential contracts with mills which want the product."

"Back to your former partner."

"Okay, sorry, don't mean to be takin' up so much of your
time. I heard he was in Frisco and plannin' on leavin' for
South America at the end of the month. This is the first I
heard o' him in five years. It's my only chance, now that I
know where he is, for a few weeks at least. He said he was

gonna leave the country. Least that's what I heard. But listen, he don't give one shit about that farm." Her hand was diving down into her handbag, fingers searching the corners of a satin grosgrain lining. "He won't give you no trouble. I can tell you that for certain. An' I certainly don't need him horning in on what has been a very labor-intensive venture!"

"What exactly do you want me to do about it?" I looked at my watch. Blackmail time. I put my hand reassuringly on the cell phone clipped to my belt. The standby light blinked.

"Find him, find him, Emma. He's here in San Francisco. I cain't do it, I dunno the city and I'm only gonna be around for a few days. I gotta get back to the farm. Carla says you can find a needle in a haystack. You find him and you git his name on the right piece of paper and make sure it's legal—"

The phone rang.

"Excuse me," I said, sliding out from behind the table, Kimilar's suitcase of a purse at my feet was blocking my way.

"Oh, sorry!"

The phone rang, insistently, the bigger gig, the bigger gig.

"Here! Oh, hell, it's stuck! No. Wait; there!" Kimilar struggled with her purse as the buckle snagged on the rung of a chair. I was practically vaulting over the table when it rang again; I didn't want to be hearing the mechanical voice against the background of conversation.

Ring. Ring. I punched the button.

"Hello? Wait a moment please."

"You-will-bring-the-money-" The nasty voice leaked into the Cafe Flor.

"Wait!-"A hellish static played through the earpiece. Weaving through the tables, past the cappuccino line and onto the deck, through the portal onto the sidewalk. I finally stepped outside into the cold, velvet darkness where I could concentrate. The voice of a different kind of businessman, a parasite with a faulty sound track. His breath caught with hyperventilation. He was nervous. Or asthmatic. Across the street a noisy group of diners arrived at Cafe Med, couldn't get in, a maître d' appeared; they had to wait outside. I turned my back, facing a fence.

Trying to place his voice, the background noise of a television, the kind of static from a cordless or cellular phone, I
clutched the receiver. That was the voice. That was the man
that I wanted. Phone glued to my ear, nothing would come
between us, my blackmailer and I. Nothing except his careful planning and probably a lot of experience in his factory
of fear.

"You-have-the-money?" Gravelly tones of late middle
age, the all-American accent from anywhere through a voice
altering apparatus of some kind. A woman's voice falsely altered? Keep it on the line.

"Yes. Just the way you wanted it."

"Unmarked," pause, *"bills."*

"Yes. Hundreds, it's what you wanted, right?"

*"Drive-out-to-the-Cliff-House. Be-there-in-half-an-hour.
Park-in-one-of-the-spaces-on-the highway. Walk-up-the-hill-
to-the-Visitors-Center."* Pause, hand over the speaker. *"Go-
down-the-staircase-and-turn-left. Walk-fifty-feet. In-front-
of-a-small building-you-will-see-a-pay-telephone. Wait-there-
for-your-next-instructions."* Click.

I turned back toward the street. The little group was being
ushered inside the restaurant now. I ducked back under the
portal and past the boys to where Kimilar's tan seemed to
have faded and her expression looked grim. Staring at her
surroundings, she jumped at me arrival.

"Oh, hi! What was that all about?"

"Business," I said. "Now, if you'll just give me the name
of your ex-boyfriend, and tell me just how you came to be
convinced that he's in San Francisco, I'll be on my way. And
it would be really useful if you had a photo."

"Got one right here, all ready for ya. John C. Osbourne."
Kimilar reached into her bag, and found an old color snap-
shot. "Here. Here's his picture." A shiny colorful square
came my way.

A white man, not in the best condition, not in the worst
condition, a man in his mid thirties, was closing the rear
hatch of a Jeep Grand Cherokee with a red and white license
plate, a star centered above it. The rear of the car was loaded
with camping equipment. He was struggling with the lock,

his hand seemingly stuck to the key, a look of surprise on his face as the photographer shot the picture. He didn't look angry. He might have even laughed, close-set eyes squinting with the flashbulb. Glad to be going on vacation. Testing out the roll. John C. Osbourne was working on a goatee, and the sandy blonde hair on his head, what was left of it, looked very fleecy.

"How do you know he's in San Francisco?"

"I have a post office box number."

She opened her handbag and took out a Xerox copy. On the face of it two registered receipts, scraps of paper which showed gray where they had curled up against the glass of the photocopier. I took the Xerox out of her hands and looked at the address. It was the kind of zip code that meant a grimy morning. Letter drop blues.

"You think he received these letters," I murmured, looking at the Xerox, the cramped and careful handwriting of Kimilar Jones.

"That's what the PO receipt says. But I never heard back." She shut the purse firmly. "I sent him a letter about the farm and a copy of the title. Never even got it back. Who knows why he's not answering me? He's probably just busy. We didn't end on good terms either."

"Do you know his Social Security number? If I can't find him at his post office box I'll have to try and find out if he's working."

"Yeah, I do have his Social Security number." She bit her lip. "I think." Her hands disappeared deep into the bag.

"What are his habits? Why would he choose to be in the area?"

"If he's employed, it's in a garage. He knows foreign cars pretty good. Special detailing. His Social Security number," she read off a paper still in the bag, out of sight, "seven, thirty, forty-four, fifty-eight, twenty-eight."

I wrote the number in a small notebook. "Good. Listen, Kimilar, this is what I'm going to try and do for you. You need a quitclaim." The blue eyes looked at me hard. Was I able to get her farm back? Was that the question they were asking, or was there something else?

"What's a quitclaim, Emma?"

"It's a kind of deed through which the owner, or co-owner in this case, releases all title to the property. If there aren't any problems or other claims upon the land, back taxes and so forth, there shouldn't be a big problem from the legal aspect. Finding him and getting him to sign are something else. You seem confident he doesn't have an interest in the property anymore. He might develop an interest if he knew you were on the brink of a successful business enterprise."

"Hell, he's got bigger enterprises himself." Kimilar seemed to reassure herself as much as me.

"How do you know?"

"Dumb bastard's always up to something. Hard work was never his thing. Ah kin tell you that the farm is still one helluva lot of hard work. I really don't think he cares."

"I'll see what I can do. Say I find him and get him to sign the quitclaim, what are you offering me?"

Kimilar was ready for this part. She hauled the big purse onto her lap and clutched the silver buckle earnestly. "Emma, I'm prepared to offer you five percent of the next five year's profits if you find him and get him to sign whatever it is that he needs to sign so that my farm is finally mine and I can get on with fucking business."

I thought about it. I thought about Kimilar's profit and loss statements and the piece of lightweight fluff in my hand and the deep velvety darkness of Kimilar's sweater. Ten days. "I have a program with a quitclaim on my computer. But I don't want five percent of the profit for the first five years. I want one percent profit for the next fifteen years."

"Well, well, well," Kimilar chewed on her lip for a moment before she smiled. The blue eyes sparkled; Kimilar liked to deal.

"You plan to be in business a long time. So do I," I said.

"Deal." She clutched her bag tightly as if it might get up and run away from her.

"And I'll need a two-hundred-and-fifty-dollar retainer," I told her. "Do you have a copy of the title?"

"Sure, I can ask Blue; she's down on the farm." Fingertips rode over her face.

"Are there any outstanding documents? Proration of taxes? It would be nice if I had the previous bill of sale."

Kimilar was nodding."Taxes are paid up. Ah'll ask Blue about the previous bill of sale," she said, counting out two-hundred-and-fifty-dollars onto the table in fifties. I watched the money land there, hard earned money. I didn't want to touch it yet.

"By the way, how'd you get the box number?" I asked.

"How'd I get it?"

"Yeah."

"Why you wanna know?"

"In case he's not there I can work the original source."

"I dunno about that." Fingers raked the flaxen hair.

"Kimilar," I said, "don't tie one hand behind my back. Clients that can't reveal their own sources are just making the trail twenty times harder to follow. After all, time is money. Your money."

"I-I cain't. The person is—" Kimilar's chin might have trembled, it might have been a trick of light. "The party who gave me the post office box number is day-ad. I'm sorry to say. So, Emma, you see, I've given you all the information I have." Her lips closed as finally as the silver knot on her handbag. We both stared at the money on the table. Hard-working hands and a good business on its way, held up only by a jerk who never paid into the mortgage. "I'm staying at a hotel with mah brother, Jason Jeeters. Here, the Clinton Arms." Her fingers found a card in the pocket of her suede jacket, folded and crumpled."The Film Festival put us up, mah brother and I. They are so nice." She pulled the suede jacket over both shoulders and shivered. Zipping it up with a short jerky move, the black fleecy sweater disappeared from view. "And Jason's been working so hard, this is his big chay-ance." One by one Kimilar picked up the bills and then held them out to me. "The farm is everything to me, Emma."

I counted and folded the bills and put them deep into my pocket. My coat was just that much heavier, lined with a little more of that special cotton and linen paper from Crane and Crane. "Having a good time at the Festival?" Time for a little chit chat while I made out a receipt. Flipping to the back of my notebook, I started printing in the date and the amount of retainer.

"Well, there's a lot of queer movies, no pun intended. Movies that sometimes don't tell no story at all! Not like Jason Jeeters. This is Jason's big moment and I don't want to miss a second of it." She stood up, pawing in her bag again, she came out with two tickets to the Castro Theatre. "*'Pale Refugee,* that's Jason's film. You don't wanna miss it. It's closing the Festival." She handed me the invitation. "Jason plays some great guitar and the goats are really cute."

PALE REFUGEE

A FILM BY
Jason Jeeters Jones
Starring Martel
CASTRO THEATRE
SUNDAY, NOVEMBER 5, 1995
RECEPTION AT 8
SCREENING AT 9
CATERING BY BRIDGEWAYS

I squinted at the italic writing while still making out the invoice, my hand automatically making my signature at the bottom.

"Here's the number of the hotel. They can page me at the pool at the hotel. Jason Jeeters said there are Hollywood agents lookin' for talent! I tell you, I don't mind hanging out with a buncha guys that don't look my way twice." Her hand nervously grasped a hip. "But the gay girls—I had no idea! Why, there's just all kinds, ain't there?"

"Yes. There are all kinds."

"I don't mind tellin' you, it ain't my thing, but as long as everybody's lookin', I may as well too. But as soon as I get me that quitclaim signed I'm heading back to the hills where I belong." She grinned, all those big teeth looking like tomb-stones in a churchyard.

I peeled the receipt off the steno pad and tucked it in the

breast pocket of her jacket. "I'll get back to you," I said. "When I have something on Mr. Wonderful."

Kimilar tripped merrily away, the little silver bells on her boots tinkled and the leather fringe feathered in the wind. A businesswoman, Kimilar was having a blast, but it was no time to give away the farm.

CHAPTER FIVE

CAMERA OBSCURA

The Camera Obscura is a large camera, an amusement from a former century when optical illusions were considered worth the price of admission. When I reached Point Lobos Avenue I rolled down the window. A sudden whip of wind slapped me in the face; eucalyptus buttons clattered onto the ground, their sharp-edged leaves sticking to the windshield. The brittle trees were not native to California. Their long branches, curving over me, tended to snap in the fierce wind that blew off the ocean. I kept the window open; the cold wind would keep me edgy. I thought I heard the ocean, the roar of a distant monster.

I caught sight of the Golden Gate Bridge; the road swooped downwards into darkness. I downshifted; there was salt in the fog; the roaring of the ocean became louder. Point Lobos Avenue brought me straight to the edge of the world. A greasy spoon called Louie's claimed the spot, along with the concrete ruins of the old Sutro Bathhouse. Usually there were hordes of hungry tourists and lines of dinosaur buses lined up at its curb. Tonight the place was a tomb.

I turned left as instructed and surveyed the offering of thirty or forty empty parking spaces, ninety degrees to the ocean. I parked smack in the middle, cut the engine, and

44

took a look around. Behind me was a dark hill, propped up with erosion control concrete, made to look like rocks. To the right the Cliff House beckoned, its windows darkened.

Looking out Romea's little windows I saw no one. No other car was parked within sight, nothing moved, except the ocean, roaring and crashing at a frantic pace just beyond the seawall. Just below the Cliff House was a promenade where the twenty-five-foot-square building that was the Camera Obscura was visible. I could just see the big block letters, GIANT CAMERA.

To the right, the white concrete cliffs of the old baths shone, snakes of rebar crawling out of their sides. Six huge pools, three acres of public amusement that was now nothing more than a dangerous concrete sarcophagus, boiling with cold salt water. Every year one tourist was sacrificed to the Pacific, a sneaker wave carrying them away without a trace as they naively strolled the ruined parapets, not that I hadn't prowled the old baths a few times myself, a low tide promenade.

Behind me and to my left were cranes and a hillside of heavy construction, twelve-foot-diameter piping and so on. The remains of Playland were still being torn down. The freak shows and shantytown vendors were being replaced by a series of seaside condominiums, silly modern pseudo Victorians that had been built along the shore on the graveyard of Playland. All gone now.

Beyond the condominiums the flash of streetlights ended and the black stretch that must have been Golden Gate Park was a dark void. At the end, by ocean's shore, two windmills were etched against the sky, one shorn of its blades. They were a present to San Francisco from one of a long line of Dutch queens.

I pulled on my lightweight leather gloves. Thin, an extra skin, they would keep my hands warm and supple. I'd practiced with them at the range and they gave me a sense of confidence aside from other advantages. I pulled them tightly over my hands as I got out of the car.

Playing for time, and to an invisible audience, I walked over to the seawall on the edge of the cliff and looked over the awesome boundary, the end of a continent and the beginning of the mightiest ocean in the world. I opened my coat and took a deep breath, trying to assess quickly the possibilities afforded to me, to the blackmailer.

The front was breaking; the gray blanket of fog was pierced. A crescent moon brought everything into focus. Seal Rock, a hundred-foot promontory, jutted out of the ocean like a bad tooth. Waves were throwing themselves at the stone surface, assaulting the rock as they had done for many thousands of years, slowly eroding it away, never giving up, ravenous white foam glittering like a row of fangs in the moonlight. It was time.

The wind whipped my coat, the leather flapped like bat wings as I fought my way up the hill. My body, bent at an impossible forty-five degrees, kept a steady pace. Mist filled my eyes. The Cliff House offered the darkened window of its gift shop. Golden Gate Bridge ashtrays, tea towels with the mostly extinct seals, and shot glasses with Cable Cars climbing halfway to the stars.

It was a good choice of location. The parking lot and the Camera Obscura were both spots which could be easily monitored from a distance. Numerous shrubs and hidden pathways wormed the hillside, providing perfect hiding places and avenues of escape. The constant noise of the ocean would cover up anything, a cry for help, a gunshot, the breaking of a heart.

I went down the stairway as instructed, the noise making me feel terribly vulnerable. Anyone could have ambushed me. I reached the bottom of the stairs. The wind hammered away, trying to lift me up, skid me along the pond of its mist slicked concrete, insulted that I would venture so close. The metal of the railing had been gnawed away by the sea and the salt and the wind. Why did people persist in building these unnecessary addenda to natural beauty? What strange hubris worked here? What would make blackmail an attractive occupation?

The long promenade howled with wind and I had to grasp the rusty railing to make any progress. I rounded the corner at the bottom of the stairs, past the Mechanical Museum.

There was fifteen yards to the little blue and yellow building. GIANT CAMERA.

I saw the big letters emblazoned across the top, the cupola which held the double lens. Flayed by wind and sea, a jaunty striped flag flapped desperately. A small lamp shone over the door marked ENTRANCE and created a circle of light. Five feet in front of it was the phone booth. Next to it was a wooden post and a mounted box. CAMERA OBSCURA information: 25 cents.

The concrete lay before me like an exposed catwalk. The ocean lunged from time to time over the rails, laughing, ready to suck unsuspecting nature lovers into the ocean where they would be tossed mercilessly until they drowned. I wondered who was watching and from where as I stepped into the light.

This was it. Nervous acidic sweat ran to my waist and collected there in a caustic rivulet. My back felt exposed to the ocean and any monster that might emerge from it. I walked on tight, steely legs. I reached the phone booth. The light had burned out or someone had broken it. I looked at the receiver. The phone number itself had been ripped off the dial.

I picked up the horn. There was a dial tone. It worked. I replaced the receiver and looked awhile at the phone booth, as if I should do something with it.

The moon was brighter and the wind had a sharper edge. I looked behind me; the Camera Obscura could have afforded me shelter from the wind, but I would have to stand there like an idiot in the cold moonlight with thirty-five grand in my pocket, the gun feeling like a useless lump of metal. I imagined a cross draw, ran through the movements in my head as I waited for the phone to ring. What would Frances the physician say if she knew I was packing? But we weren't exactly speaking anymore.

I took a quarter out of my pocket, dropped it in the little wooden box, and pulled out a flyer. Frances and I visited the Giant Camera when we first moved to San Francisco. It was our one-year anniversary and we paid our dollar to a drunken ticket taker who let us in, waving his hands extravagantly. We went inside, the only ones in the center of a darkened room, fifteen square feet. We stared into the shining parabolic disk in the center of the room.

"Camera Obscura' means darkened chamber in Italian," the brochure explained. *"The basic mechanics of photography, the projection of an outside image onto an opaque surface, is accomplished by light filtered through a lens, or a series of lenses."*

I remembered looking over the shining disk at my love. Frances. A woman who looked through microscopes for a living, she had shelled out the two bucks for our admission. Five feet wide, the curving bowl gave to us the ocean outside. We seemed to merge there, together in the presence of the mighty ocean which was trapped underneath our fingers on a magic platter. Frances had explained to me about refracted light. Standing next to her, I needed no explanation of miracles.

I looked at my watch and followed a few sets of lonely headlights as they made their way up the hill and disappeared into the groves of eucalyptus. Time was measured in crashing waves, the deep distant throaty sound of a foghorn, and the memory of a kiss. I folded the brochure and put it in my pocket.

The foghorns are an illusion too. The boats used radar now. Romantic San Franciscans insisted that the foghorns not be silenced and so they still hooted, just for effect. I was, in fact, standing on the edge of the world and listening to a sound effect waiting for a phone to ring.

I thought about how nice it would be to light a cigarette. About what kind of person made a living with spying cameras, Peeping Toms with bigger ambitions, slimebuckets who couldn't make it any other way. Time crawled by, leaving a chilly wake; the big arm of the ocean reached out and shook me.

The phone rang. My hand flew through the wind and yanked on the receiver.

"Walk-back-up-the-hill. Cross-the-street. Walk-through-the-parking-lot-and-up-the-path-past-sign."

I knew the location. The hilltop garden was created as an

ocean viewing area, another project of the nineteenth century eccentric millionaire Adolph Sutro.

"*At-the-top-of-the-hill-you-will-see-stairs. At-the-top-of-the-stairs-stand-in-the-middle-of-the-large-open-area. You-will-see-a-light-blink-three-times. If-you-do-not-see-the-light-come-back-tomorrow-night. If-you-see-the-three-blinks throw-the-money-in-the-direction-of-the-light. Stand-in-the-middle-of-the-area-for-ten-minutes. If-you-have-followed-instruction-the-video-will-be-back-at-this-phone-booth. Return-to-the-same-phone-booth-tomorrow-night-for-further-instructions. If-we-are-satisfied-we-will-continue-business. We-still-have-the-most-interesting-piece-of-the-product-to-offer-you. Same-price,-same-cash,-same-phone-booth-at-the-Cliff-House. Only-the-action-gets-better. Come-alone-or-you-and-your-politician's-career-goes-to-hell-in-a-hotel-room.*"

We. The two locations. The phone booth, the walk across the Great Highway. This plan was designed by two people. That was good news. Two people doubled my chances of finding one of them. I set off on the latest treasure hunt where I was going to throw thirty five-thousand dollars into the bushes.

I was familiar with the ruins of the once formal gardens, the grove of pine, the parapet that the voice on the phone had described.

I walked up past Louie's and crossed the Great Highway. There was no traffic. The curtain of fog had been completely drawn away. I could read the letters on the brown national park sign which bordered the pathway. The two stone lions lounged at the entrance, their expressions somewhere between a yawn and a growl, their manes held their perm sculpted in concrete, their tails curled around useless stone testicles. I walked past them onto the overgrown path.

Long green arms of Monterey pine impeded my progress, snapping behind me, their big wet brooms brushed my cheeks. Water leaked between the sole and leather sides of my shoes; they were squashing as I made it to the crest.

The meadow grove greeted me, an elegant gray forest of Monterey pines. Sixty, seventy feet high, they formed an arched roof over a field of mud that had once been a huge carpet of flowers. Hundreds of statues, characters from mythology and popular Victorian culture, had inhabited these grounds, given a fresh coat of white paint every year. Only a few were left.

On an elevation, facing the carriage turnaround, stood a statue of Diana, the huntress. Figure of equal opportunity on Mount Olympus, Diana had been an affront to all men as she had been named head of all hunters. Curling her arm upward in a modern gesture, she let everyone in the park know who ruled. Her ponytail kept the hair out of her face, the northern side of which was green from mold. The look on Diana's face was all business, dirt dripping from the corners of her mouth made her look completely grim. The gangs had put their monikers in spray paint on her plinth base, and somebody had torn the front legs off of her deer.

It was said that when women died a swift and painless death they had been slain by Diana's silver arrows. She was making good getaway time in those concrete sandals, too. Her stone eyes seemed to look right into my soul as I passed her. I walked further up the path, to a little cookie cutter gazebo that some history-loving hand had kept in white oil paint. Someone named *"Schizo"* had left their mark on spray paint there too.

I saw the first wall of a raised parapet. The terrace hung over the ocean like a seagull. Rising about twenty feet off the ground, Sutro had built an elevation of landfill. The northernmost set of stairs would be concealed in brush. Blotches of shadows played on the ground as the big pine trees bent in the wind. I hurried down the path, left arm tight to my side, keeping the gun steady. I scoured the low black shadows for movement. Squish, squish, squish, the ocean came closer.

A break in the shrubs revealed the stairway. *Thunk!* My footsteps echoed on the lid of a manhole cover, a hollow metal sound indicating a drainage system. The ceiling of trees parted for a moment in a stiff gust of wind and I saw more clearly the break in the shrubs and the stairway which would lead me to the top.

Slightly breathless, toes numb, anxious, eager to complete the deal, I fought through the fog and found the rough-hewn steps. When I reached the top the city lights cast an ambient glow that made it easier to see. Eyes scouring the large flat area, half concrete, half broken stone, I saw only succulents and freeway flowers climbing through the cracks. Tortured cypress trees, embattled by fierce conditions, twisted on the edge of the hillside. Perhaps that was a broken sundial or the leftovers of a fountain in the center. There was nothing and no one about. I walked into the center and stood next to some unidentifiable rubble, a big lit-up target that followed instructions. I wondered from where the light would come.

Ready to do business; come on boys, come on. Blink the light, dammit.

My green coat glowed in the moonlight. The white streak in my hair was an exclamation point riding over the top of my whitish winter face. My left foot started jiggling. I stopped it. I looked back at the side of the parapet facing the grove and lawn. The rear wall consisted of three angled sections, each section cut out and supported with four decorative diagonal buttresses.

Blink, blink, blink. The light came from the east. The ocean growled and a wave crashed behind me.

This was it. The blackmailer was lurking underneath the concrete wall facing the lawn; I must have walked by him coming up the path.

Throw the money.

Throw.

The money.

I took the packet out of my wallet and looked again to where the light had flashed. Middle section, fourth diagonal. I squinted.

Blink, blink, blink.

I almost smiled. Anxious, are we? Three giant steps forward and I hurled the bundle of plastic wrapped cash ov the wall where it must have landed in the shrubbery be Perhaps I heard a scurrying in the bushes. Perhaps it the bursting of a million bubbles on the edge Whatever it was, I couldn't follow my inclinati chase. I couldn't retrieve. I backtracked to the center of the circle and made myself completely still and completely visible as I checked my watch.

In between the crashing of waves I thought I heard a clicking, its rhythm shifting from time to time. A ten-speed bicycle making its way below the terrace and behind my back. A confident pedaling, happy with his harvest. I hoped. Then there was only the relentless crashing of waves.

It seemed that for hours to come I would contemplate strange, shifting sights and sounds, murmurs on the wind, flickerings of moonlight that could have been flashlights, the squeal of doves or of a blackmailer discovering the money had been marked.

I looked through the cutouts of the wall into the deep shrubbery and the moonlit lawn beyond, imagining Victorian ladies, black and gray dresses dragging over the confetti of flowered carpets, pansies planted with precision. Dammit. You'd better get a grip on your nerves or you won't be long for this kind of business, the business of bigger gigs.

I had been so careful with the powder, I thought. The tiny bits of dust were barely visible, the bills were so highly distressed with any number of random pen markings and thumbprints that I was sure they would not notice the powder.

I didn't want to ruin the deal. I wanted to get the video back. That was my assignment. That was the most important thing and to catch the crooks. Not the money. You took one chance too many, Emma. You shouldn't have marked the bills. I checked my watch. Two minutes.

A series of breakers hit the coast, probably pounding the ruin of the Sutro Baths below, followed by something new. A banshee sound that was riding on the wind. I looked at my watch. Eleven minutes had passed. I started my walk back down the hill.

I didn't have to worry about the powder after all. Or the warning on the curling lip of a wave. I reached the phone booth by the Giant Camera, and there, flapping in the ocean ~eze, was an envelope. I looked for the chunky rectangular shape of a video. But no. The envelope was far too light; the wind played with it.

Teasers. I opened the envelope. A negative rested there. The still made from the video, the hotel room image Xeroxed onto the blackmail note. The lower right-hand corner was clipped off, just as it had been on the contact print. *"The action comes later, with the second payment."*

Grasping the film by its edges, I held it up to the light of the Camera Obscura. Yes. Willie's politician client spread-eagled on the sheets, her white legs black, her black hair white as a seagull. They hadn't given me the video, but I did establish contact and they were happy with their money. My invisible quarry had thirty-five grand in used hundreds. I had five pieces of original evidence and had passed off the bills as unmarked. The stage was set for the big buy. So far so good. But the worst mistake you can make is underestimating your enemy.

I took out my lighter with a quick slight of hand. I started a flame under the fragment of film and hoped, from wherever my business buddies were watching, that they didn't see me smile.

Of course I didn't burn my recently acquired merchandise. No, *that* negative had been returned to its envelope and was tucked safely in the breast pocket of my coat.

I was burning a different negative, one taken last summer. Two women laughed and clutched each other as an automatic timer caught them kissing in a tent underneath giant redwoods. I brought the negative along as a dramatic gesture to an invisible audience.

As the flames melted the plastic, the negative image of the two women extruded; their heads became little dots on the end of long figures that vanished into a toxic puff of smoke. It was time to go to the movies.

CHAPTER SIX

LATE SHOW

The Castro Theatre, the gay temple in the gay neighborhood in the gay mecca of the world, was brimming with the Festival audience. I had never gone to the movies with a gun. The concealed weapon was lethal secret hidden from everyone else. Mona was off getting popcorn and I had that ego-inflated, serotonin-boosted high of someone who had just thrown thirty-five grand over a parapet and scored the first point in the bigger gig. It was the kind of chemical brew that could lead to mistakes. Mona Marie had a sparkle in her eye that could go both ways. Somehow I was in the driver's seat, with no idea of where I wanted to go. I took a deep breath and looked around.

Hollywood Babylonia, Mission Alhambra, call it what you will, the place was decked out with paintings of faux gardens, forty feet high. The Mighty Wurlitzer was already throbbing, risen from its pit, as it had done seven nights a week, three hundred and sixty-five days a year for as many years as anyone could remember. Both sides of the stage were graced with a Gibson Girl cameo portrait; done in pale oil paint, the women had vague smiles and flowers in their big hair.

It was one big merry-go-round of faux effects until the lights darkened and the show started. The Castro had a new sound system, but, I thought, shifting on the lumpy cushion, you could tell the seats were original.

The house was sold out. Fourteen hundred and fifty people roamed the aisles, searching out friends, finding seats. I opened up the program and found the index of directors and their work. *Jason Jeeters Jones, Pale Refuge, page 48.*

PALE REFUGEE

We are very happy to be presenting a documentary-diary from first time director Jason Jeeters Jones. From his upbringing in the Ozarks, his family's trek across the great suburban malls, into the arms of Martel, the raw story of his life, hustling, drug addiction, prison, and return to his rural roots, is a journey you will never forget. Townsfolk and drifters, from Rib 'n Rack waitress, Shauna Delight to farmers in the neighborhood whose sexual practices are hardly mundane, *Pale Refugee* is the documentation of a farming community and a compelling relationship. *Vanity Fair* critic A. Sapphire Poore lauds *Pale Refugee:* "A compelling story from the forgotten realms of America. From shit to shepherd, the survival saga of one tough piece of trailer trash is an American epic of the twentieth century, with Jason Jeeters Jones as the queer Paul Bunyan and Martel as his darling companion."

I looked up at the picture of who I assumed to be Jason Jeeters. He was a huge man, a big white man who made it through a state prison with most of his jaw and nose intact. He was bending over an electric guitar in what looked like a wrenching gut spasm. His ballooning biceps stretched the ribbing on his T-shirt sleeves. He'd been out of prison long enough to grow his hair, which hung in tangled raggedy clumps to his shoulders. Two goats, considerably better groomed, looked at the camera from between a split in Jason Jeeter's massive thighs. Their round eyes, so close together they nearly crossed, had the strange goatish pupil, an iris split up the middle. A little black fringe of bangs had been combed between their floppy white ears. Someone had put rhinestone collars around their necks. Kimilar Jones was just visible in the background, posing on a stepladder, draping herself in a fleece creation on the aluminum rungs. You could see her big teeth flashing from twenty feet. Slimy divorce cases indeed.

I stood up to let two people pass in the row. I perused the crowd and didn't see Kimilar or her brother anywhere. Waiting for Mona, I looked above my head at the big tented ceiling. The two-story fluted chandelier, looked like a hand grenade. I wondered who screwed in all those lightbulbs.

"You can meet everyone you know at the popcorn line, including half of Margo's campaigners." Mona's voice was like butter, smooth, rich; her wrists were thin with birdlike bones. Her dark, shingled bangs brushed against the rims of her red glasses. A small golden cross at the base of her throat bounced between delicate clavicle bones. Mona slipped gracefully into the seat next to me. "We waged a ground war for voter turnout in the Richmond District. We must have done fifty thousand door hangers last weekend for Villanueva. Mayor Villanueva, Mayor of the Neighborhoods."

"Too bad about Market Street though. All the Los Angeles franchises."

"Politics, Emma. It was the trade-off. Watch all the playgrounds get fixed up."

"She's bucking the old-time Democrats."

"Saying we should keep the two-party system simply because it is working is like saying the *Titanic* voyage was a success because a few people survived on life rafts."

"You are no doubt quoting Aunt Rose."

"Aunt Rose quoting Eugene McCarthy. I grew up at her kitchen table, remember. I know all the rules of politics."

"Like what?"

"Never write anything down, rule number one."

"Could have saved a lot of politicians. Go on."

"Set aside time to flatter people." The little cross glittered at the base of Mona's throat. "I have seen Aunt Rose puff people up, never knew what hit 'em. Flattery is the easiest of the political arts, she used to tell us.

"I remember afternoons sitting around the kitchen table

after school with my two sisters, cousins and George, Rose's baby son. I can still see the pale pink chrysanthemums on the lime-green background on the oilskin tablecloth. And the plastic rice spoons, the little ceramic rests. The tea and cookies.

"Aunt Rose would be checking our homework, doing the dishes, listening to the radio newscasts, and reading five newspapers in three languages. "Always be the first with good news," she'd say, picking up the phone and bringing someone up to date. She'd be shamelessly collecting debts while doing the dishes. Of course I didn't realize what was going on at the time. But Rose's involvement has made me interested in government, has made me believe in electoral politics."

"You'll go far, Mona," I said into the steady, dark eyes behind the red rimmed glasses.

"Except I'm an electrical inspector, not a politician." Mona had turned in her seat and was speaking extra-earnestly. "Not that I don't shamelessly collect debts. But there are people who can make a difference. We have to believe in democracy."

"It's a nice sentiment, but even before term limits the politicos were trading jobs between themselves. Without term limits it's even worse. Now there's not a chance in hell an actual public servant could make a go of it, not without the millions it takes to mount a campaign. So where's Villanueva getting hers?"

Mona's eyes went flatter, slid away under those lids and back again. "We're all doin' what we can." I looked down at her fingers, delicate, dancing fingertips played with the Film Festival catalogue. "Hey, know how many lightbulbs there are in that big pineapple? The Castro Theatre used to be in my district." She pointed to the chandelier with her free hand; balanced above the crowd the lamp looked like a huge silver dreidel. "One hundred and thirty light-bulbs. My chief had me check every connection personally. Ever since the Alhambra burned down. A lot of these old palaces have wiring that have been mainly a mouse meal for the last sixty years."

"So what kind of shape is the Castro in, anyway?"

"I did an inspection on this building not too long ago." Mona arranged her blazer behind her on the seat, some kind of soft material brushing my shoulder; turning around she popped a kernel into her mouth, chewed gracefully. "They say those Gibson girls keep all the bulbs burning long after their dark date. And when the house lights fade, if you watch closely, their eyes slide towards each other."

"I'll watch out for that one."

"The popcorn people say a lot of things, but the hard reality is that bringing the wiring up to code in this place cost them a fucking fortune."

A crashing major G chord boomed through the theatre, the Mighty Wurlitzer moved up an octave; the back of the organist became especially animated, his feet and hands working all the pedals and stops. Mona's hand slipped back into mine as easily as a pair of needle nose pliers. Her hand, like a small bird, came to rest in mine.

"I did a lot of hours here, cut them a lot of slack on the timing. The place is such a big antique. I'm glad the whole thing is up to code. I think there was a variance for an extension cord up in the balcony for some of the lighting instruments. The place was built as a silent movie theatre, but the original screen and proscenium is back there. Except for what the seats do to your ass, the place is as safe as the triplexes over on Geary. But they don't have any ghosts over there."

"Ghosts?"

"The house manager did like to talk. Maybe he filled my head with too many ideas. Maybe I saw things I didn't see. I put in a lot of hours, and the lighting can be pretty dramatic, especially when you're all alone here. I saw things, heard things, things that couldn't exactly be explained by the electrical code."

"Like what?"

"Remember Mel Novikoff? You know, the guy who turned the Castro into a rep house, saved it from triplexing?"

"Yeah."

"When he died they say all the doors and the windows upstairs in the mezzanine flew open. The Castro sign blew a fuse and the letters went out for five minutes. People working concessions heard footsteps on the stairs, footsteps without feet."

"The Castro has soul."

"And lost souls. If you believe the popcorn people, the Castro is a virtual haunted hotel. Let's see, there's a lady in blue, and a child who always sits in the same seat in the balcony. But, those long skinny windows in the mezzanine would let in any kind of noise that bounces off Twin Peaks. Noises come into the theatre, seemingly from nowhere. I've spent enough time in here to know. You should go back behind the screen. There's another screen there—and a whole golden proscenium. Another castle, two feet deep. Behind there you can hear pile drivers and car wrecks. The whole neighborhood seems to reverberate through the boards of this old place. The velocity of the fog coming through Twin Peaks is enough to shake all the glass panes in the leaded windows. Sounds like a xylophone. Spooky, but not unexplainable." Mona Marie's little hands landed back in her lap, folded complacently.

"You don't believe in ghosts, Mona?"

"I believe in human imagination. And electricity. They used to think that was magic too. Until Ben Franklin flew his kite."

"Ben Franklin," I murmured, thinking about the many times I had seen the inventor's cheeks, powdered them extra white. "So you never saw anything you couldn't account for? All voltage, wattage, and ambient noise?"

"Sure, I saw something. But seeing isn't believing."

"You're such a rationalist. What did you see, Mona?"

"It was nothing, really."

"Mona, give."

"Why?"

"Because I'm curious as hell, Mona."

"Okay, okay. I'll tell you." But Mona was looking at the ceiling. I found myself admiring the line of her chin, the straight shininess of her ebony hair, the way she had to search for the moment that rocked her world. "It's something I haven't really thought about. But just keep it mum, okay? Besides, I don't want any rumors going around about the Castro. While fire dangers in theatres are a real threat, a panicked crowd can be the most significant factor in loss of life—"

"Yeah, yeah, yeah. What did you see, Mona?"

"The people in concessions had been needling me about this supposedly spooky fire hazard. Spook citing, ha ha ha."

"And you saw it."

"I didn't see anything, Emma. It's all done with mirrors, no smoke."

"What happened, exactly?"

"Okay, okay. I forgot you work for a lawyer. There was that one time I left my tools behind the curtain. Actually, it was just about a year ago. December. You know how you go into a matinee and afterward when you leave it seems so dark, like you've lost a whole day or something? They'd been doing remodeling after the earthquake and the place had been closed for a few weeks, so they took the opportunity to bring some of the electrical up to code. They were in a hurry to get it done for the Christmas season. All the construction was finished, the ceiling had been repainted, the place was pretty as a palace, as a present. Everyone had gone home kinda early, the holiday season and all that. I finished my last inspection, pretty much alone in the place. My last day on the job; the Castro was ready to reopen. I remember I came outside. The marquee looked all bright white, they were putting up the big plastic letters. *The Women* was happening the next day. Stores had been offering Rosalind Russell shoes in size sixteen for the evening, you know. Christmas in the Castro. I had my own holiday stuff to get together and in the rush I had forgotten my tools. Who knows, maybe I wasn't ready to leave the Castro. My district became Pacific Heights. Don't know how many gourmet kitchens with indirect lighting and appliance islands I can take anymore."

"And your last night at the Castro?"

"Okay, so I'd forgotten my tools and I had to get back inside. Tod, the house manager had the keys, he was letting me out when I told him. Fine, he opened the door, but he wouldn't come in with me. He just turned the key and said, 'Be my guest.' Now, usually the guy accompanied me everywhere, he was the house manager, right? But he wouldn't go in. I thought maybe the guy was ribbing me, you know? I called him a chicken and he invited me to come back tomorrow. Suddenly it wasn't so funny. But, hell, I needed my tools and I'm hardly superstitious. I thought maybe Tod was just giving me a good rib. So I went in by myself." She took a deep breath. "No doors flew open. No footsteps. I opened the door to the theatre, kind of giving a quick look to my right and my left, you know? The chandelier was glowing that dark red cherry color, just like it is now. There were no ladies in blue or laughing children. I was almost laughing myself as I looked over all the rows of seats toward the stage, where my toolbox was sitting." She bit her lip for a split second. "That's when I saw it." She squinted her eyes and looked toward the stage again. "And man, I did see it. Just like they'd all said. The flaming seat." She rubbed the side of her mouth with a paper napkin, hard.

"The flaming seat?"

"Yeah." The easy laugh faltered for a second, the corner of her mouth was bright red where she had smeared her lipstick with the napkin. "Yep! Right in front of the orchestra pit. Third row, center aisle, just like they'd said." She shrugged her shoulders, her blouse moved against her skin with a whispery sound. "Flames. One of the chairs was on fucking fire."

"Flames?"

"Yeah, you know, those yellow tongues that make a whole lot of heat and can roast an auditorium or cause a stampede in ten seconds? Flames, just shooting up from one of the red velvet seats in the Castro Theatre."

"What did you do?"

"Honey, I'm an electrical inspector. There was only one thing to do. Inspect. I went down the aisle to see what was happening."

"And?"

"No smoke. No flames. As I came closer I didn't see anything. No fire. No smoke, heat, sparks. Center aisle, third row, middle seat was just so much velvet and creaking springs."

"What did you do then?"

"I could hardly issue a complaint, could I?"

"Did you pick up your tools?"

"No, Emma, I didn't. I went back outside and told Tod I changed my mind. I came back the next day and sat with a whole lot of faux Rosalind Russells and picked my tools up from Tod's office."

"San Francisco, open your golden gates
San Francisco, I'm coming homeeeeee....."

The palace throbbed until the final strains were sung. The big hand grenade chandelier faded and the eyes of the Gibson Girls seemed to slide towards each other from either side of the stage and the memory of Mona's encounter with the paranormal faded away into the magic of Cinescope.

CHAPTER
SEVEN

UNDER
THE MARQUEE

"Great flick."
"Highly derivative."

Mona and I walked up the patterned carpet out into the lobby letting the critiques of others hit the carpet like old pennies.

"Well cast, except for the cousin."

Outside, wind and mist was a slap in the face; the marquee was bright as a new moon and a thousand faces lined up for the Late-late Show outside. Fourteen hundred and fifty people out, and fourteen hundred and fifty people in.

A small group clustered around a blonde dinosaur of a man. As he looked around him, flashbulbs started popping. It must have been Jason Jeeters Jones, the filmmaker.

Even larger than he appeared in the photo, Jason was wearing old blue jeans and a plaid shirt, sleeves torn off and raggedy on the edges. Men, three deep, gathered around him, staring at his overly developed arms. The brute appeal was selling well at the Castro.

I could make out the barbwire and rose tattoo on his arm. A small constellation of pimples gathered around his neck. Perhaps Jason took steroids to achieve his hyper-muscularity. I could smell his body odor as we made our way out the door. Mona and I walked directly behind his back. Jason was holding forth. I pulled closer to listen.

"Do you mind hanging out here for a moment?" I asked Mona. "I have to do a little professional eavesdropping."

"Not at all," Mona replied, and I pulled her hand through the crowd which boiled under the bright lights of the marquee. A. Sapphire Poore barreled through the crowd, a photographer behind her. In a flash they were joined by two reporters, their press passes slung around their necks, and a gaffer with a portable lighting pole. Cameras started whirring and clicking as Sapphire asked her questions.

"How do you like the Film Festival, Mr. Jones?"

Jason beamed. "Every visitor to San Francisco must feel like they done made it to heaven. But I never thought it would be like this. Could be like this. The Castro Theatre is a palace and my film is goin' to be shown there. The Castro neighborhood is like coming home. It kinda makes you realize you never had a home before."

"What did you think of tonight's film, Mr. Jeeters?"

"Thay called it a prison film." The big man laughed derisively. "But something was missing. It made me think that whoever made that film ain't never done time in the school detention, if you get my meanin'. Ya know, ya gotta be there. Ya gotta spend seven years looking atta chain link fence topped with razor wire and bein' scanned by nine gun towers. Nothin' against the other guy or anything. I mean, the technical values were really good and there was a lot of good information. I hope, I really hope, that *Pale Refugee* gets across just what prison life feels like to the people who are in it."

"You have been lauded for the cinematography, particularly the landscapes in Pale Refugee—"

"You gotta know bein' locked up to appreciate bein' free, lady. There's nothing like the look of an open field to me," Jeeters' basso voice was smooth and had a visible effect on the curious gathered around him. "Nothin' like it."

A stunning young man had joined Jason by his side. He looked as delicate as Jason did robust. He wore Bermuda shorts and a Madras shirt, a droll cherub in fraternity garb. It had to be Martel.

"Hi, honey, how ya' doin'?" Martel looked at Jason lovingly.

"We'll go soon. I'm just gonna answer a few more questions," Jason reassured him. "Everybody, this is Martel, star of the film," he announced.

"Costar darling."

"Not according to the press release, hunny-bun," Jason beamed at him.

"Mr. Jeeters, is it true that you were a gang member in prison—" a print journalist piped up.

Suddenly everything changed. Jason's chin hardened into cement; his mouth narrowed. As his big barrel chest filled with air, Martel held on to his arm, looking as powerful as a flea.

"You gotta get the perception, man," Jason said after a pause. "It isn't *your world.* Let me tell you, there are guys in there, why, prison is not too much different than where they grew up. The straight timers, they're in for life. It don't matter too much to them what happens, you dig? You don't know people like that, in your lives with houses and roofs always been over your head. Look around here in front of the Castro. You see a lotta people sleepin' on the street and more every year. Watch my film. You'll see how I survived in prison. There's more of us in prison than there are in your college system. Yeah, I was a gang member. And that's all I'm going to tell you about it."

"Can I have your autograph?" A pencil and paper came Jason's way.

"Don't worry about it. Jason Jeeters gets a little excited about his gang history," Martel confided to the journalist in whispered tones. "You know, in the joint, they used to call him Eskimo Nigger."

"Uh—what does that mean, exactly?" the journalist asked.

Martel just snorted and rolled his eyes. "We wanted that to be the title, but the distributors said, *"Eskimo nigger? No, no, no!"* Martel laughed and turned back to Jason. "Now

honey, take me home please. I'm tired. Where are the girls?"
They both looked around at the crowd.

And then I saw her. Kimilar Jones stood in the shadow of
a big bottlebrush tree. She wasn't alone. I could see her
white boots. She was on tip toe and a taller woman was
holding her close, kissing her. Then the woman in overalls
bent Kimilar backwards, her mouth pressing harder and
harder against hers. Overalls was giving Kimilar a deep
throat kiss that was even taking *my* breath away.

"Is that her?" Sapphire pulled on Jason's shirt and pointed
to the pair in the shadows.

"Yeah! There she is! That's my sister!" he confirmed, ob-
serving the steamy kiss under the bushes. "Go for it, lil 'sis!"

"I *thought* so!" Sapphire snapped her fingers as her cam-
erawoman aimed at the bushes and flashed. The kiss
stopped. Kimilar's face shone in the darkness like a deer in
the headlights. Her blue eyes, lit up with the new-found
wattage of a female affair, flashed aquamarine. Her mouth
was red and swollen from being kissed. Overalls, laughing,
pulled the duck bill of her hat over eyes with one hand, hiding her face. Together they emerged from the shadows.

"And, Ms. Jones," Sapphire's voice took on the inter-
viewing tone again. The white lights suddenly hit Kimilar's
face, flooding away the rugged lines. She blushed as Sapphire stuck the mike near her big teeth. Kimilar looked like
she would like to bite it. "Your farm is actually the setting
for the film and you make some appearances."

"I just walk around in the background, really."

"How did you find the film this evening?" Sapphire continued.

"Well, let's see. I guess I didn't quite get the way the film
ended," Kimilar stated.

"Speak up!" Sapphire thrust the mike closer.

"Kimilar lives on a farm; it's a *cyclical* thing, she don'
know nothin' 'bout narrative," explained the film director.

"I know how your evening's going to end if you don't pay
more attention to Martel," Kimiliar warned her brother quietly. "Can we go home now?"

"And how are you finding San Francisco, and the Castro,

Ms. Jones?" Sapphire's microphone moved back into Kimilar's face. Kimilar turned around and shrugged her shoulders back at Overalls. "Whattamy supposed to say?" she asked. Overalls came up behind her. Slowly, methodically, her lips dove into the brown suede collar of Kimilar's jacket and travel down her neck. We all watched as Kimilar squirmed and her mouth dropped open for a minute. The microphone stood waiting; the crowd watched her.

"Okay, lady, I gotta statement for ya," Kimilar slapped her knee as the microphone returned. "I been one lesbian virgin for too long!"

The crowd roared in response. At this, Overalls tipped Kimilar over and their lips met again.

"Okay, okay. Let's go now girls," Jason had taken Martel's hand. "Hey, everybody, we gotta go now," Jason waved at the crowd. "Bye y'all."

"Bye-bye!" Martel chimed in, garnering a kiss from Sapphire Poore as he left.

I observed the strange pride of Martel, Jason, Kimilar, and Overalls as they regrouped and disappeared into the fog that hung on the edge of the Castro marquee. I tried hard not to applaud the performance as they disappeared. A. Sapphire Poore was scribbling furiously in a notebook, as her photographer packed up her equipment.

A noise by my shoulder took me elsewhere.

"It's been fun, Emma."

Mona stood there, a slightly puzzled look on her face. Her mouth moved towards mine. As much as the public kiss of Kimilar and Overalls had been dramatic, Mona's kiss was understated. I felt her bangs brush my chin as I felt a moist brush of lips. "I'll see *you* later," Mona promised and then, she too, walked away.

The crowds were lining up for the late-late show. I looked into the distance. Mona was but a thin shadow moving down Market Street. Why Mona, I thought, I never even saw you lick your lips.

Just on the other side of the Twin Peaks bar, caught between the glow of two street lamps, a small rag tag group huddled, passing things between them in the dark. A large figure was easy to recognize as Jason Jeeters Jones. The group was busy. Little things with which they were very careful, precious things in cellophane envelopes, were being passed back and forth.

Time to take the brother back to the farm, Kimilar. I looked around for the fluffy flaxen hair, the white boots, the lanky figure of Overalls, but the two women were nowhere to be seen. The crowds pressed behind me, a stretch limo pulled up in front of the theatre, and the street throbbed with blue and white neon.

All in all, a most successful evening. Thirty-five grand was being counted out by happy blackmailers and I had a nice cache of evidence. Jason Jeeters was doing drugs, and maybe that had been Kimilar stepping into the stretch limo. The two Gibson girls *did* seem to look at one another when the house lights went down, and nobody noticed the lump under my arm. Mona's lips had been relaxed, not asking for anything, just there for the ride, with only a hint of promise.

So far, so good.

Everyone, absolutely everyone, was satisfied.

CHAPTER EIGHT

AMATEUR PHOTOGRAPHY

Unblinking the security system, I stuck my foot in it, anticipating Mink's need to escape. The front switch had been wired so that a light in each room came on when I turned it on. I never had to come home to a dark house again. Before I went to bed I reactivated the system. Let a thousand power stations churn, I was in for the night.

I tried mollifying Mink's dignity with high protein kibbles. She quickly nosed a few kernels off the dish and ate them from the floor. Friend was still outside. I called her to no avail. Some damp eave was cozier, no doubt. I made myself an avocado sandwich and went into my office. I couldn't wait to examine the evidence: two envelopes, a contact print, a ransom note, and the main merchandise, the negative itself.

Clearing away a space on my workbench I covered it with white paper. A fresh pair of cotton gloves fitted tightly. I turned on the high intensity light, with a magnifying glass, the kind modern ladies use nowadays to finish their needlepoint or to build bombs. The small radio was tuned in to KQED.

"In Villanueva's strongholds, mainly Noe Valley, the Haight, the Castro, and Upper Market, Calvin Smith never got less than twenty-four percent. In those same precincts

69

Shay never got more than twenty-one percent and sunk as low as five percent.

"Treblain Steward, a Castro District resident, said, 'The questions that Villanueva supporters ask themselves is, "Should I vote for Villanueva or Calvin Smith?" Not, "Should I vote for Shay or Smith?"

"Darlene Fell, co-director of the Human Rights Campaign Fund, a national gay political lobbying group, said, 'People are still looking for a sign Villanueva can win. They are asking "Who will be the best mayor for San Francisco?" And the answer that keeps coming back from the lesbian and gay, Latino and other neighborhood associations is Villanueva can get the job done and bring people together. San Francisco's gay and lesbian population accounts for an estimated fifteen to twenty percent of the electorate and is a block which turns out on Election Day.'"

I pulled open a small drawer with the fingerprint powder, dragon dust, in its two-ounce jar. This particular batch had been bought in Chinatown. The fine red powder was ground from the dried sap of the dragon tree. It was cheaper in price than the photocopier toner powder that I'd previously used and it didn't destroy a spot of landfill for a few thousand years.

I loved fingerprints. As a child I coated my fingers with Elmer's glue. I remembered peeling the delicate dried tissue off my fingertip, looking at the exact duplicate of that intricate pattern that only belonged to me. I knew even then that fingerprints were the ultimate identification, they still beat out DNA evidence in any courtroom.

I examined the envelopes, contact print, and ransom note under the light to check for any visible fingerprints or identifying marks. The envelopes were standard letter size, both the same. Pristine, unfolded. A random blue pattern printed inside rendered them opaque. These types of envelopes are available in thousands of drugstores and discount malls in California.

There was nothing inside them and no markings of interest. If I had a DNA lab, maybe I could analyze his spit. The only way to check for prints on paper is to fumigate them, a

time consuming method which I wanted to get out of the
way before I started on the more interesting negative.

I brought out two tubes of Superglue and an old metal
cookie jar with a tight fitting lid. I squeezed the contents of
the two tubes onto a piece of aluminum foil. Contrary to all
manufacturer's instructions I put Superglue inside of the air-
tight cookie jar along with the evidence. Envelopes, ransom
note with the collaged headlines would all be fumigated
with whatever emanated from the Superglue. If I was lucky,
in about twelve hours the fingerprints would be described in
a white deposit on the paper. I pushed the lid on tightly and
sealed the edges with black electrical tape. Superglue was
good for a lot of things, including headaches to die from. I
turned the exhaust fan on to high and examined exhibit A,
the main attraction.

The negative was my biggest hope for a fingerprint. The
hard shiny emulsion surface was the ultimate in delicacy,
and the closest thing to glass. If I could lift a print off the neg
it would save me twelve hours waiting for latent prints to develop. If the guy had any previous record, I could find him
through my own sources. I pointed the light in various directions on the surface. No print was visible. I brought out
the dragon dust.

I fluffed out the bristles of a fine sable brush; twirling it
between my palms I dipped the tip of the brush into the powder. The negative lay on the counter, the incomplete square;
its corner had been snipped off in a straight line with something like an Exact-o knife.

Softer than Frances's lightest touch, the bristles moved
over the negative, leaving their trail of powder behind.
Bingo. There, up in the right hand corner, a thumbprint. Toward the core it had two long ridges and a short ridge. In the
center the lines converged into a characteristic concentric
circle. A whorl. My quarry was a whorl. About thirty-five
percent of all fingerprints are whorls. That narrowed things
down to about twenty million U.S. citizens.

I moved the powder in the direction of the flow of the
print. I brushed some strains of powder away and laid a piece
of tape over the pattern. The fragment of fingerprint lifted

cleanly off the surface as I pressed the tape onto an index card. There. I looked at the mark of my quarry. A fingerprint written in the sweat of a cameraman without a conscience. I had been holding my breath for minutes. There it was.

Unless someone has a record, it's very difficult to locate a person who doesn't have a previous relationship with the victim. Serial killers, contract hits, you have to locate the guy first and use whatever you've got as evidence later. Of course, any evidence I had was going to be rendered inadmissable by my workshop tampering, but I was hardly worried. The glow powder would nail him, if only I could find him. The only value of this negative was going to be historical, indicating where he had been and who had let him get there.

I looked at the negative fragment through the magnifying lens and read its contents in reverse. I tried not to focus on the victim, a real woman, with hips that rolled, and breasts uncontrolled, a woman without a silk scarf to hide the neckline while she talked turkey in the back room. I didn't want to see her in this way, the most relevant thing about this woman in this moment *was* her nakedness.

It was time to make a positive from the negative. A positive which I could carry around in my wallet, a totally benign print.

I cleaned a pane of glass until its surface squeaked and slid the negative of the hotel room scene underneath it. I screwed the clamps tighter and adjusted the lens of the camera, watching the scene take shape on the viewer. Broadcasting beautifully onto the tray of the enlarger, I brought the negative into focus. The hotel room was as readable as a map. The detail was astounding. I could read the campaign posters in windows of houses on the hill. I could see the nick on the edge of the windowsill, the rose petals printed on curtains that blew on foggy breeze. The curving backbone of a gargoyle was attached by a big piece of angle iron to a decorative terrace outside the window.

A set dresser couldn't have done it better. An open handbag and a newspaper on the dresser which might yield a date. The dinosaur-shaped humps of particular hills lurking on the San Francisco skyline. Two feet of Twin Peaks tower were just visible; that placed the room north and east of the tower. The view was almost as good as a map.

The lower edge of the window showed the curving gable of a brownstone roof, somehow familiar. A clock radio to tell what time it was, and a corner of sheet with a black dot the size of a spider. Many present features. All except the figure of the man who made her arch in ecstasy on the rented sheets.

I turned on the red safety light and brought out a piece of photographic paper. Turning on the enlarger I started to expose the image. As the light poured through the negative, I moved my hands quickly through the air, over the body of the woman in the hotel room. Dodging her image out, the hotel room scene was re-created minus its startling star.

Who was the co-star?

While the print was drying I cleaned the workbench, putting the original into the safe. I called Rose and left a message. "I'll be by in the morning to pick up the info."

It was, in fact, already early that morning. When I got the print out of the dryer, I was seized with a yawn that threatened to split my head in two. My eyes were blurry and full of sand. My hands were shaking, but I didn't care. I would have my hotel room. I would find my man. All I needed was a magnifying glass.

I walked past the browning avocado sandwich, the photographic print warm in my hands. I drifted out of the office, reminding myself to lock the office door. I found myself in the bedroom. The room was slightly spinning as I lay down on the old coverlet. Little patterns of aprons started turning in front of my eyes. I coughed and took the magnifying glass, peering at one of the prints. Wow. The little bug on the sheet was just as I'd hoped it'd be. Two initials. *"MH."* Mark Hopkins. Bingo.

Eyelids sagging, I saw it was five-thirty. Dawn in an hour. I pulled the lid off of the Superglue chamber. The blackmail note and the envelope appeared unaffected by the fumes. I put the lid back on as I soaked a few cotton balls in sodium hydroxide. That would speed up the process and the toxicity. I would have to keep an eye on it.

I would also need Willie's expense money for the handmaidens.

I would be just that much closer to him and I would find my quarry's foxhole. Closing my eyes I saw the white lobby of the Mark Hopkins Hotel. I should arrive at noon, just at checkout time, when the pink collar workers cleaned the rooms.

I hit the pillow, just for a moment, automatically pulling Grandmother's wedding ring quilt up over my long tired body. Such a long day, from commuter plane to queer cinema, from cash to kiss. I closed my eyes just for a moment.

The quilt seemed to jump into the picture, wedding rings spinning, wheels of ancient aprons and cast-off housecoats twirled, the kaleidoscope cleared and I saw her. The politician was making love on my grandmother's quilt. She was wearing my grandmother's apron and she was making love to me. She was going to tell me an important secret. A state secret. She was going to invite me into the territory between her thighs. But she didn't speak English when she used the telephone. What was she going to do with the telephone? I woke up and grabbed the real receiver, hard plastic in my hand, squinting against the harsh light of day.

"You die, you slimy bitch!" snarled across the line, the noise, low and animal, with a grim delight found my ears and entered my head. The deadbeat dentist had found me.

I put the phone down and looked at the plastic device, a techno design that Frances had picked out for the bedroom. The dentist must have been pretty clever to get the number. Must have had some connections that put him beyond the root canal crowd.

I was unlisted. I had been unlisted for years. The sour smell of sweat, photo developer, and dragon dust emerged as I threw off Granny's quilt. I'd have to change my phone number. *What are you? Some kind of animal?*

A wind from the Valley was tossing the City one of those hot San Francisco fall days. The print had blown off the bed. Had I opened the window? I stood up, hanging onto my head, the razor sharp San Francisco sunlight pierced my optic nerve.

The office door was open. I locked it, sliding the dead bolt home with finality. I could hear the hungry exhaust fan still sucking up the fumes. I hadn't smelled a thing. The avocado sandwich was a relic. On the other side of the front door the Saturday paper waited, a slim thing.

The headlines, however, were huge. The Defense of Marriage Act has passed by a huge margin in the Senate. Eighty four members voted for it. Among the fourteen who voted against it were California's Democratic Senators, Dianne Feinstein and Barbara Boxer. And now the Defense of Marriage Act would go to the White House.

A studio enlargement featured a cute group in a convertible. Calvin Smith had bought a new Porsche from a local dealership in Bayview Hunter's Point. After church he gave some of the local Christian ladies the ride of their lives. Laughter and hands holding on to veils and feathers as they laughed like girls in Calvin Smith's convertible. On the back page a box mentioned that a synagogue had been burned down in Holland. *Holland.*

I took my toothbrush into the shower and began the cleaning ritual, head to toe, washing my hair three times and leaving the conditioner on while I scrubbed my knees, ankles, and in between each toe. When I was done I took a deep breath and reached for the hot knob and turned it off. In a sudden freezing burst I was coated in an icy sheet that cleared my lungs and woke me up enough for the next long, hard day.

HUM OF A
DISTANT VACUUM

The avocado sandwich landed in the garbage, green slime over coffee grounds. I made a cup of coffee with one eye and read the paper with the other. Things were bad on the international front: skinheads on the rise in ex-east Germany. The Japanese Diet had passed strict security measures limiting the freedom of information in that country. Closer to home the mayoral race was getting nasty. Antonio Shay was smearing the memory of former state comptroller, the deceased Joseph Villanueva.

Calvin Smith took to the high road, vowing to dump the police chief and Roberta Stanko, executive director of the problem-plagued Housing Authority. However he lost some goodwill when he invited the Rev. Gene Bumpkin to share the stage with him. Rev. Bumpkin was fired from the Human Rights Commission by Shay when the minister said publicly that sodomites were an "abomination" and should be stoned to death.

Villanueva had commitments from Hollywood friends. Among the entrepreneurs who were ready to wage war on the homeless of Market Street were a Planet Hollywood, and Blues Brothers Bar, Madame Tussauds, and Music World Rock Videos were all lined up to sweep away the cardboard shelters and take in the tourist dollars.

I turned the page. The number of women on death row in the United States had just topped two hundred. Bridgeways had just won a design award. Bridgeways, the high-profile pilot drug rehabilitation program built on the Bay, looked like an Italian village. One of Supervisor Villanueva's biggest successes, it was hailed as a model program; several documentaries had given Bridgeways, and Villanueva, national notoriety. A statewide, even a national model was discussed. A fluffy coiffed First Lady, a former college roommate of Supervisor Villanueva, made a special appearance at the christening. She flew into San Francisco with fifty suitcases in Hairforce One and kept the society editors and the gadflies buzzing for weeks.

Straight for Life, everybody called it, as the rehabilitants worked their way from selling Christmas trees to the kitchen of the Bridgeways restaurant. Captive votes? Page two mentioned that school lunches were going to be cut despite a veto promised by President Collin. Let them eat cake. They probably did at Bridgeways, even if it was the customer leftovers.

Local astrologer Joan Green predicted an easy win for Smith, saying, "The City will be a showcase for the rest of the nation with many diversified groups coming together creating a new social order. The chart of Calvin Smith shows a powerful Pluto positively aspected, ensuring dynamic leadership ability. Just like Charlemagne!" Who was she voting for? Oh, she would never say. But she did wink in the photo.

Charlemagne vs the Madonna of the Neighborhoods! I threw out the paper, finished my coffee, rinsed the cup, grabbed the keys, a big raincoat, and the enlarged print, and made it out the door. The weatherman had been right.

A moment of summer in November; the dark and foggy night was a million months behind me. One corner had a surprising burst of color. Four reverse cactus dahlias, burning pinwheels in the garden, had managed to open up in the warm air. I snipped them at the root with my shears. It was 11:45 when I backed Romea out of the garage.

I was far, far behind schedule. That was why I almost for-

got about calling Willie's answering service for my backup.
I delivered the message precisely as instructed to the bored,
distracted male voice on the line. And I added a special note
to Willie to alert the former Mrs. Harlan Knapp. Deadbeat
Dad was turning into a stalker, the kind of loose cannon that
just might be loaded.

The Mark Hopkins Hotel is located on the top of Nob
Hill. A pink and green palace built with Gold Rush money,
torn down by an earthquake and rebuilt and recently acquired by the Intercontinental Hotel Chain. The old place
has a cheerier ambience than its dark marble sisters on the
other three corners.

The interior was tropical colonial and so was the employment arrangement. Looked like a lot of Central Americans
who were keeping their eyes downcast as they cruised underneath the curving fronds of potted palm delivering
drinks. They didn't take orders. They just put the drinks
down and it never mattered if they ever spoke English. The
white uniforms and half bows fit right in with the bamboo
furniture and pedestal tables, walls of fake latticework.
Right at home on the banana farm, it made me want to reach
out and swat a mosquito.

Noon. The hustle and bustle of checkout and not a hotel
dick in sight. Where to start? Where would the picture
have been taken? Some kind of suite. Swanky hotels sometimes offer a second elevator, a special diplomat service.
Or a penthouse suite. Or something completely ordinary.
Certainly there would be a house dick. I looked around and
didn't see anyone who fit the bill.

I thought back to the photo and wandered past the bell-
boys, who hovered at attention, their gleaming brass carts
loaded with luggage and hangered clothes. At the front desk
people were busy paying their bills, opening wallets, the
screeching of dot matrix printers churning out invoices.
Keys cast over the counter by Japanese men in black and
gray, shopping bags from Saks Fifth Avenue and Gumps
filled with last-minute presents. The braying of Midwestern
tourists in matching red nylon jackets, caught their attention.

I picked up a brochure and checked out the various possibilities in suites.

The Honeymoon Suite, the Penthouse Suite, the Jacuzzi Suite on the fifteenth floor, and the Junior Suite. The Junior Suite was low-end, nothing like the big windows and gargoyle in the photograph. I opened the brochure and looked at the photographs of the rooms. The black marble bedside table was standard in each room. Was that a house dick peering around the side of a rickshaw flower cart?

I sidled up close to the elevator and took a discreet look at my black-and-white enlargement of the room. There, just beyond the stripe of woodwork. Marble on the walls. The Jacuzzi Suite. Fifteenth floor.

The elevator was opening. I stepped through the tide of fur, Chanel, and Armani into a deep mahogany box. I pressed fourteen. There was no fifteen.

The doors opened onto the fourteenth floor. Signs informed me that rooms 1501 and 1502 were located to the right and left of me via two separate stairways. The hallway of the fourteenth floor was empty, but three doors were open. I heard bright Spanish chatter coming from the rooms. I thought about the view of Twin Peaks and checked my bearings out of the windows on each floor, imagining just which room would have the view I was looking for. I turned right. North. Hurrying down the hallway I found the stairway to the first Jacuzzi Suite of the fifteenth floor.

The location within the hotel would make this an ideal suite for diplomats, politicians, or executives in sensitive positions. The small curving stairway would make for easy security, monitoring the comings and goings from the suite. The hired simian types could lounge in a little alcove in the hallway, in between the Ming vases full of orchids.

I heard a door closing behind me and a sharper voice, barking orders. I hurried up the stairway. Lines indicating a door on the right-hand wall were just visible, except for a small utilitarian handle. Ahead of me was the door to the suite, a solid walnut job, inlaid in ebony stripes. It was open. I stepped into the Jacuzzi Suite.

I could have been stepping into the blackmailer's photo-

graph, only now it was in color. The quilted bedspread of
leaves was silvery gray in color. The carpeting was a soft
green. The curtains had tiny flowers, and the view was the
northerly view of Twin Peaks. Outside the window I saw the
back of a gargoyle. A hefty piece of angle iron held him fast
to the concrete balcony. The bolts were as big as my fist.

To the right of the bed I could just see into a marble room.
I turned back to the bed. That was the bed. That was the
exact view. I brought out the photograph again. I focused on
the hills outside, the angles of the buildings. I could just see
the curving brownstone roof of the Pacific Club jutting out
from the windowsill. A club, a private club, that didn't admit
women. Oh, this was the place all right. That had been the
moment that was worth all the money, and the lens, I
thought, turning around, the lens would be located directly
behind me.

The wall featured a painting of two turn-of-the-century
beauties enjoying a Roman bath together. And just underneath the picture frame, hard to see from any farther than six
inches, a slight change in the pattern of the surface of the
wall. It looked as if there had once been a hole in the wall.

"What you doing here?" A small brown woman stared at
me indignantly, without fear. Strong arms gripped a big
stainless steel cart full of clean folded towels, and a cornu-
copia of shampoo and body lotion samples. She had a mustache and wore a sparkling white nylon uniform and worn
white mules on her feet. She snorted at me, the muscles in
her arms tensing on the cart. "You guest here? You get out
now, you!" Her face swelled, became red. "I call security!"

"Wait, I don't want any trouble."

"I call security! I call!" she said, but her voice was a
slight degree softer. Slowly I reached for my wallet.

"I just wanted to take a look around the Jacuzzi Suite,
that's all."

"I don't know nothing." She wasn't talking about security
anymore.

"I just want some information on somebody else who
might have been interested in this room."

"I dunno the guests, lady, I just clean the rooms."

"How long have you worked here?"

"Two years." Her eyes squinted as she looked at my wallet. She could have licked her lips and I wouldn't have been surprised.

I held out the picture of Ben Franklin in front of her, nice, kindly Ben.

She grabbed for the C note, but I held it just away from her fingers. Her little black eyes became hard, there were little glimmers of thought there. What she would tell, what she could tell. I had my woman all right. I had my link.

"The Jacuzzi Suite here is very popular," she began. The gargoyle perched outside the window turned up its nose at the traffic fumes. "They like the white tiles. The guests."

"I didn't come here to talk about the tiles."

"What you wanna know, lady?" She stuffed her hands in her pockets.

"I've been told that someone had a particular interest in the Jacuzzi Suite. Four, five, maybe only a few weeks ago. He wanted to stay here. Hang out here. Someone had to give him entrance. I know that he came to this particular room." Ben Franklin made his sudden appearance, again and her fingers literally twitched in her pockets.

"Maybe, maybe not. I could get in big trouble." She sniffed and put her hands back on the handle of the cart. "No hundred dollar worth it, lady."

"How about three hundred?"

Fingers relaxed, eyes traveled over the glittering gems of plastic shampoo bottles loaded on the cart. The little mouth traveled sideways and returned to the middle.

"Five hundred." Two black raisin eyes met mine for the first time.

"I don't want to rent the room, I just want some information." I turned around and started toward the door. She let me get halfway there before she stopped me.

"You no tell?"

"No. I won't tell anyone. You won't lose your job on account of me."

"You won't tell nobody. You swear."

"Yeah."

"Gimme." She held out her hand, her chin hardened under tight lips and her little black eyes looking frightened.

"Last, uh, July, I think." Her fingers twitched.

"You were approached by a man, who just wanted to look around."

"Yeah, he wanna look, some guy, I dunno."

"I want a description, okay? No bullshit."

"A little guy," she said. "White skin, he sorta sweat, sick, like. He don't breathe so good. He don't give me no name. He want to see everything. He want to be alone in the room. He's strong. A strong man. I don't know what he do. I come in. Everything okay. He don't do nothing bad. I don't see no problem, so when he come back I let him in again. He was an okay guy, you know? Lots of people here have money, do things. I don't know. I don't understand nothin', lady. I just do my work."

"Tell me more about what he looked like. Big, small? Here? Here?" I held up my hand.

"There," she shrugged. She held worn hands at shoulder height, the glint of fear was still in her eyes. "I toll you. He little guy, maybe five feet two, three. He come up maybe to your shoulder, lady. He wear jacket, light brown, pants, black, I think. Oh, yeah. Strong man. Big. Big arms. Walk like a monkey, you know. Banana arms. Strong. He have no hair on top. He kinda bald. Oh, yeah, he have a big bandage on his chin, you know, like he cut hisself shaving."

The bandaid was an old disguise saw; it is a detail that can be instantly altered. So far all I had was a balding, white, five foot two or three male.

Noise picked up in the hallway.

"Did he have a high forehead, low forehead, mannerisms?"

"I dunno, lady. He chew on toothpick. Yeah, it wasn't like he was a regular Mark Hopkins customer."

"He was not so big. Strong."

"You said he came back."

"Came back?"

"Yeah, you said you let him back in again."

Her lips pressed shut and her chin tried desperately to grow into her neck.

"Look, I don't want you to lose your job. But you have to come clean about just exactly what happened."

"Yeah, once. I let him back in. That's all. Now I gotta go, lady. You let me clean." She turned her back.

"Another hundred dollars to let me into that closet at the top of the stairs?"

"The—the linen closet?" the hooded eyes opened slightly. She was scared. Bingo again. I held out the hundred-dollar bill.

"Why not?" I said. "You let him in there, didn't you?"

No reply.

"You knew he was here for a whole weekend, didn't you—"

"Listen, lady, I dunno who you are, I dunno who he is. I let a man into a room. I let you into a room. Now you get outta hotel or else."

Two Bens gave her pause. "Ten minutes," she said. "I dunno why everybody is so interested in that closet!" She shook her head and lumbered down the circular stairway. But she knew. She knew there had been a high security weekend. And she was the only person who could identify the face of my blackmailer. A little strong guy, just like Napoleon.

I thought I heard the turning of tumblers, the click of a latch. A voice was barking orders down a hallway at what must have been a few other maids. At the foot of the stairs the squeaking of cart wheels, the opening and closing of the service elevator at the end of the hallway. The overwhelming whine of a vacuum cleaner, a whine which would continue for ten minutes, and blanketed all noise.

I moved down the stairs to the thin door; she had left the door to the linen closet slightly ajar for me. Inside the closet, pink and white towels lined the shelves of the linen cabinet. A trolley with a cloth bag for the dirty laundry took up most of the room in the closet and hid the wall behind it. I pulled it aside, and examined the Sheetrock. Four tiny slits scored the plasterboard, describing an opening big enough for a small person to crawl into. A doorway carefully and almost invisibly cut out of the wall.

I put my penknife in the slit and pulled. A thin square of Sheetrock tilted toward me. My man had been quite a neat little carpenter. The maintenance staff of the Mark Hopkins wouldn't make a door like this, unfinished. And on the back of the sheetrock a tiny hole where he could have inserted a screw, or something to pull it closed behind him.

There it was, the darkened hole, the lair of my photographer. I bent down on all fours and crawled inside. The vacuum whining became muted. I stood up and felt above me. A ventilator shaft made a hollow sound. Crouching, I flashed my torch around the space. I saw that the Mark Hopkins was in no way plumb. The wall studs were not flush, and everything looked crooked. Wiring wandered in and out of the studs threatening to trip or strangle me.

The narrow corridor would extend maybe twelve feet into the darkness, I guessed. Galvanized piping elbowed into the darkness at the end of the stretch. That would be the Jacuzzi plumbing. Bending down again I inserted the tip of the corkscrew from the knife into the sheetrock door. I pulled it closed, just like I was the animal who had holed up in there.

Immediately the air felt fetid, and damp. Dark walls closed in on me. I stood up, careful not to hit my head on the ventilator shafts over me. I stilled my heart as my eyes searched the wall for a pinprick of light. Fingers moving over the surface I found the little pimple of caulking material. As I picked away at it, a chip fell out and a shaft of light burst into the hole. I bent down, keeping my spine along the wall, imagining having a miniature video camera in my hand. I myself would be a sneak and creep device, moving closer, squinting, bringing the scene on the silver bed into focus. The thigh with the tiny crinkle of cellulite would even be visible through his telephoto lens. And the invisible partner who may have been kneeling at the foot of the bed.

If the VIP was VIP enough there would have been an advance security detail which would have checked for any bugs. Mr. Baldy must have checked into his sweatbox, and, when the guest was out of the room, drilled the hole. I took out a Kleenex and wiped my brow. Tiny lights danced in front of my eyes. They told me to breathe where there wasn't any air.

I turned the flashlight back on instead. Trying to relax and slow my breathing, I searched the crevices at the base of the studs. I tried not to imagine what it was like to cage yourself in this sweatbox to get a beaver shot. I moved the light around. Mr. Baldy, what kind of animal are you? I brought the light closer to a hole drilled in the stud to facilitate the electrical wiring to a wall sconce on the other side. A burr on the edge of the hole, a chip of wood that was too bright. That wasn't a burr at all. It was a toothpick. His toothpick.

The narrow sides seemed to close in on me; I could smell his smell. I could feel his breath in the fetid little coffin where he lived for a weekend. My stomach turned and the vacuum was silenced. I picked the toothpick up with a Kleenex, folded it, and put it in my pocket, got back on my hands and knees and backed out of the hole. As I left, my shoulders coming out of the hole last, I took a last look at the little pinprick of light. I wondered if anyone would notice the hole on the other side of the wall. The next advance security detail for a VIP. And they would wonder, just like I did, who had booked this room on the night in question. But that, I thought, brushing off the accumulated lint and sawdust off of my black jeans, wouldn't be so very difficult to find out.

I replaced the little square of Sheetrock, making it appear nearly as invisible as I had found it. I shoved the laundry trolley up against it, turned out the light, and closed the closet door. It locked automatically. I moved noiselessly down the stairs. No one strolled the fourteenth floor. I took the stairway route down, the long concrete stairway full of air and light. I flew downward, gulping air, leather wings flapping, falling through space and a time far away from that dark and ugly hole.

CHAPTER TEN

TRIP
TO NOWHERE

I had always wanted to go to Paris. Frances and I had made many vacation plans, but I had never understood that vacations were a fantasy for physicians. The plans were the reality. All Frances needed to do was talk about vacations. And now she was gone. Slimy divorce work; if I wasn't doing it one way I was doing it another.

I walked through Union Square looking at the imported shoes gleaming like diamonds in the window. Leather gloves that looked like something a murderer would wear. Just around the corner, three blocks west, would be Unique UniGlobe, according to the numbers, a downscale address. I passed the window of Paradise Travel Options and saw the posters of faraway places. The third world for sale. Bubbles tickling your toes, a margarita cooling your throat, a lovely picture when you didn't know there was cyanide on the Pacific Reef.

The receptionists, efficient Mercuries, via strands of cables and bleached smiles, will speed you on your way. And thus the hordes were delivered around the earth, delivered out of their stuff boxes and into the sea. If the wholesale destruction of the culture you visit doesn't give you indigestion, then the food will.

Unique UniGlobe Tours wasn't there to service the work-weary with glossy packages. The sidewalks were polka-dotted with blackened bubble gum and puke. Just a few blocks from Macy's I saw a big plastic sign with do-it-yourself plastic lettering which had been slid onto a grid. Unique UniGlobe Tours, whose *s* was slipping off its track. It looked like a one-way ticket to hell, but so did the neighborhood.

The windows were plastered with signs. PHOTOCOPIES FIVE CENTS and cut-rate tickets on airlines you never would want to hear of again. If you believed them, you could tour the world on a dime. A dime was what paid the rent on UniGlobe Unique Tours.

A fan listlessly moved the air while one harried clerk was harassed by an octopus of phone cords. Bells jangled and it sounded like he was speaking Spanish, Portuguese, and English all at the same time. Mid-forties, sweating under a white nylon shirt, strands of black hair stretched across his pate like greasy streamers. He had a turtle face, a sharp nose curved over a tight v-shaped mouth; pieces of information reluctantly emerged from the tiny coral lips.

His eyes, nestled in folds of flesh as deep as shopping bags, never looked at me, although I knew he had registered my presence. A sitting area featured two folding chairs and a stand ashtray between them, tilting at approximately the angle of the Tower of Pisa. A large, half chewed cigar butt rested in the narrow trough. Click. The man behind the desk hung up one of the phones and wiped his brow. He still didn't raise his eyes above the counter.

There weren't any travel folders, glossy beaches, white women in red bikinis on black sand beaches, the usual tit and butt show. There were just a lot of xeroxed flyers with a badly reproduced cartoon airplane flying across the top. In some of the prints the cartoon had been distorted, after several generations there was only a gruesome leer stretching across the cockpit. Click, and a machine gun spatter of what sounded like Portuguese. I sat down and looked at where the linoleum didn't quite cover the concrete floor to the right of my left foot. Click. Shuffle. Grunt.

The place made you want to travel but provided no image of destination.

Two teenagers, tall and short came inside the store and looked around, baggy pants, baseball caps, and a rectangle of white paper in hand. Counterman's eyes flickered briefly over the counter as they read the copy machine directions. They lifted the lid and put the rectangle of paper on the glass.

"Don't slam the lid!" Counterman yelled, barely skipping a beat in Spanish.

The boys did a little invisible footwork and their mouths tightened a degree as one of them very, very slowly closed the lid. The shorter one popped the nickel, and we all watched the green light pass back and forth making the copy. When the copy was made the taller one extracted it and the original. His protruding eyes searched the copy for defects as his hand rested on the still raised lid of the copy machine.

"'Don't slam the goddamn lid!" Counterman yelled.

The jawbone of the tall one worked now, his long strong hand poised on the lid. His eyes never leaving Counterman, he brought the lid down with a final crash. The beige plastic lid split along one end and he smiled.

"'Get the fuck outta here!" Counterman yelled, climbed off his stool, short legs ponderously bringing him to the front of the counter. He had nothing on adolescent footwork; in seconds they were long gone.

"See what they did! See what they did!" he said to no one in particular, racing over to the machine, running outside. What was out there brought him back in even faster. "Goddamn bastards," he said, and his fingers found what was left of his hair. Returning behind the counter, he took his seat and looked up at me. "What do you want?"

"A trip to Hawaii."

"'We don't do vacations. We just sell surplus airline seats. You want packages you go down the street to Paradise Tours, Unions Square, lady."

"How about information?" I smiled and held up the hundred dollar note. The man looked at the note. He looked at Ben Franklin's face as if the Founding Father was an old chiseler who never did anybody any good. He went for a snatch and I pulled my hand back.

"Tell me who has post office box number four seventy-five."

"You're not a cop." He looked me up and down, and found the idea unbelievable. "Are you?"

"Please," I took out Ben Franklin and passed it over to the man. The bill disappeared into a drawer.

"Okay, okay, I'll get you the name." His eyes narrowed. I should have known. Plane tickets, post office boxes, and everything else would be for sale. "George C. Welter." The man opened up a book. "Want to know when he opened the box?" he asked cooperatively.

"Yeah, I'd like to know that."

His hand bent toward me, palm outstretched, fingers curled toward his chest, Esperanto for "Give." I brought out a twenty and watched it disappear into his pants pocket.

"He opened his box four weeks ago and closed it yesterday. He came in regular, once a week. But he's leaving town." He grinned; he could have won a Miss American contest. The phone rang and he picked it up. Speaking a mixture of Spanish and English, he managed to ignore me as if I had discovered the secret of invisibility. *"Lo siento, lo siento,"* and he hung up. The smile came back.

"Do you have a forwarding address?"

"Lady . . ." The man leaned forward so close I could count the strands left on his head. "Like I *said*, he's leaving the country." He leaned back and smiled, clasping his hands behind his head and showing off the absorbent qualities of nylon. There weren't any. Sweat was collecting above his belt. He leered something truly terrifying.

"How much?"

"Two fifty."

Two hundred and fifty. "Out of my range." I turned and started walking. It was all of Kimilar's retainer and I didn't want to spend it all in one place.

"Two," I heard from behind me.

"One fifty," he tried again.

"Okay. One fifty. Now, tell me about George Welter's

travel plans. I want a copy of the ticket," I said, holding tight on to Ben.

"You sold this ticket two weeks ago Monday," I said after he handed me the Xerox of the ticket and I handed him the money.

"Yeah, I sell that ticket."

"The name on here is George Welter."

Varis International was written across the top. I peered closely at the restrictions. "Unique UniGlobe Tours." I squinted at the Xerox, at the codes and dates stamped which would have originally been in red carbon ink. "These are open tickets for the whole month of November," I said.

"Yeah, I know."

"Why would he use an alias?"

"You're asking me?"

"The man who bought the ticket, do you remember what he looked like? Long hair, sandy blonde? Close set eyes?" I brought out Ben again.

"Open ticket to Rio. Yeah, yeah, I remember a guy who bought one of those tickets. Sure. We had a special surplus seat sale on Varis because of the riots in Rio and that kidnapping off the beach. Yeah. I sell a guy this ticket. He don't know when he wants to go, I make a special effort to get him an open ticket. But the sale ends end of November."

"And what are the reservation procedures?"

"Well, he can just show up at the gate anytime, standby. There's three flights a week. Monday, Wednesday, Sunday. Flight leaves at eight P.M. Arrives at nine. Gives you an extra day on the beach."

"Can you describe this man?"

"Yeah, let me think." He eyed the bill. I put it down on the counter between us. "About six feet tall, two hundred and fifty pounds, a big guy. Brown hair, long sideburns, big square chin, a nose that had been broken a few million times. Don't tell him I put you onto him, okay?"

Keeping my hand on the bill I pulled out the picture of Kimilar's ex-boyfriend behind a Jeep Grand Cherokee. It was impossible to tell how tall he was, but the Jeep gave a sense of scale. You wouldn't want to meet him in a dark alley, except that he looked for all the world like a guy who just enjoyed camping.

"That's not the guy." He waved his hand and put it in his pocket, holding the bills close.

"What do you mean?"

"That's not the guy." The bill slid out from under the heel of my hand. "I'm telling you."

"It wasn't this guy'" I asked.

"You deaf? It wasn't this guy. The other guy had darker hair. His face was totally different. This guy has a fat face. His nose is like a baby's. All in one piece, see. The guy who bought the ticket had a long skinny face and a nose that looked like it had been personally braided by Joe Lewis. Believe me, it wasn't this guy."

"I believe you," I said, believing him. "Did he give you any kind of forwarding address?"

"No. The ticket is as good as cash."

"How did he buy it?"

"He bought it with cash."

The phone rang behind him and the man picked it up. Reaching over the counter I pushed down the button, disconnecting the line. "He bought an open ticket with cash. Didn't that seem a little odd to you?" Lights started blinking on the phones.

"Lady." He batted my hand away with a controlled violence and lifted up a receiver. "*You* seem odd to me. Now get outta my face, okay?"

Walking outside, I thought about what I could and couldn't do for Kimiliar. And what it was going to cost her to find out why someone was impersonating her ex-boyfriend, a man whose nose had been braided by Joe Lewis.

Now I *really* wanted to go to Paris.

TOURIST
ATTRACTION

I had just enough time to head out to the ocean before I constructed my money parcel. Driving along the waterfront I wondered at its future.

If Antonio Shay remained mayor the area would sport the Mission Bay project, or, if Calvin Smith were elected, a new baseball stadium, surrounded by acres of concrete parking lot would be Villanueva's Market Street redecorated by Warner Brothers. Villanueva's face was shining from phone poles as I drove past Bridgeways. The facility looked exactly like an Italian village built yesterday. Welcoming wreaths were still tacked to the door, in honor of the First Lady's visit. On the second and third stories, rows of dark glass windows, lined with antiqued shutters, afforded the recovering addicts a decent view from their rooms. Flower boxes lined up under the windows proclaimed white geraniums and the logo of the establishment.

Past Pier 39 and the rackety tourist trade, up Clement Street, around to the Presidio, I was glad to be under the arching eucalyptus trees, fragrant in the warm air. Point Lobos Avenue brought me to the Cliff House.

Busloads of weary tourists crawled out of double-decker buses, cameras and cardigans slung around drooping shoulders. Behind the Cliff House restaurant gulls screeched and dive bombed into the ocean. Three tourist buses pulled up and farted as they parked, scattering red winged ravens who roamed the gutters. Video cameras and diaper bags. Squirrels scampered away from a flock of elderly men and women in red nylon jackets with the words "Roto-Kill" silk-screened on the back. It was the Mark Hopkins crowd, the same tourist group I had seen at the hotel. Now they huddled together against the chill of the fog.

I pulled on a large, loose-fitting overcoat raincoat, fitted a flowered silk scarf over my head, knotting it behind my neck, letting the tails trail down under the collar along my back. A big pair of dark glasses nearly obliterated my features. I draped the cord of a cheap Kodak instamatic over my head and drifted past the crowd. The concrete stairs looked just as shabby as the evening before, but the Park Service concession was open and the Mechanical Museum cranked out a hurdy-gurdy tune, lending a false gaiety to the scene. I waited until the deck was full of tourists before I went to the phone booth and pretended to make a call.

Turning around, I pretended to speak into the receiver. The blackmailers undoubtedly could have followed my progress from the phone booth up the hill from just about anywhere along the coastline. The construction site was roped off. The Sutro Gardens was up behind a bluff. But the Camera Obscura telephone was most clearly visible from the shrubby hillsides or the condominiums built on the former Playland.

The phone booth itself was accessible from the concrete stairs or an asphalt path which led to a historical marker and a second parking lot. I hung up the receiver and walked over to one of a line of pay telescopes. Plugging a quarter into the slot, I fitted my eye to the brass ring and saw darkness until the ticking started. I trained the scope out to the sea. I heard the voice of a Park Service ranger behind me. "Seals quickly dwindled in number as hunters sold their whiskers for pipe cleaners and marketed their genitalia as aphrodisiacs."

I swung the telescope along the surface of the rocks to where the public pets of San Francisco basked. Their skin

slicked like India rubber, they wallowed, turning themselves over in the sun and braying. I let the lens rove over
their bodies. At the edge of the foaming ocean a lone black-
slicked surfer clutched a board and paddled into the horizon. The waters off San Francisco were far too cold and
treacherous to be hospitable except to the hardiest of
surfers. Most surfers would prefer Mexico, Hawaii, or least
southern California. Riding this part of the Pacific was
treacherous at best. I watched the surfer paddle out farther
and farther, stifling a vicarious anxiety. The world was full
of foolhardy people climbing hundred-story sheer-faced
buildings, jumping from bridges attached to elastic cords,
and floating around in hot air balloons and calling it fun.
The surfer had turned around now, aiming the board toward
shore.

As the Roto-Kill tourists approached, I swung the telescope behind me and peered between the nylon jackets and
up the hill to Sutro Heights. I read the brown informational
signs, white letters in focus announcing when the park
opened and closed. Farther to the right, the blades of one of
the big old wooden windmills cranked to the hum of the
Coast Highway traffic. I squinted into the treetops and
along the rows and rows of blank gray condominium windows. At one end condominiums were still under construction and I could finally make out a large grinning clown
face, toppled on its side, what had once been a ticket booth.
Aiming the telescope higher, above the construction dig, I
found a cliff top snag and a curved beak. A peregrine fal-
con? A flap of wings and I attempted to move the scope further on its pedestal until it wouldn't go any further. Tourists
didn't usually look behind them.

But I did, pushing through the flocks, retracing my steps
back up the stairway. Everyone else was going down. I
pushed up against the stream of people, past the cable car
tea towels and Golden Gate ashtrays out onto the Great
Highway. I crossed the Highway at Louie's and found the
parking lot and the path which led up to Sutro Gardens.

Last night's moonlight walk was today's crowded urban
park. Accompanied by a group of five on mountain bikes,

superseded by two joggers, one with baby cart, I hiked up the asphalt to where the grove of cypress stood. The grass was drying up, and the benches with sun had sitters, the benches without sun had pigeons.

Mounting the same steps as I had the night before, I reached the top and walked to the viewing platform. Now, in the daylight, benign groups of tourists milled about, looking around them curiously, wondering what they were supposed to see.

"Sutro named this balcony '*Dolce Far Niente*' or 'Sweet Nothing'" a park ranger was saying. Sweet nothing was right. I looked at the parapet wall. I looked again to where the light had flashed. Middle section, fourth diagonal. I squinted. I sprinted. I jumped directly over the stone wall, causing only a few heads to turn, and made my way to the spot where I had thrown the thirty-five grand the evening before. It was gone. *Niente*.

"It took eleven gardeners and thousands of dollars to keep the twenty acre park groomed and blooming, but Sutro's folly did not stop there."

Nor did mine. I was crawling on my hands and knees through Sutro's botanical bonanza finding only the traces of tourism underneath the wall. Gum wrappers, plastic bags of peanuts, Coke cans, and a condom. Further on the debris thinned out. A carpet of eucalyptus buttons was hard on knees and hands; my palms held the imprints of thorny stars. Keeping my eye on the place where I had thrown the money, I backed up to a tree trunk. The thick green Yankee points, an impenetrable shrub, had grown up around it. I had thrown the money to the right of the tree trunk. I moved carefully along the ground to the other side of the tree. There was a small nest of cigarette butts there, underneath a blanket of pine twigs. I smiled and picked one up with a penknife.

Benson and Hedges, smoked right down to the filter and stubbed out so hard that what was left of the butt was nearly broken in two. Five little butts, bent into a V shape. I never saw a glowing light. He would know just when to put it out. Cellular phone and no footprints on the carpet of needles and buttons that Mr. Sutro had sown. Benson and Hedges. The oral boys. Toothpicks and cigarettes while they waited. Cameras for eyes and poison-pen letters for tongues.

The fog was starting to close in; I wiped my dampening face with my sleeve and buttoned my coat up tighter. As I left the park, I placed the flaming dahlias by Diana's feet. I was one step closer.

CHAPTER TWELVE

THE
BIG JACK

The workroom smelled like a fake fingernail factory ready to explode. I opened the window in the living room. In the office I turned the exhaust fan on high before I opened the sealed barrel. The papers rested inside, strangely translucent. Yes. Something was there. Fingerprints on the papers. White swirls on white, just like snowflakes, no two alike. I blew on them gently. Perfect little replicas, a history of how the paper was handled. Carefully, again and again. Thumb, thumb, thumb. Bingo! I couldn't wait to call Rose. I turned out the lights and turned on the red light again.

I slid the print under the stand camera arrangement and made a photograph of the whiter than white thumbprints. As the film was developing I fed the cats, inside and out. I phoned Varis Airlines and found out that the George Welter ticket had, as yet, not been used. I made myself a dinner of tortillas, cheese, and salad, right out of the refrigerator and onto the burner. The television screen offered a kinetic art, almost soothing when on mute. I finished the quesadilla and picked up the phone to call Rose.

"Baynetta Security Services," a professional voiced lilted. Rose had a secretary now; I kept forgetting; we were all that grown-up.

"It's Emma, put me onto Rose, please."

I waited for the connection. Rose's voice came on the line after a few moments. "Sorry, Emma, I had to get rid of some suits."

"Very uptown, Rose."

"I've got a whole portfolio of Villanueva cuttings. It fills a few phone books and somebody had to stay up and feed the laser printer."

"You bought the store, stop whining."

"I'm not whining."

"I have some more business and a favor."

"Start with the business. I figure that's the bit that pays."

"I need an operative to watch the San Francisco International Terminal on Monday, possibly through the end of the month."

"Long time.' Rose checked the calendar. "Pricey."

I gave her the details of the open ticket, the gates used by Varis Airlines. "The bill will be taken care of," I said.

"Oh, Lord, it's not another one of Carla's creepy friends again, is it, Emma?"

I said nothing. Rose always knew if a case involved Carla. Carla was Rose's ex. Carla was a lot of people's ex, but she was first and foremost Rose's ex.

"Well, don't sleep with this one this time Emma. It would just make your calluses thicker."

"Spare the sermon and just get somebody out at the airport, okay? Here's the favor. How would you feel about backing me up tonight around ten-thirty, eleven o'clock?"

"A little sneak and creep would do me good." I could hear her smiling. Rose, paralyzed from the waist down, wheelchair bound, had a four-wheel-drive jeep that took her places most people could never go. "Where exactly might this gig be?"

"Across from the Cliff House. Sutro Heights, on or just below the pediment, the terrace called Sweet Nothing."

"What's coming down?"

"A blackmail gig. A two-man job. I've got bogus bills that aren't going to make them happy. I'm expecting backup, but I might just want some backup to the backup."

"Careful, girlfriend. Sounds like a limb to me."

"Trouble pays."

"Okay. We'll go out and have a drink at one of the Irish bars, after it all works out." Rose agreed to wait in the parking lot, bringing an old beat-up van with a lot of beadwork in the windshield. The homeless hippy camping in the park routine had worked well. Rose's sweet New Age patter was totally opaque and she'd memorized all the nonsense rhymes from *Alice in Wonderland*. The third round of *Jabberwocky* kept the cops off her case; they would just figure it was best to leave her there for the night and not haul her in on a 10-31, psycho.

"Here's the big favor part. I've got some fingerprints," I said. "If, for some reason, these guys don't show I'm hoping we can track them down that way."

"Fingerprints, Emma, you're asking something now."

"I said it was a favor."

"So you know Blake is back?" Rose asked.

"Yeah." I knew Rose's young prodigy had been recently set free. "He was released last week; I read it in the papers."

"Okay, so you know what you're asking. He's on parole, Emma."

"I'm hoping everything goes completely according to plan. I just wanted to know if there was a possibility."

"Baynetta Security, land of many possibilities. We'll talk about it later. See you at the parking lot, girlfriend." Rose hung up the phone.

The film had finished developing; turning on the red light I made a ten-inch enlargement of each of my blackmailer's thumbprints. And, as I became more familiar with the pattern of ridges and deltas, it looked like it was only one thumb, the right one.

I dried the prints with the hair dryer and listened to the radio. Politicians were revealing a whole lot of nasty secrets about each other and nobody could remember the days when the buses ran on time. The Bay Area Rapid Transit would not run to the airport. Villanueva came out in support of national identity cards. But she went to a gang member funeral, a gay wedding, a bat mitzvah, and a Japanese tea ceremony with board members of the French/American school.

I put a piece of tracing paper over each of the prints and traced the pattern of the thumbprints in black. Then I rephotographed them, reducing them to their original size. Nice prints, complete little life histories. The life line has just gotten a little shorter, I thought, bisected by the river, as in, up the.

Next I set about replicating 35,000 dollars in sixty-pound bond paper. One piece of bond paper would net me three pieces of paper the size of a dollar bill. A ream of paper would net me three 500 stacks that would have approximately the same weight, and size as cash.

When I was finished, it all fit neatly into a Gladstone bag, a cheap overnight affair Frances used to take with her on trips. I would be glad to throw it over a balcony on its last trip. A soft, rhythmic sound caught my attention. Mink was batting a hundred; the balled up piece of paper, the exact size of a hundred-dollar bill, sped across the floor again and again. Mink, jealous as all cats are, would appropriate anything that held my attention for more than a few minutes. In her expert paws, a counterfeit bill acquired a life of its own; her claws were deep into the paper now.

I got the gun out of the safe, checked all the chambers and the safety, and put it in my shoulder holster. The leather handles of the Gladstone bag fit into my palm like an old handshake; Mink looked briefly at me and then redirected her attention toward the counterfeit bill.

I decided to see it as a good omen. The spirit of the cat would be with me when I took the bag of false goods to Sutro Gardens tonight. Mink had spun the bill into the kitchen, ice hockey or just a great huntress. I wondered about the moment when my business partners opened the bag and found sixty-pound bond instead of money. But Willie had taken care of all that, I told myself. Mink had bared her fangs now and the fluffy paper ball lay lifeless on the floor, shredded.

CHAPTER THIRTEEN

ROAD KILL

I reached the ocean at ten-thirty. I parked on the highway immediately across from the parking lot of Sutro Heights. I walked down to the telephone booth and got the call. I hiked back up the concrete and crossed the highway just like the night before. I passed Romea, yellow, the color of caution. I liked the thought of Rose, camped down in the parking lot.

Criminals. I knew what happened when people didn't follow through on the goods. Willie's client would be flashed in a supermarket tabloid. I could wind up shot in the head, backed up against a tree with a big wad of stage money stuffed down my throat. So what was there to get so excited about? My heart was pounding. Backup, Willie, you promised.

I walked across the parking lot and wondered at any number of eyes I couldn't see in the darkness, any number of eyes trained on me. Raccoons, rats, and a pack of wolves. A lone gray cat and a Tac squad. A few friendly boys from the sneak and creep division would keep me safe once I delivered a whole lot of bond paper to a couple of blackmailers. And if I die before I wake I pray the coroner won't make any really bad jokes over my corpse. The cororer never hears anyone's prayers.

There wasn't a sound as I walked through the parking lot.

The lumps of paper were heavy in my coat pocket, almost as heavy as the lump in my stomach. Suddenly I was feeling very alone. And I really didn't want to be.

I stopped at the beginning of the path. For some reason I thought about Kimilar. I saw her on the farm, hauling bags of feed and hoisting bales of hay into the barn. Shearing goats and holing up for the winter, smoking a pipe, and, as Kimilar said, taking a book. For some reason that kept my feet moving through the muck, up the asphalt, damp branches clawing at my coat. The grove was empty, misty moving up the asphalt. I turned right and walked slowly toward the parapet.

I stood again in the center. One of Sutro's used up statues.

With nothing but a bundle of white paper and a pistol. Target practice for anyone with a grudge or just out on the rampage. I had to get out of the moonlight. I had to get out of the park. I had to get the video. Come on, boys, blink your lights. Let me throw my bundle and the cops can close in. Blink the goddamn fucking light. Or did you find the glow powder on Bennie's face?

Come on, boys, you wished on a star. I'll make my toss. Carry moonbeams home in a jar. Come on, blink, dammit. Just a little button, a flasher button on the side of an aluminum flashlight. Just a little twitch of the finger. Three times, remember.

Fuck. Dark all around me. The stone walls seemed to close in. The grove beyond seemed endless. Trees assumed twisted shapes, hands on hips. A seagull with insomnia screeched and chuckled. An especially large wave crashed on the shore at the bottom of the cliff. Somewhere on the other side of the world those waves were warm and people were riding them on polystyrene boards, a special vacation package, the one you're never going to take. I checked my watch.

Nothing. No sale. No deal. Sorry, lady, we have no bananas, no video, no executions today. We saw the cops. We found the fluorescent powder. *Dolce Niente* and after twenty minutes my feet were falling asleep and I was shivering with cold and the certainty of failure. I had a whorl of fingerprint and I'd lost the thirty-five grand. The gig was up.

I prepared to walk down to the parking lot where I expected my backup to say good-bye. Or whatever backup does when it never backed anything up. The paper was a damp lump by my side. Blink, blink, blink. What? Little lights swam in front of my eyes, the result of looking too long and hard into the darkness while holding my breath.

I was hallucinating now. I would leave. Twenty-five minutes. Thirty. There was no light. Gig's up, Emma. Give it up. You blew it. And yet something drew me to the parapet wall.

I looked again to where the light had flashed the night before. Middle section, fourth diagonal. The tree trunk with the big shrub skirt. Where someone had lain in wait. Somebody who sucked on cigarettes and tamped them out, grinding the burning stubs into the ground, breaking the Benson and Hedges filters in half.

I peered at the shadow of the tree. A stately lady, petticoats of shrubs, branches for arms, lifting up the delicate skirts to show, what? The thirty-five grand? Something that might make Smokey the Bear angry? Face it, Emma, you blew it. Yet surely there was a patch of inky darkness, a hole, a pit in the slight silvery edges of leaves.

I sprung over the wall and went into a crouch. I held my breath, the ocean crashed behind me, the tide was coming in and it was almost possible to be inconspicuous rustling through the bushes. I felt the garden around me; would there be a SWAT team ready to close in? I kept close to the ground, inching forward, keeping my head lower than my shoulders, developing a stiff cramp, but not wanting to get down on all fours, a position from which it would be too difficult to defend myself.

I found what seemed to be the tree where I had thrown the money the night before. Its twisted shape was in the form of a question mark. I felt around on the ground. Something sharp—no warm, the surprise of it made me jump back. A cigarette butt. Crushed deeply, twisted in two as it was stubbed out. I pulled my hand away and peered through the bushes, my eyes adjusting to the darkness. There. On the

edge of the spill of shadow on the lawn. The little grove a darkened curtain and a long lump lying on the ground. I didn't
want to cross the open field, but I did so anyway. And it was
more than a lump. It was a Coca-Cola can with a hand attached to it. A hand that wouldn't let go. A hand attached to
a body lying on its stomach under the Monterey pines.

A horrible stench rolled up from the earth, warm, fetid,
steaming, it filled my nostrils, and I instinctively backed
away, then put my scarf up to my nose and came closer.

Mr. Coca-Cola's hand was warm and slack. He had no
pulse. Someone had gone very carefully through his coat,
his pockets were turned inside out, and someone had even
unbuttoned his shirt to the waist. And stopped.

I touched the ground to make sure it was there; I held my
breath and listened like I had never listened before. Listening for a murderer that might be near, just behind the tree
trunk, back by the shrubs under the wall. Mr. Coca-Cola was
fresh, warm. Someone could be waiting and watching. I
heard nothing and let my eyes roam over the corpse before
me.

No signs of struggle. No branches broken. I listened again
to the night and sent up a silent prayer to that faraway statue
on the other side of the park. Who had killed him? The
searcher who stopped his search at the waist? Diana, the
huntress, help me out here. I turned on my flashlight on
micro. For some reason, the visuals helped me to overcome
the stench; Mr. Coca-Cola's sphincter's had relaxed and the
contents of his bladder and bowels had been lost underneath
that custom-cut suit. Nothing below the waist.

The hand that clutched the Coca-Cola was pale, threads
of dark hairs on knuckles. The skin on the back of his hand
was loosed, stretched, lined with veins. There was a flashy
insignia ring on a thin finger, a large diamond with two long
bevel-cut diamonds on either side and an initial I couldn't
make out. The cuff of his shirt was clean, starched. From the
look of it, he could have put it on for this occasion. Excuse
me, ma'am, may I have the pleasure of this blackmail with
you?

I looked along the length of his gray flannel arm to a full

head of dark hair that didn't match the lined, aged look on
his hands. There was no exit wound that I could see, but a
pool of blood was slowly leaking out from underneath his
chest. A noise. A rustle in the bushes. I turned off the light
and saw the shape of a cat race across the floor of the muddy
grove and disappear into the fog.

Time to meet my business partner. I grasped the hair on
top of his head and pulled. It came off. A toupee which revealed a balding head and a few hairs struggling along the
top, flattened down by the toupee which had been riding
over it. There was no way around it now. I took the back of
Coca-Cola's collar in my gloved hand and hoisted the front
of his body up and shined the flashlight directly in his face.

He was a white man, about forty-five, maybe fifty, a horrible grin stretched across his lips. What was he expecting at
the moment of execution? Not this punch line. He must have
fallen face down in the mud, felled like a redwood. I guessti-
mated him at six feet tall and a hundred and sixty pounds of
pretty good shape.

He was not the man who had crouched in the hotel wall.
This guy was big. I looked at his fingers. He was a smoker.

I met his eyes, the blown pupils of death that didn't react
to my flashlight. Veins had burst inside his brain and filled
the rigid confines of his skull with blood, compressing the
brain and causing the pupils to blow. A long, thin nose
pointed to two generous, wide lips stiffening into a permanent grin. He had shaved recently and the sweet smell of his
aftershave mixed with the product of his bowels and my
own sweat, beginning to rise out of my leather jacket. Underneath his lip, most of Coca-Cola's jaw was missing.
Jesus, someone prowling Sutro Heights with a shotgun?

I gave another yank, pulling Coca-Cola's head up higher,
and found what I had expected. There. It had been done
close up and dirty, execution style. There was a gaping hole,
a star-shaped wound, raggedy, almost two inches across,
soot around the bullet hole and a long scarf of blood running
down his neck.

The hole itself was small. A small .22 caliber would do it
nicely. The bullet is too small to create an exit wound be-

cause it lacks the velocity to penetrate the bony skull. It just bounces back and forth within the skull causing hemorrhage and nearly instant death. Blood was dripping out of the neck wound onto the top of my hand. Warm polka dots that turned my stomach and still no negative. *Splunk!* I let his head drop back into the mud, wiped the back of my hand on the leaves.

I pulled his shoulder and rolled him over in the nest of twigs and did what I was paid to do. Opening the sharp edge of his double breasted jacket I slid my hands along the inside of his coat, the second person to invade the territory tonight. Nothing. No wallet. No car keys. No gun. *Dolce Niente.*

I took off one of my gloves and ran my naked fingers along the inside of his coat. A stiff breeze came up, providing olfactory relief. Down along the edge of the hem where the lining met the wool, where things could be hidden, trapped. Dammit, dammit. No negative. No money. I felt along the back of his pants where his pockets would be. No lumps of money, no wads of cash. Just the last bowel movement of Mr. Coca-Cola. The bigger gig was disgusting.

Before I said good-bye I picked up one of his paws. I dragged the limped fingers through his own blood. Then I grasped his thumb firmly and pressed it several times on a piece of white index paper. The hand fell back onto the ground with a soft thud, leaving me some pretty good prints. I waited but a second for them to dry in the moonlight and folded the paper and put it in my pocket.

I brought out the black light that would reveal the presence of any of the glow powder. I turned it on. The gruesome tableau glowed in a cold green light, a night-of-the-living-dead portrait with no special effects whatsoever. Mr. Coca-Cola lit up like a billboard and he was real.

Glow powder, on his suit, even on his smiling lips, on the grass, even on the trunk of the tree, where someone must have laid a hand at one point. I opened his suitcoat. The inside pocket was alive with fireflies, chemical powder, no cash. I replaced the toupee and rolled him back over into the grass in his original position. His body, sluggish, would soon be stiff. I walked away over the grass, saying good-bye to the soles of his feet. And I returned just as quickly. One of the soles of his shoes was ajar, skewed.

They were old, but well polished shoes. Old fashioned, elevator heels, multilayered in leather and wood. Only one little piece of rubber on the bottom. A piece that had been peeled off.

There was a mark on the leather, a knife blade perhaps, swiping through the shoe polish. Someone had pried open the heel of his shoe. I could see a small hollow in the heel of the shoe. About an inch deep, the three by three inch hollow would easily hold a miniaturized video. But the secret compartment was empty. I put my fingers inside just to make sure. All gone now.

Squish! The shapes of trees were merging in the grove. I crouched closer by the tree. The feet of Mr. Coca-Cola were lying at an angle to the ground, the result of my turning him over too quickly. Nobody fell like that.

A shadow moved slowly across the lawn, a low, crouching thing, one arm inside his jacket. Big square shoulders, bowlegged, crab walking from tree to tree. A figure that stopped when a cloud moved away from the moon and revealed Mr. Coca-Cola on his stomach. I drew my gun and waited. Nothing.

I pulled back behind another tree. Whoever it was wanted to be in a more advantageous position, preferably away from the source of his interest. The body. When the wind came up I took advantage of the cover sound to move back toward the wall and along behind the shrubs where I had a good view of the body and the entire grassy field, and, unless someone was on the wall directly behind me, I was safe.

I looked at my watch. I sat there for a half hour. I sat there until my butt went numb. I sat there until I was sure that whoever, or whatever, I had seen on that grassy field was nowhere around. Creeping along the wall whenever the wind came up I saw no one approaching the body. The figure must have been unrelated. There were houses just beyond the Diana statue. It was not impossible that someone might be walking through the park. That someone might

have seen the body and just walked away. Another drug
dealer.

I tried to keep my confidence level low, I didn't want to
make any mistakes as I made my way down to the parking
lot, to get into Romea and get on my way. Perhaps there was
a video floating around the world somewhere now. A horrible video that might or might not ever see the light of the
screen. Thirty-five grand had been picked off of my blackmailer after he had been cleanly executed. Thirty-five that
he really had no reason to carry around. Unless, of course,
he intended to walk away with the goods, double-crossing
his partner. It wasn't my kind of company and it wasn't my
kind of job anymore.

A small pop exploded into the night and I felt something
breeze by my cheek. A dull thud in the ground behind me
got my adrenalin pumping fast. I moved away from the
shooter, from the trajectory of the bullets. I backed away
like any animal, keeping out of the big open spaces, skirting
the edges until I could get on a switchback path that would
lead me to the parking lot and Romea in her darkened corner. A clickety-click made my heart stand still. He had a bicycle. There was only a steep cliff next to me. He had
thirty-five thousand dollars worth of motivation, a bicycle,
and about a hundred pounds of solid muscle over me.

I could hear the shifting of the derailleur on the edge of
the parking lot, where all of Willie's backup was supposed
to be waiting for me. I moved quietly, keeping low, the path
was dirt and gravel. The clickety-click stopped and a heavy
foot dragged along the gravel and only the sound of the
waves could be heard.

Waiting, the Gandhi method; the cat meowed. The trees
around me lurked, their inky low branches providing a lot of
cover off the path. I waited until the noise of the waves picked
up again and started climbing. I wanted a look at the enemy.

Then I saw him. Small, five foot four or five, and built
like a small utility building. Blond crew cut and black
sweatshirt, he walked in slow tight circles, an animal in a
cage but there were no bars to see. The bowlegged walk, the
ultra-developed torso set off bells in my head. Bubble boys.

Steroids and the attendant psychological profile. What did they call it in the Castro gyms? Roid rage. Muscle man with some bad side effects. He was looking from side to side, confused by the crashing of waves. He got on the bike and drifted down to the end of the parking lot. His foot dragged the gravel as he stopped and stood by my car. Rose's van was clearly visible. He looked at it for a moment, and walked over to Romea and put his hand casually over the hood. He was such an easy target. Come on, Emma. It's you or him. Sometime you will have to have a little cold blood. I took out my gun. Always aim to kill, girl. I put him in my sights. And pulled the trigger.

A return volley split the night air, bullets whizzed all around me. He had hit the ground in an instant, and he had more firepower than I could have imagined. I started moving around behind him. The revolver was warm and heavy in my hand.

I had two advantages over him. I saw him and he didn't see me. Other than that I was outgunned. The rest would be brains and endurance.

Figuring how fast the bicycle could move, and how quickly I could cross the road, I tried to figure how far down the street I could I make my break to cross the road safely. There were plenty of hidden spots in the Sutro Baths where I could hide and put my remaining bullets to their best use. Furthermore, I wanted to lead him away from Rose. I went through the layout of the Sutro Baths in my mind; all the walks I had taken there, the exact placement and depth of each one. I would lead him into an unfamiliar maze, circle back, and get the hell out.

Moving carefully along the edge I waited until the bicyclist was a fairly small figure, then I sped across the road, immediately attracting his attention. A bullet burst from the end of a flame, and just past the curb hit the ground behind a sign. The clicking started immediately, came closer. I scrambled over the edge of the cliff, tennies causing a rock slide; I kept my balance, rubber soles riding dirt; I was a dry skier going down, down into the dangerous, boiling waters of the Pacific Ocean and the concrete pits of the Sutro Baths.

The sound of the chain slipping onto the sprockets was slow, regular, confident. He was crossing the highway, close behind me. I moved east, along the rabbit paths. There were several weaving paths, which intersected and went up and down steep hills. One path could only be reached by racing through the obstacle course of the Sutro Baths. I knew how deep the old pools were. There was low tide and ladders on either side. He might be strong, but he wasn't agile and he probably didn't know the territory.

Crouched behind the sign, I listened to the clickety-clack coming closer, the chains loosening, catching on a large wheel. I sprung forward and down the cliff, enough rocks to grab the tennies, staying low and moving along the first low ridge of a concrete wall. He must have seen me. I crouched and waited. Come on, come to me, leave the bike.

Wish coming true, I heard footsteps on gravel and I began my own apelike crawl. Rusting rebar and concrete thrust out like question marks from the walls along the labyrinth of old swimming pools. The walls were higher, I was running on sand, a grunting of frustration, confusion behind me, my feet sped faster. Some kind of animal. I knew I would be out of audio soon, the waves crashing, foam tapping on our shoulders would obliterate any sounds.

The mist was hitting me already, green coat slicked, jellylike, feet thudding along a path and down into what looked like a deep well. One of the former baths, at low tide its ground was only five inches of the salty brine. A series of metal loops supplied a ladder. There were four concrete boxes between me and the trail. I had to get through them, up and over the fourth wall before he saw me. He followed, his progress would be much slower, those stocky muscle strung legs having trouble finding the footholds, the gigantic arms would pull him up, but only to go into the next bath, the bottom of which would be as black as hell.

Foam bubbling away at my feet, I heard the growl of the ocean, turned and automatically crouched as the bubbles of a wave broke somewhere out to sea. Never turn your back on the ocean, I reminded myself, looking into the series of dark pits in front of me. It was time. I paced myself.

Up one ladder, jump down, squish, the mud wasn't too bad, my hand found a ring handle and I scurried up, not looking back as I jumped the top and over into the next bath. He should be along the wall now, following me into the labyrinth.

The third bath was nearly dry: my feet knew the spacing already, the rhythm of extending, pulling on the rebar and swinging my legs over the wall, a gymnastic horse move, only one more ladder, crawl out of what could be your coffin.

The light at the top of the last tunnel. I went up more slowly, conserving that last bit of energy. I crouched at the edge and sprung out, visible for a nanosecond, and the gun burst with angry fire. He was located just where I wanted him. He would have to go through the pools to find me. The blond crew cut cocked to one side as he realized that there was no way to walk along the walls, he'd have to go in and out of each of the baths. There was a brief angry noise, his shoulders and chest seemed to swell, his jaw grew longer in the moonlit shadows, a horrible simian form, something fierce and low on the food chain. I raised my gun and aimed, but he dove into the first concrete hole.

I ran straight through a treacherous veil of branches, cutting marks on my cheeks, my feet fleeing the pursuer, wondering how long the four cubicles would hold him up. It would take him precious seconds to make his decision to jump into the darkened concrete wells, never knowing what was at the bottom. It will be worth thirty-five thousand dollars to him to make the obstacle course. My money, my life. When you use a gun, Emma, shoot to kill.

I looked back and thought I saw his hands on the ladder rungs, and finally, I reached a grove on the edge of the highway. Crouching behind a tree I saw him emerge from that first box, just like a gopher he came into sight. Standing up on his hind legs, arms curled with muscles, a menacing shape against the encroaching black ocean.

A spurt of white foam came up behind the man. He was bending over, ready to jump over the next hurdle. The thirty five thousand dollars he thought I had kept him in the race.

I dashed under the black shadows of trees onto the hard asphalt, realizing my heart was beating, like a cartoon. It tried hard to escape my chest. The realization made my knees weak and a little dance of white spots animated my sight. My arm found the bark of a tree; I leaned and felt the scrubby chips underneath my fingers, patterned like a pineapple. My vision cleared and I stretched my sight through the blackness to the ocean, whose growl met my calming breath.

I readied my weapon and said a little prayer to Diana. He was in my sights, a heartbeat away from death. I took a breath and squeezed the trigger. The weapon exploded, I blinked, and he was gone. There was only the foaming lip of a wave, curling over the edge of concrete.

I waited. He was still gone. Those simian arms would haul him out of the pit in a flash. But they didn't. There was just the gray air over the growling ocean which pounded against the ruins of the Sutro Baths. Must have been a hit. A watery grave. He wouldn't be found for days or weeks, or even months.

A hundred yards up the highway, Rose's van waited innocently. I opened the door, hands shaking. Rose spent the longest minutes of my life starting the engine. No one chased us onto the road. No one followed on foot or vehicle.

"Long time since I've been in your van, Rose." I swung around in the bucket seats and surveyed the various listening devices installed behind pink plastic beads. "You could lose the tacky leopard upholstery, though."

"You okay, Emma?"

"Yeah, sure."

I looked back to the gray horizon and wondered about all the people who had ever disappeared into the ocean. It was just like the older timers said. You can try to ride the waves, but you better not turn your back on the ocean.

CHAPTER FOURTEEN

FUCKED
UP

That was the moment that all good things began to seem bad. When a gray veil was pulled over the entire venture and all that followed would seem dogged by doom. The sunlight was soiled, every face on the street looked deeply troubled, and every laugh seemed to hold a cruel mockery. As we drove away from the ocean, Rose by my side, the din and clatter of traffic, ocean, and sirens all combined to form a cacophonous sound track, creating a malevolent feeling which followed me everywhere.

"We'll pick up your car tomorrow. When the place is full of tourist buses."

"I'm supposed to catch him, Rose! What if he's not dead? What if he is dead?"

"And what if you are? Let's not do this on his terms, Emma. Let's take him through the back door. Remember, I saw him. He's an *animal*, Emma."

"Don't insult my friends." Fleeing away under the umbrellas of trees, away from the ocean, from that moment when there was nothing to see, a spot where a man had been standing. As I stared into the cones of light ahead of me, Roseanne worked the hand accelerator, pushing the van around the dark curves toward home. I turned on the radio. *"It is our sense that God has intervened on our behalf."* I

113

reached for the dial, but not fast enough—*"and that He is invested in a victory for Calvin Smith . . ."* a preacher was saying.

"Divine Right, all right!" Rose snorted. "Villanueva's got to win, Emma. The right wing can manipulate even Calvin Smith. Everyone is deserting us, Emma. Everyone except Villanueva."

"Rose, I got a new fingerprint. I rolled it off one of the suspects."

"Once we're back at the office, don't forget to wash your hands."

"Blake there?"

"He's sleeping in the cot in the back. I'm sure he'll wake up for you. Bring your bloody fingerprint and you can tell us all the details."

"Pull over at this phone booth." I looked around at the brilliant fast-food restaurant. The *cholos,* homeboys, lounged, frustrated by barely lit booths that never rang. A convertible full of lipstick and hot hair cruised by; a minor din arose from the phone booth convention.

I dialed 911.

Listening to the endless loop of tape I was advised that if this really wasn't an emergency I should call another number. Antonio Shay's idea of law and order was building more jails, preferably giving the contracts for the prefab units to his friends in Texas. Meanwhile he forgot that nobody was answering the phone. I counted seventeen pairs of Nike's before I got a live human on the line.

"Nine-one-one, please give me your name and the location from which you are calling."

"Sutro Heights." I put my hand over the phone to muffle my voice. I heard the clicking which meant the call was being taped. I spoke quickly. "Dead male, white, middle-aged, lying right on the path. Shot at close range." I hung up and walked past the cholos. Their phones weren't ringing and there wasn't much to do since the convertible had turned a distant corner. Rose had pulled up to the drive-in window to get a malt.

Lounging at the pay phone I thought about the body lying

on a bed of fragrant pine needles. The first officers would just secure the scene and then they would all wait for the people from Photo Detail. Desk-jockeys would traipse in from the suburbs with all their cameras and fancy vests full of film.

More people would arrive with strings and things. They would take his fingerprints, and we would each have a copy, but mine was in blood. Our blackmailer would be no one important. He was just an ambitious errand boy, a small-fry, homicide of the week in an overworked department. No one would notice that the corpse had dipped his thumb in his own blood.

CHAPTER FIFTEEN

FOOTPRINTS
IN THE SNOW

Rose had rented a warehouse in eastern Potrero Hill, close enough to the freeway to make the square footage of no interest to condominium developers. We passed by the cars filing off the exit and turned into Rose's anonymous driveway, past the shopping carts and cardboard dwellings, which sometimes held some of Rose's security forces. The warehouse with the wooden storefront could have been the meeting place for Alcoholics Anonymous. Instead the initiated had to salute a video camera hidden behind a twist of blackberry bushes to gain entrance.

Rose tripped the three systems guarding the place, and we walked into Rose's idea of a security gauntlet. Three more cameras and we had to press code before we were admitted into the office park. Usually a hive of activity, the place was only humming with sleeping computers. Indoor palm trees stretched toward the night's darkened skylight. Secondhand oak furniture, wooden desks and file cabinets, heavy as anchors, were massive players in a dark football field. No wooing the clientele with a suite of downtown offices, brocade wallpaper, leather-topped desks, and overpriced lunches downtown.

Rose took her clients to little known gourmet haunts and saved money on location and furniture. The big bucks she spent on computers and an extensive private security system guarding some of the biggest art collections in San Francisco.

"Can I use your phone?" I asked, once we were inside.

"Sure. I'm going to go check on Blake."

I dialed Willie's answering service.

"Law offices," said a voice just dragged from between the sheets.

"This is Emma Victor, are there any messages for me from Willie Rossini?"

Shuffle of paper. "No." I heard the click of a light switch. "Are you sure?"

"I'm sure." There was a chirping in the background.

"When did Willie last pick up her messages?"

"This morning," he yawned.

"And she didn't leave one for me?"

"Hey, you got short-term memory loss, lady?"

"No, but I wish I did. Thanks, anyway." I hung up, trying to press Willie's warm, gentle tones out of my head. A double cross on the part of my employer? Not possible.

"Blake, you gotta go out and pick up Emma's car." Rose looked tired, a musical staff of wrinkles lined her forehead. I gave Blake the keys.

"Sure." Blake Fortier, mouth tightening into a defiant bud, was half hidden behind a file cabinet. His T-shirt was rolled up to reveal a new jailhouse tattoo, colors bright and tacky, biceps pumped up from the weight room, he still had a weight problem. Blake slumped his shoulders and crossed his feet at an angle, leaning on the file cabinet in an attitude of highly practiced lounging.

"What happened to your face, Emma? Looks like a cat got at you," Blake asked.

"I was off the beaten path." I closed the door as Rose wheeled behind her desk. "And I may be way out of my league. How long you been out now, Blake?" I asked.

"Five weeks, and damn if Rose's dad didn't pull some strings."

"Great! What kind of time do you get for breaking into Pentagon files?"

"Aw, they don't know what to do with computer criminals. Lompoc is a country club, man. The guards treated me like some kinda businessman!"

"You look good, what are your plans?"

"They wanted to send me back to the ghetto to keep the kids from hot-wirin' cars. Fine, I said, community service, let 'em learn everything I know. The world is gonna be ours. There just ain't no way to beef up security fast enough to keep us out."

"Blake." Rose used her arms to push herself higher up in the chair. "I hear there're still bars on the windows at Lompoc. That makes it a prison. And if you don't want to go back there, I suggest you go get on a Muni bus and pick up Emma's car."

"It don't run for half a hour, Rose! Listen, Emma, at Lompoc, I wired a freakin' pay phone—"

"I don't want to hear it, Blake. You hear me!"

What I didn't need to be was in the middle so I stepped into the background, stared at one of Rose's screens until the air was a little less blue. Blake was rolling a perfect joint. Rose rolled the pencil between her fingers. "I need to talk to Emma right now, if you don't mind, Blake. "

"Yeah, sure. Hey, Emma, good to see you, man."

We watched Blake's stubby body weave through the oak furniture and into the night. Tormented teenagedom, even for a genius. "I hope he brings back my car right away," I said.

"Blake's the best hacker I've ever had."

"Rose, you don't really want him following the rules, do you?"

"I just want him following my rules. I had a visit from the Feds yesterday. Someone hacking into the Defense Department employee files. It's gotta be Blake. He stayed on the line too long. And he's lying about it. A few years in prison, minimum security didn't teach him anything. It might teach me something though."

"You going to disinherit him?"

"I'm just trying to contain him," Rose grumbled. "You can help me, Emma."

"Don't think I'm cut out for motherhood, Rose. Let's get some work done. I feel like the bottom has dropped out of this gig. My seller is dead. Some unknown backup never showed. Willie is supposed to be at a conference on justice in New Orleans. She isn't at her hotel, a number she personally gave me before she left. There are no messages for me with her answering service. My employer suddenly seems not to exist, as if this job is only a figment of my imagination. The money is gone and a very touchy piece of merchandise is still floating around in the universe. All I've got is a bloody fingerprint, Rose. And the feeling that there's something funny about this gig."

"As funny as a death wish." Rose sniffed. "I smell a setup."

"I wish I could get in touch with Willie."

"Like I told you, Emma, Willie has a lot of friends in high places, they pay, but they often don't play by the rules. Which is to say, you can get screwed bigger by a senator than by a professional burglar."

"Okay, okay. We don't agree about Willie, we never did."

"The lady let you crawl out on a limb and left you there. I rest my case."

"It's totally unlike her," I said. "But any explanation eludes me, except one. There's big juice here, Rose."

"Big juice! We're talking local politics, Emma, right? A blackmail scam in a city of seven hundred thousand doesn't exactly attract the interest of the CIA."

"I don't know, Rose. There's something else, I just can't put my finger on it. I don't have enough information. I have to find Willie. I think the trail leads back east, Rose, back to Washington.'

"You've been seeing too many movies, Emma."

"Just because *your* conspiracy theory didn't turn out to be right last time—"

"Whaddaya got for fingerprints, Emma?"

"The number one gig," I pulled out the three fingerprints and handed them across Rose's desk. "Exhibit A." The fingerprints, perfect, black, tiny intricate lines.

"Not bad. You do this yourself?"

"Yeah. Penny taught me. Rose, do you think Blake could get into the FBI ASIS files these days?"

"It could happen," Rose pushed a mouse around on her desk. "But I don't want to compromise his parole. I don't want Blake's dinner coming to him through a slot for the next twenty years. So tell me, what are the stakes? High enough to take a chance?"

"Margo Villanueva," I said. "The mayoral election."

I watched the minutes tick by on the clock.

"I emit a low whistle of appreciation, Emma."

"These goons are trying to make a buck off a bedroom secret. But there's more than that. Somebody's trying hard to bring Villanueva down. Awfully hard."

"They'll always be someone."

"Villanueva's a progressive, Rose. And I've got a really, really bad feeling about the enemy."

"Okay, girlfriend," Rose assented slowly. "Let's talk to Blake. But I'm timing him. I don't want him getting carried away and locked away."

"Rose, one more thing," I remembered Rose's high fashion collection. "I'm going to have to have a go at this the other way around too," Fred still sent Rose the occasional frock; she kept a closet full of them, never quite willing to throw them away or donate them to the Salvation Army. But she didn't wear them either. "The wheelchair sort of ruins the line," she said once after a few too many martinis. It wasn't a topic I brought up often, but it was time to visit the star of the negative, the woman I never wanted to see with her clothes off. It was time to pay a visit to mayoral hopeful, and extortion victim, Supervisor Margo Villanueva.

"Rose, could I borrow one of your Paris suits to go to an A-list reception?"

"Sure, sure let me go pick one out."

"She don't have to worry about her car." Blake walked in and threw me the keys. "It's outside. But what is Cinderella gonna do for shoes? All she's got is tennies."

"Never mind that," Rose return with a black suit in a heavy plastic garment bag. I opened the zipper and took it out.

The suit was beautiful, black linen, with those long lines that would stretch my frame visually. White velvet cord had been inset, outlining the suit at the neck and cuffs, a Chinese frog knot on either lapel. Tiny mother-of-pearl buttons held the tight bodice closed. It was a lovely creation, all right. The level and style and craft were superb, a fashion plate outfit for someone who hadn't had a decent meal in twenty-four hours. I held the skirt up to my waist. Rose's father always wanted her to hide the chair. I would be a Hostess Cupcake, albeit with the wrong shoes.

"Here," Rose picked up two large folders of newspaper cuttings, organized and clipped according to year. "Take home some reading material. If you're going to a party, you might as well be informed as well as beautiful.

"Sure, give me the clippings, Rose."

"We'll let you know about the fingerprints, Emma. Good luck."

CHAPTER SIXTEEN

HAIRLESS

I drove home, my house almost unrecognizable. Never had the address felt more like a collection of two-by-fours covered with some tar and a lot of electrical wiring running around through the walls. Mink and Friend could survive outside better than I could inside. Everything was so botched. No money. Willie was gone. Some sadistic dentist had my phone number after a hundred-buck out-of-state subpoena serve and nobody was asking me if I needed to have my teeth cleaned. The work wasn't feeling long on benefits.

I parked Romea in the garage, keeping the headlights on until I could get out of the car and turn on the interior lights. I took a flashlight and went up the back stairs, checking the ivy-filled corners of the garden. Bad luck, going in one door and out another. And I'd been doing it for years. Maybe that was the problem. Up the ramp and in the back door. Mink wanted food and petting, confused about the order of her desires.

There was one message, a sour but important one, from Laura Deleuse. "We probably don't even need your vote anymore, Emma." She couldn't stifle a snicker. "They're calling Calvin Smith *boss* already. Right behind the chief's back!"

When I overcame the deep impression that the information made I began to think about my transformation. The grooming necessary to my appearance would take time I didn't have. I would work on my nails, a nice meditation that ended in short red enamel ovals, but the depilatory requirements were a drudge.

I grabbed a pretzel and looked in the mirror. My face was still covered with scratches from the dense shrubbery by the ocean. I made some chamomile tea and pressed the bag against the cuts as I read through the massive clipping file on Margo Villanueva.

The only surprise was Villanueva's vigorous stand against the right wing. She'd supported a whole investigation of the California Ku Klux Klan and their connection to the National Rifle Association.

I hung the suit on a hook behind the bathroom door to steam out the wrinkles. Testing the water, I hovered for a moment, adding lavender oil. Villanueva was a dedicated public servant. Her history didn't belie anything else.

I took off my robe and sat on the edge of the tub and put my feet inside. The water was hot. Looking beyond my breasts and belly, down to the foamy clouds which floated in the bathwater, I thought I saw patterns that weren't there.

Villanueva's husband, Joseph Villanueva, had been a moderate Democrat, a number cruncher who became state auditor. Much older than Margo, he made a name for himself quietly cleaning up a lot of government waste. On a visit to San Francisco he met and later married the San Francisco Mission High School principle, Margo Villanueva. When he won the state comptroller election, they established two residencies in Sacramento and San Francisco. I inserted a new blade, blue black and evil, into the engraved steel holder.

I got out a small boar gristle shaving brush and a big bar of soap, tacking the articles up on the bathroom wall.

Margo Villanueva ran for School Board president, won in a landslide four years after the death of her husband Joseph. Villanueva supported lesbian and gay teachers way before it

was known that we had an electorate. She had supported the
Rainbow Curriculum and a lesbian and gay youth counselor
for the District.

San Francisco wasn't always a gay mecca if you lived
with your parents, it was a nightmare. Teen suicides were
up. Bashings in high schools. Villanueva in her infinite wis-
dom, had understood this. I hadn't heard the word lesbian
until I was eighteen. Maybe I'd been lucky. What a thought!
My fingers ran satisfied, over my smooth marble calves.

When Joseph Villanueva died of a sudden heart attack,
Margo Villanueva's career pushed into high gear, Supervisor
and now possibly mayor. Hardly a career widow, Villanueva
proved her personal mettle. And, of course, upon Joseph's
death she inherited an instant constituency and a nicely cul-
tivated power base. State comptroller had its blessings.

The caulk was coming off in long rubber lines on the edge
of the tub. Boy did I need a week off, I thought. The big jack
could be just around the corner. Keep two steps ahead of it
and the money would be mine and there would be hot grains
of sand between my toes for weeks to come.

CHAPTER SEVENTEEN

nO
ANSWER

Sunday morning in the Mission. There was no suspicious activity, no activity at all. The population of the Mission was evenly divided between people locked up in church or locked in sleeping late. Precita Park, at the base of Bernal Hill, had the few dog owners, wandering with their plastic bags in hand.

I looked up the address of Willie's answering service: 1471 Rhode Island. That would be Potrero Hill, not far from Rose's. I looked into the mirror. The chamomile had done its work; the scratches had faded to a pink webbing.

Put yourself in the mood, Emma, but what was the mood? I wasn't sure anymore. I closed my eyes for a moment. Love. Friendship, Beauty. Lust

I heard something. A clunk. Someone's faulty transmission down the block? Something closer? A penny, a shoe, dropping? I looked around me. Stucco housefronts, old Victorians, bleached pale in the colorless San Francisco sunlight. Curtains drawn, a group of children down the block screaming hysterically. A bee busy on its errand.

I went into the darkened garage and turned on the lights immediately. I went into the root cellar, the dirt floored area where all the bulbs were stored. There, in the corner, where the shovel and hoe rested behind an old bag of cement. I moved closer and jumped at my own shadow. Nothing. I activated the security systems and left, happy to be backing Romea onto the sunny street, a street where no one seemed to be living or breathing. In a moment I was shifting up the steep hills of the Potrero neighborhood.

The last in a series of Victorian row houses, 1471 Rhode Island occupied a corner overlooking the industrial parks that cluttered up the landscape in front of the Bay. Cookie cutter dwellings, with bathrooms and laundry porches tacked onto the back. 1471 was bougainvillea-pink; the woodwork was outlined in black and green. The wail of a baby came from inside.

Two pieces of galvanized pipe served as a railing to the front door where everything was reasonably kept up. A terra cotta planter housed happy-faced daisies, and cherry tomatoes had been carefully trained up a bamboo pole.

But when I rang the doorbell, neither the man who answered it, nor the baby on his hip had a happy face. The man clasped a glass bottle that was nearly empty. The fat-faced, bald baby was maybe eighteen months. Except for his blazing black eyes he was a dead ringer for Dwight D. Eisenhower. He stared at the nipple of the bottle in his father's hand as if to will the milk to come to his mouth.

"Yes?" the man asked, his black eyes flat, cautious.

"Emma Victor, sorry to bother you." I handed him my card. He put the bottle down on the stoop. A thin, slight man, the baby seemed too much for him.

He held out his hand. "I'm Jose Carquinez. This is Alexander. What can I do for you?"

"May I look through the messages that Willie received in the last twenty four hours. I'm her employee and this is an emergency. I seem to be unable to reach her.'

"I don't know if I can—"

"Here, will this help?" I said, showing the man one from my Ben Franklin collection. "It's a legitimate request, but the college fund can always use a little help." I nodded at the infant in his arms. The baby turned. His eyes ate me. I folded the bill and held it out; the man took it without reluctance, proudly. The baby turned and looked back at the door. The man who I presumed was his father showed me inside.

The house had the typical shotgun layout. A small hallway was decorated with family photos, older relatives, old-fashioned jobs in portraits covering the peels of wallpaper. I could see through the parlor, back into the kitchen, two closed right hand doorways would be minuscule bedrooms. The man showed me into the parlor. A sofa was covered in an Indian print tablecloth. A big table dominated the room. Piles of newspapers and diapers waiting to be folded kept company with much loved stuffed animals. A breakfront held numerous paperback novels, romance novels, light-weight stuff. A calendar held an image of an angel just over a television where muted soap opera faces leered at us.

"Come in my office." he put Alexander down in a playpen. The baby sat up, looking like a startled Buddha, narrowed his eyes, and then started to wail. Jose bent down and turned him over on his stomach, shook a few toys in front of his face and patted the cotton T-shirt on his back. Alexander quieted down, and Jose led me to a small room off the front door. Twelve by ten feet, dominated by a large desk and a PBX system, headphones, and a remote extension, handy for when Alexander needed a change.

A row of clipboards in bright plastic colors were evenly spaced on the wall above the desk, names of clients written in Magic Marker on the silver clips. Most of the clipboards had a flurry of messages clamped down.

The room was filled with the chattering of two parakeets. The little blue and yellow budgies were grooming each other, oblivious to Jose. A bank of gray filing cabinets lined one wall. A window looked out upon a roof and beyond that the top of a big avocado tree and a nice hunk of sky.

"Wendyl and Linda, they love the noise, the sound of me talking on the phone. And they kind of keep me company," he explained. A series of clipboards were organized in a metal divider and the rest of the place was filled with filing cabinets. A light sprinkling of birdseed covered the cabinets and the hardwood floor.

"My wife died when Alexander was born," Jose explained. "Her mother had started the answering service and passed it on to her." That explained the old battered cabinets. "I used to take over sometimes, it's an-all night business, as you noticed." Jose's eyebrows rode a little higher on his face. "It's great and the only way I could be with Alexander. He's got a full-time Daddy. We get groceries delivered, and a gourmet pizza to celebrate a new client. We get along."

"Willie's calls?"

"Oh, yes, sorry." He brought down a clipboard. The parakeets fluttered in their cages. "They're arranged chronologically."

I looked over the hastily scribbled but legible notes on torn paper. Friday evening, somebody's estate business, an invitation to a symposium in Washington, then Saturday morning, a message from Willie's dry cleaner and her son-in-law in Idaho. I checked back to Friday night. My message to Willie about the flower delivery wasn't on the clipboard.

"My message isn't here."

"What?"

"You know, the one I called in Friday night?"

"Friday night, Friday night, remind me . . ."

"I left a message about a flower delivery."

"I remember." Jose took the clipboard and leafed through the notes. "It's not here. I don't understand. But I remember it; about the flower delivery, right? Some restaurant I never heard of."

"The message isn't here, Jose." I squinted at the edge of the paper; it was irregular like deckle edging, but it wasn't. In the cage, the birds were grooming themselves, feathers floated in the air. The window sill was polka dotted with their black and white droppings.

"Jose, do you ever let your birds out?" I asked.

"Oh, oh, only once or twice."

"And they probably like to hang out on the window sill, the upper sash, here, right?" I asked, walking over to the window.

"Well, yes . . ."

"Look, Jose." I bent down to the floor and picked up a nearly completely decimated piece of paper directly underneath the windowsill. Only the words *'flowers'* and *'sutro'*, in Jose's hasty handwriting were left.

"Ohmigod, I'm sorry, I—" He looked into my face, his eyes frightened. Alexander had awakened in the other room, a confused cooing. The parakeets chattered over him. "This is terrible, I never have had, I swear!" Jose's hand ran over his cheeks, his chin.

"Don't worry about it." It was far, far too late for worry. "Here's my pager number and phone in case Willie calls or anything else comes up."

"I'm so sorry."

I wrote down a new message for Willie. *The flowers are dead; call immediately. Inform client, the former Mrs. Harlan Knapp re: very negative subpoena reception and possible danger.* "Will you give this message to Willie when she calls?" I handed the message to Jose. He read it without asking, a worried look confirming on his face.

"The flowers," he breathed, "I hope it wasn't a big problem."

"Hey, Jose," I sighed looking at the parakeets, "shit happens".

The yellow-crested bird was pecking at its image in a mirror, seeking false company. It was a compulsive, misguided routine that would never end.

A HARD
OPINION

Russian Hill is one of the ritziest pinnacles in San Francisco; every house is a fiefdom, an architectural example of the power and income of its owner. Here was a French chateau and there an Elizabethan Tudor. Supervisor Villanueva's house was a modern, poured concrete job, somebody probably pounded forty feet of pilings into the rock to keep it stuck on the side of the hill. Two valets stood at attention at either side of the entrance. Behind them, jasmine, honeysuckle, bougainvillea, and ivy covered the concrete abode of the mayoral hopeful.

"Park your car?" A face leered into my window, squinting at the note I was writing on the back of my business card. I cranked the glass up, finished the note, folded it and put it in a sealed envelope. *Supervisor Villanueva. Urgent. Personal.* I wrote on the front. I put the envelope in my black handbag and climbed out of Romea, opening the door for myself. Long legs don't fit well in cars and so I don't enjoy getting out of them. And I really don't enjoy anyone watching.

The stooped figure in a white linen coat extended a claw-shaped hand. I handed him the keys and squared my vision on Margo Villanueva's address.

"I don't know how long legs fit in little cars," he said.

"I didn't think parking jockeys came with opinions about

the guest's anatomy." I straightened out the suit, got ready for an early entrance.

"Dat's all I got, lady, that and five fifty an hour for parking your car. Maybe I don' even have no opinions anymore. Who knows. Nobody listens anyway. But I tell you one thing. I don't think you're no guest."

"I knew it. Even Coco Chanel can't put the ritz on me."

"I'll take care of your car real good, though."

"You do that." I handed him a five and looked past his linen coat up the walkway to Margo Villanueva's house. The portico, bluebirds on white tiles covering the interior was cheerfully Mexican. Inside the hum of a vacuum cleaner let me know that I was way early.

I slipped into a dark vestibule, papered in olive-green silk and covered with dozens of small oil portraits, nineteenth century miniatures and more recent copies done in the same style. Adults in the grim black of Spanish formality looked stern; children, sober in lace, worried about the Inquisition. Rose's Chanel suit fit right in. Peering closer I saw that some of the children had modern clothes; Villanueva must have commissioned portraits of children and grandchildren to fit in with the old family portraits. I hung in the vestibule, peering around me at the rest of the place. Supervisor Villanueva's house inspired the ease and grandeur of a hacienda, and her property taxes would probably pay my mortgage for a year.

A large living room stretched a good thirty feet to my left. Long overstuffed, magenta silk couches snaked their way around a big plate glass Bay View. The sun shone on the water and the white folded sails of docked boats. A big half round stucco fireplace took up most of one wall. There was fresh wood stacked on either side, and a half circle of smudge indicated that the fireplace was used frequently. Rough beams spanned a sixteen-foot ceiling, and a spiral staircase led to a gallery full of books which topped off the room. Their spines glittered, gold on red moroccan bindings.

Underneath the gallery the walls were decorated with masks, naive, gruesome, inexplicable. Carnival masks that leered and had the number "four" painted on the cheeks and forehead. Masks with separate heads coming out of their mouths, replicating and regurgitating themselves; skeletons winked with their one promise: *You are this too.*

To my right, the dining room was being readied for the reception. Women and men in white uniforms were spraining their wrists with marble platters of cheeses and silver platters of seafood.

A wrought-iron chandelier, five feet in diameter, spilled prisms of question marks over the table. On one end of the room a breakfront the size of an Oldsmobile Cutlass held seven antique globes and numerous hand-painted plates. To the right, the door to the kitchen swung in and out, starched aprons, dead expressions, and the humid kiss of a palm print on the brass doorplate; the Bridgeways inmates glided smoothly and efficiently, spotting each other as the door swung back and forth, green ovals on their backs with flowing white script, *Bridgeways,* door open, next course, never missing a beat, all thought of that happy world of heroin far, far behind them.

The marble floats landed on a huge old mission table not quite as big as a football field where a caterer was arranging sprigs of herbs and fresh wildflowers between the platters. A series of French doors opened onto a terra-cotta courtyard where caterers were busy opening a sea of estate-bottled Chardonnay. White lights glittered on topiared orange trees, reflecting on all the bottles of wine, vodka, whiskey, cognac, bourbon, beer, and soda pop.

Niches in the garden wall were filled with Latin American saints. Four bright polychromatic angels knelt into the middle of the courtyard. They all bore gifts, just like the people that were going to pass through the portal. And they all expected something in return.

A noise from the kitchen got my attention. A pillar of nervous white silk with whippet hips was giving orders. She was holding herself back from going ballistic. I looked at the suit. Its surface shimmered with the fineness of its threads; the crabs and lobsters of the table just begged to drip upon it.

It could only have been Dee Dee Hammerman, the palace

guard, the woman who Willie had trouble getting past on the phone. She dressed boldly, her small features, eyes and mouth, were lost in the big boned Slavic face. Veins stood out on her hands as they gripped her hips.

She was about five eight, large chunky gold earrings matched similiar big beads and baubles on her neck and wrists. Her fingers ended in dark red, vampirish nails. I tried to remember her background, but failed; she wasn't a local blue blood. While the progressive wind might have smelled sweeter to her, she still treated the help like help. A young Hispanic woman was nervously chewing her lip as she explained a problem in the kitchen.

"Don't come to me unless it's a crisis," Dee Dee hissed at her. Her helmet hair, a short pageboy, was shiny as a penny. Three mother-of-pearl buttons the size of Mason jar lids were sewn to the front of her suit.

"But, miss, the—" a young woman in a nile green suit faltered in high heels.

"Is there blood on the floor?"

"What? No, I—"

"Well, it's not a crisis unless there's blood on the floor. Get it?" Dee Dee Hammerman pirouetted on a spiked heel and left the room. Her patent leather pumps had been shined to a mirror finish; you could fix your lipstick in them if you curtsied deeply enough. I put her at forty-five and pushing a little hard at the exercise routine. The tendons on her neck stretched as she tried to hold her temper. Maybe she wasn't used to Bridgeways, the Democratic choice of caterer.

Dee Dee Hammerman approached a portly man who'd also arrived on time. He was concentrating on the caviar with an exquisitely quizzical look. His arm decoration, was a young woman who looked exquisitely bored. She sighed and looked at the food. He sighed and looked at her.

"Dee Dee Hammerman," Another cadence altogether, all treacle, but the glint in her eye was as hard as her acrylic nails. Dee Dee's eyes moved up and down the man and his escort, trying to place the face. "Tony Lenner, Kaiser Permanente," she confirmed.

"Yes!" The man with the beefy cheeks wrapped his fingers around a dripping prawn. He wiped his mouth with a napkin vigorously before extending his hand. The white suit moved safely away from the table, from him.

Dee Dee Hammerman's smile played a little broader across her face. "How was lunch with Margo last week? Wednesday at the Cyprus Club, wasn't it?"

"Those desserts!"

"Yes." Brittle smile. "Decadent."

"I have to say, I was very impressed with Margo, Dee Dee. Calvin has all the connections, of course, a career politician—but after lunching with Margo I have to admit that I'm not sure Calvin Smith is the right mayor for San Francisco. Never thought I would say that either!" They bobbed heads in joyous communion. "After all, Calvin can pull so many strings, he could do a lot for San Francisco, but Margo is a girl from the City!"

"That's right, she knows every neighborhood block club, and she's committed to keeping hospitals open and profitable in the city."

The man stroked his chin. "Margo's a progressive who understands the marketplace and its role in health care," he nodded. "The labor problem, the labor problem, and the labor problem. Margo's got some creative ideas. The Bridgeways facility is a marvelous example of the community and the health care system getting together."

"Not to mention the penal system," Dee Dee Hammerman murmured.

"What?"

"Please." Dee Dee pointed out the green bottles glistening on the wet bar. "Please help yourselves to refreshments. Excuse me." The downy flanks of her shoulder blades twitched and the iron smile fell off her face as she bolted across the room. Dee Dee Hammerman was a woman with a lot of plates in the air. And, I thought, as I saw her approach a blond man in sunglasses, their twin kisses on either cheeks, she had a lot of faces. Right now this new face was beaming, but conspiratorial; acrylic nails raked a pattern into blondie's shirt. I moved closer through the crowd and he came into focus. Five foot six, heavy to stocky build; the guy was a walking brick chimney. He didn't look like any kind of tycoon, union or corporate, that Margo Villanueva would want to court. He clutched a pony glass, taking small, measured sips of whiskey.

His chamois shirt had the fork pattern of Dee Dee's nails across the front. What was this designer dude doing at a Democratic wingding?

Dee Dee and the pale one huddled together; I had to interrupt them to get to Margo Villanueva. I remembered Willie's words to her secretary when I was lounging in her office. "Can't get ahold of Margo! Still! It's that damn press secretary," she had sighed. "Keep trying," she had instructed. A perplexed goatish shake of her white head.

I huddled behind one of the Mexican baroque pillars, the profiles of cherubs keeping me hidden as I heard their words.

"When do I get to see Margo?" The questions sounded like an order.

"Soon," she promised. "I've got you a slot right before the speech."

"I hope you're right about that." Chamois wrung his hands slowly together, something aggressive, some anger was deferred into the gesture. "Do you think Margo's . . ." he paused, "ready?" The rest was lost in the drift of ambient conversation.

"I need a hard opinion, Bert. Something's come up that is beyond me. I think all the horses have bolted the stable."

"But I thought the stable was locked!"

"Sometimes the barn catches fire," Bert growled. Dee Dee drew closer to him. She swallowed and licked her lips and told Bert something he didn't really want to hear. The only visible change was the shift in the big lantern jaw. He ground his teeth as he listened, his fingers gripped his glass tightly. Bert held more cards than Dee Dee in some game in which Villanueva was a potential pawn; I was sure of that.

"Let's not talk about that now."

"It's a lovely home, isn't it?"

"Do you know the architect, Sam Fong?"

"Excuse me." Their two faces looked up blankly at me.

"Wasn't Sam Fong the architect who did the Papparizi Hotel in Genoa?" I asked.

"Genoa, Genoa." Dee Dee rolled her eyes. " I don't know the Papparizi, uh, have we met?" Dee Dee said, not quite placing me as the help, but not as a donor either. The Chanel suit didn't do it. Her eyes started to travel down to my feet when I got her attention again.

"I'm here to see Supervisor Villanueva."

Dee Dee let a light laugh of derision escape. "I'm sorry, but the Supervisor is a little bit busy." She waved her hand at the crowd. Bert lounged under the overhang in the shadows, his chamois shirt fading into the stucco, his glass empty.

"I'm Emma Victor, but my name won't mean anything to you. Could we speak for a minute in private, Ms. Hammerman?"

She stole a look at Chamois. They exchanged the glances of old friends, looks which carried too much content for a party.

"It's very important, really."

"Margo's busy." Her lips barely missed a beat.

"Not too busy for your old friend, *Bert*. He seems to be getting an audience with no problem. I'd like to rip off your friend's sunglasses and check his pupils."

Dee Dee's manners fell into some chasm from which they did not return. Under the shiny pageboy her face seemed to transform into a variety of personas. A cold fury underlined her words. " *I—have—a-a-a-a-a-a-a-a-a-a-a-a MINUTE*!"

A sudden din from the kitchen seemed to underscore her words.

"What did they train you on? Raw meat?" My remark was lost when something crashed onto the floor in the kitchen and several Bridgeways trustees fled for cover behind the swinging door.

"What did you say?" Dee Dee's eyes found Bert's for a nanosecond. Bert put his glass down on an end table and his right hand crawled across the chamois shirt toward a shoulder holster. Or maybe he just had an itch.

"Let's not get off on the wrong foot here; the Supervisor

will *want* to see me," I pressed. "I promise you." The clock ticked, the guests tittered around us.

"There's an extremely urgent message from her attorney, Willie Rossini. Give this to her." I handed her an envelope. I sure would like to pat your friend Bert down for any heavy metal he might be carrying, I thought.

"I'll give her the message." Dee Dee took the envelope and put it in a blind pocket between the side seam of her skirt. There was a ruckus at the door and she turned her back on me. The cash cows began their stampede, and Dee Dee Hammerman's face didn't register anything but the glow of ready money coming her way. I melted back into the crowd and hoped for the best. Chamois Shirt leaned against his pillar and watched the press of people fill the vestibule.

Overwhelmed by the smell of perfume, the tickle of satin, the waterfall of giggles, and the brush of mink coats, I loitered amongst the oil portraits and watched Bert. Around me the faces of Villanueva's grandchildren looked like vicious pug dogs in black velvet. Seven o'clock and the money flank attacked the monster groaning board with relish. The faces were familiar, the names were familiar, used only among the initiated.

"Planet Hollywood, Jay Shaeffer, Jay Shaeffer, Planet Hollywood." Dee Dee was introducing a ponytailed executive to the clots of old money. The place was filling to capacity. A two hour reception and the Supervisor should be making her appearance soon. Happy recognition noises filled the air. The pundits, the sharpies, the financial priests, high-profile pooh-bahs, they all knew each other, and they were all showing up for Villanueva.

The crowd was getting high fast, Villanueva had come up in the polls, and the champagne was good. If things went her way the place would be pumped full of endorsements and money. Villanueva was strong, stronger than I thought. Enthusiasm and money was present. How could Supervisor Villanueva lose?

Easy. One scrap of negative and, according to Willie, Villanueva could kiss it all good-bye. I took a position by the kitchen door where I could follow Bert with my eyes and then with my feet. He ducked behind another pillar and I was convinced I was making him uncomfortable; but I had only just started my work. I passed the groaning board, tagged a piece of broccoli, and cornered him by a polychromatic Jesus, bleeding profusely from his Roman perforations.

"I don't believe we've met."

"Bert Lubbers," the pleasant webbing of wrinkles around the eyes was deceptive. He was looking at me with a strange intensity through his sunglasses, his hand was rough, damp.

"You work for Supervisor Villanueva?"

"No, I'm in the restaurant business."

"Oh. The Market Street development plan. You want in on Disneyland Way."

"There's a lot of tax dollars and employment there."

"That's the argument Villanueva put up for that hotel consortium. For a progressive she sure gets her signals crossed sometimes. Two years ago two hotels and a tourist loading dock almost landed on the waterfront. Supervisor Villanueva fought for them."

"If you knew the facts, if you looked at what the economic impact—"

"Yeah. A lot of service jobs and nobody gets to look at the sky anymore. I'd rather see a factory."

"You don't know what you're talking about. You ever work in a factory?"

"Yeah, I've worked in a factory. But let's talk about *you*, Bert. Where is your restaurant business based exactly? In California?" I asked. The pink skin didn't have red blotches. Bert Lubbers stayed inside a lot, inside a lot of dark restaurants, maybe. "Where are you from?"

"Back East," he said and something about the way he said it made me know he was lying. Despite the designer clothing, his hands were rough, scarred.

"You have a family?"

"Yez, a wife and two children. Excuse me, I—" words slurring, but not with alcohol, the little blue eyes burned behind the glass, as if they would melt the lenses.

I beheaded the broccoli with my teeth. "Where are you from *exactly*?"

"Bethesda. I told you."

"No, originally, I mean."

"Bethesda, Washington."

"Oh." I stared at him, right through the dark glasses. I spun a cauliflower in cheese dip and let the moment draw itself out.

"How long have you known Dee Dee?" I asked.

"Just the last year." His smile was breezy, damp. "Since she's been working for Margo Villanueva. I'm interested in doing some business in San Francisco, the Market Street rejuvenation plan sounds great. Development, that's where San Francisco tax dollars are going to come from," Bert reassured me. "Now, if you don't mind . . ."

He was nervous. I had it right. So I raised my voice and moved in a little closer to see what he'd do. "I think Supervisor Villanueva wants to sell off Market Street to developers, that's what I think." I pulled in tighter to Bert; he backed up against a wall. His right hand had that itch again, crawling across the front of his shirt. "Is that why you're really here?"

"Actually, my company is starting a branch out here."

"What company is that?"

"Braemar Foods. We're thinking of moving our whole operation to the Bay Area."

"Braemar Foods? Never heard of it."

"Split two for one last year, but they like to keep relocation quiet, you know."

"A lot of people like to keep things quiet. Did you tell your wife? Are the kids excited to live in California?"

"Yes, of course. They will love the weather. Too bad about the Pacific Ocean. You can't even wade in it. And the kids love to swim."

"Do they? Maybe they swim all the way to Germany and back?"

Bert Lubbers took but a second too long to react. But that second spoke volumes. "What are you talking about?"

"Look, Mr. Lubbers, there's something about you that's

not quite kosher. You're no man from the suburbs, I'll tell you that. By the way, Bethesda is in Maryland, not Washington."

"Very interesting." Bert Lubbers laughed, but the air was weak coming out of his lungs. "You are playing at some kind of psychic game, eh?" I stared at his right hand. Small scars had been stitched across the tendon between his thumb and forefinger. His pinkie was crooked and he kept his palm hidden. This wasn't a guy that had jabbed himself with a screwdriver; I was ready to bet that sometime in the distant past Bert Lubbers had nearly blown his hand off. And after that he'd worked hard, hard enough to be able to use a weapon again.

"Excuse me?" Bert was backing away. "It's been a pleasure."

"*Guadalajara!*" The mariachi band had released their tremulous, bright voices into the night. Bert was winding his way through the crowd as trumpets and saxophone fused their brass sounds. The infusion of music seemed to change everything. Rounding out the rough edges on the businessmen and women, it made the hips of the power matrons twitch the melody. The music swelled with a sentimentality that was bright and cheerful, something you could almost believe in. I sidled over to the end table where Bert Lubbers had put down his glass and slipped it into my handbag.

"*Polly Parhmar, Warner Brothers; Warner Brothers, Polly Parhmar,*" Dee Dee Hammerman's voice rose on notes higher than brass. The band's sound built to a bleating crescendo, and all the help started clapping and whistling expectantly. The money and success and power stopped their schmoozing. And then came the woman who made it all possible.

Supervisor Villanueva entered. Her face was radiant. Smiles of recognition set off sparkles in the Supervisor's little shoe button eyes. Eye contact, eye contact, eye contact. Her teeth shone bright white as she beamed and her constituency was misty-eyed with the tears of anticipated victory. Small hands flashed diamonds, a strong neck bent to hear personal greetings; sturdy little legs supported a hard bullet body. With heels she was five foot seven. Her poppy-red suit was superbly fitted to her, the long coat glittering with a double row of military buttons, the flashing of her smile as bright as the gold braid which marched around the cuffs and neck of the jacket. She'd let her black curly hair go salt-and-pepper. The small, complacent mouth over a neat little chin smiled, emphasizing her broad cheekbones, The beloved Supervisor, the widow, the deal maker, Madonna of the Neighborhoods.

There is a moment when you know you are in the presence of power. There was nothing of rehearsed confidence in Supervisor Villanueva. She came forward through the crowds, remembering names, looking people in the eye, tilting her head, listening and then segueing onto the next person with total ease. A broad-beamed man of thirty-five, a grown-up version of one of the pug-faced portraits, must have been Villanueva's son. Thomas Joseph Villanueva shared the neat little mouth; a spade beard hid a weak chin. His eyes, however, were larger, almost bulging, perhaps from a thyroid disorder. Hadn't he just been appointed to a Federal bench? He offered a confident handshake learned at his parent's knees. The blond male aide who I'd seen earlier and a few other souls also stoked the racket that followed in Villanueva's wake.

The air was full of speech ozone. I wanted to get out of the courtyard. I wanted away from the groaning board with all its seafood and politics, compromise and promises. I wanted away from all the hoopla because soon I would be talking to the Supervisor and I didn't want any flashbacks of her thighs on the bed of a Mark Hopkins Hotel.

I waded, unnoticed, through the living room carpet. Someone had started a fire in the fireplace, real logs crackled and burned the way real logs do. And it wasn't even cold. As I walked around the big sectional sofa, the festival masks stretched their tongues out at me and the fire warmed my legs to an unnecessary degree. The plate glass window, cool and black, offered the world beyond. Seven hundred thousand lives and a lot more from the suburbs, driving, eating, playing, fucking, fighting. They *would* be served best

with Margo Villanueva as mayor. But would she make it?
Villanueva had assembled an impressive crowd tonight. But
maybe all they were doing was eating food.

The Marina stretched before me, a green stripe. To the left
the spires of the Golden Gate Bridge pierced the encroaching fog; I could see the cars backing up on the bridge. Crossing bodies of water in cars was a major Bay Area pastime.
Cars crawling back and forth over the spans as regular as
waves, their commute as perpetual as the sun's revolution
around the earth. Just out of sight was the Cliff House, Sutro
Gardens, the windmills of Golden Gate Park and the condos
built on Playland.

Supervisor Villanueva's speech was going on, and on. A
foghorn sounded an alarm and the mariachi band started up
again. The living room behind me came into view in the reflection of the plate glass windows. Over my shoulder I
could see the wall of masks, and Dee Dee Hammerman
came striding in. She had Bert Lubbers on her arm and she
stashed him alone in a room. She didn't notice me stretched
out on the sofa. I was feeling practically invisible by the
time the Supervisor walked past me, a red stripe on her way
to do business.

CHAPTER NINETEEN

KILL THE MESSENGER

There was the chirping of introductions and the high tones of the pitch, the pitch that came from Mr. Lubbers. "It's an excellent opportunity to further the rehabilitation effort," he was saying.

"Bridgeways, you're talking about Bridgeways?" Margo Villanueva sounded skeptical.

"Yes! A series of Bridgeways. A huge labor pool, uh, an opportunity for rehabilitation that has never been met by any society in history. It is within our reach now. Breakthroughs in brain chemistry—"

"I heard you the first time." The Supervisor's voice was tight.

"Look how much prisons are costing us now. And with inmates in for longer terms. We're not talking about violent offenders, stalkers. Just the legions of illiterate, poor, drug-addicted. Don't you have the First Lady's ear?"

"You're connecting this to the Market rehabilitation plan, aren't you?"

"Well, yes. Yes, of course! That and other inner-city revitalization schemes. Look what's happening in Georgia, in Southern California! Chain gangs are already working the highways, men breaking rocks, breaking backs that could be better—"

"Not to mention the advantages of chemical controls, is that what you're going to tell me?"

"In Bridgeways you've got the perfectly controlled environment. There are already a number of products on the market now which show real possibilities for behavior modification without any side effects—"

"Thanks, but no thanks."

"Please, take some time to think about it. Supervisor, real lives could be saved, why look what's happening at Juvenile Hall, in your own district."

"I've already thought about it. And I've already been approached a number of times. One would think there was an EEC plot to take over San Francisco. This city seems of great interest to the Europeans, Mr. Lubbers. We've got French pay toilets that don't flush right, German buses with faulty transmissions, Dutch electronic switches which have wrought havoc on BART cars, and the Swiss have been lining up to drug the inmate population for quite some time. I'm an *elected official*, Mr. Lubbers. Your plan won't wash in San Francisco, Mr. Lubbers. You can take your mind control schemes to Orange County, if you like. But not in San Francisco."

"I'm really sorry that you don't see the possibilities of this."

"I see the possibility of fascism. That's what I see, Mr. Ludders. Now, please leave my office. Dee Dee!"

"Beats tough love for the poor, Supervisor!" Lubbers hissed and let the door slam.

"*Dee Dee*," the Supervisor barked. I drew back to my position embedded in the sofa.

There was a fluster and bustling and Bert Lubbers shot out of Villanueva's door like a bullet. He shook Dee Dee Hammerman's arm off of himself, strode out through the party, caused a stir as he bumped into a Bridgeways caterer, stopped, took a canapé and walked toward the vestibule.

"Jesus Christ, Dee Dee, keep this kind of vulture away from me, will you? I appreciate the short-end money you've brought in, but I've got to handle this thing right. This is San Francisco for Chrissake!"

"I'm sorry, Supervisor."

"I've got guests, Dee Dee. Is Jodie coming?"

"No, I meant to tell you, she—"

"Excuse me." I emerged from the upholstery, slipping on my heels, holding out my hand. "Supervisor, I have an urgent message for you from Willie Rossini."

"Of course," Villanueva said, just like that. In a moment I was in her office. Was it Willie's name? Why did she need a palace guard? Did someone want Dee Dee to put a wedge between Villanueva and her attorney?

An octagonal room had been completely done up in white, with a wall of flowering geraniums. The carpet required a breaststroke to reach a white silk settee where Hammerman was pointing. Dee Dee stood guard over me.

"Excuse me, I have to speak to someone; I'll be right back." Villanueva caught my eye and disappeared.

"*Sit down.*" Dee Dee Hammerman pointed at the white settee. I sat on it.

"Once I get my way, I'm very obedient," I smiled.

"Just stay that way, Miss Victor." Dee Dee closed the door carefully behind her. I stood up. In the middle of the room a rococo desk, curvy legs, outlined in gold, had a matching chair tucked underneath it. A white leather blotter took up most of the tabletop and didn't look like anyone had ever written a thing on it. White Roman blinds were folded over the sash windows. I fought the snow blindness and made out a very few books in a built in bookcase and a small grouping of photos on the wall. In front of the windows was a wrought iron half circular planter holder. Red geraniums spilled over the edges of the clay pots, a wall of flowers, something that you only saw in Mexico.

Two Chinese silk screens hid a second desk, with overflowing IN and OUT trays, three phones, and numerous numbered binders. Three gold metal Rolodexes were closed and locked.

I checked the drapes and the telephone, peered inside the lamp, underneath the lamp bases, under the telephone, inside the telephone receiver. No bugs on a cursory sweep.

I walked over to the portraits. Joseph Villanueva, hands

folded on the desk in front of a flag. Thomas Joseph Villanueva, the Federal judge, was also suited, desked and
flagged. An official portrait of President Collin and the First
Lady in a photo with the First Dogs and First Children, all
now grown. A smaller oval picture of a much younger First
Lady, famous for pranks during her college days. I remembered the hijinks leaked to the press by the housemother of
their sorority. A campus made white by toilet paper in trees.
Those were the days.

Barbra Streisand shook hands with Supervisor Margo Villanueva in another photo. Jerry Brown enjoyed a handshake
too. There were other politicians, movie stars, a gallery of
vote getting. The band wailed in the distance as I turned to
Villanueva's desk and pulled the drawer open. Three pens and
a checkbook. Opening the cover, each check was inscribed
Margo Villanueva for Mayor Campaign Fund. There were
checks to caterers, deposits from supporters, corporate and
private. San Francisco and Washington, D. C. Bank of America. Bechtel. Warner Brothers.

A movement, a stripe of shadow moved along the space
under the door. I closed the checkbook. I was just sinking into
the ivory settee when the door opened and Margo Villanueva
walked in, her face a fury. She looked at me like an unfortu-
nate stain upon her upholstery. The skin on her forehead was
gathered together in a big knot over her eyebrows. A knot that
moved. Dee Dee Hammerman was planted by the Supervisor
like a bodyguard. I stood up. Dee Dee Hammerman strode behind the Chinese screens and started working the phones. The
locked Rolodexes were sprung and I heard the wheels of
names turning.

*"We have a little misunderstanding here, George. We
thought the endorsement was all set up for tomorrow. Hey,
George, does Brown have a direct line number? Give it to
me."*

"Emma Victor." I held out my hand; Villanueva shook it
mechanically. "I am sorry for having to bother you, Supervisor." I bent my front knee slightly and looked at the carpet as
if admitting that I had just sold the family cow for six beans.

There was a pause, the ivory room seemed a bit muted and the mariachi band stopped playing.

"He's an ally, George. We want Willie Brown. Willie Brown! Just get ahold of him, will you?" Dee Dee's voice cut across the room like a knife. Villanueva twitched. She wanted Willie Brown's endorsement badly.

"I will try to be very brief," I promised.

Villanueva's forehead unbunched but only slightly.

"George, you owe me. Now, look, they're totally bunked in at headquarters. What? Sure. I'll hold."

"What can I do for you?" Villanueva breathed, and I realized she was studying the ivory velvet piping on my suit as she followed Dee Dee's conversation.

"Ohmigod. Yes. That's wonderful!" Fingertips moved around the screen and a panel folded back. "We've got it, Margo! We've got him."

Villanueva folded her hands in prayer, looking just like a Madonna, and under her lowered lids I saw that her eyeballs rolled toward the heavens.

"The lighting trees won't fit in there, the ceiling is too low Willie hates bad lighting. The angle would kill him in the morning. How about the afternoon?" Dee Dee's voice came from behind the screen.

"Supervisor Villanueva, could we speak privately, please?"

"Oh, yes." Villanueva was barely with me. She stuck her head behind the screen and murmured to Dee Dee. I could hear the whine of protest.

"Really, Margo, we should do this on a hardwired phone. You know, it isn't good to use a remote. Why anyone could pick up the signal and scoop—"

More murmuring. More whining. A stronger tone, Villanueva returned, and the phone behind the screen was in its cradle.

I looked at the traces of Dee Dee's footprints on the deep carpet until I was sure the door was closed and the dark stripe that was her shadow had melted away. Villanueva sat at her desk, turned sideways to face me. She'd just gotten Willie Brown's endorsement. Margo Villanueva was almost there. She could feel it and taste it. Mayor of San Francisco. Willie

Brown's endorsement. Margo Villanueva was a made woman. Her hands folded themselves on the white ivory blotter, keeping her fingers from fiddling too much, and I wondered how I was going to break the news.

"As you may or may not know, Supervisor, I was instructed by Willie Rossini to buy a videotape on your behalf." I kept my eyes lowered, lower than my voice, aiming the words at the deep carpet between us.

"No. I didn't know." The eyes became flat, distanced, the little red breast of her suit filling with air. "That is, I didn't know it was you. What's the problem?" The suit deflated, an invisible sigh, otherwise Margo Villanueva's face was a mask.

"The problem is, Supervisor . . ." I looked over at the portraits on the wall. The husband who left her widowed looking noble, deceased. My head swam with the power of that room, of Supervisor Villanueva, and my errand that could be the mistake that sunk the career of a mayoral candidate and Willie's client. "The problem, Supervisor," the words sounded squeaky on the strained air between us, "is that one of the blackmailers has been—" I aimed the word into the ivory carpet, "—murdered."

"Murdered?" Her jaw set, the hands flew apart like birds and returned folded across her chest as if to contain her swelling body in the red suit. Her little black pumped feet curled and uncurled at the ankle until they landed on the floor and the Supervisor was propelled out of her chair, facing me, leaning so close. I could count the freckles on her nose, the wrinkles on her forehead, the votes she would never get again.

"Why do you come to me with this shit?" she hissed. "I hire Willie to keep this kind of trouble away from me. Far away. Not bring this—this—garbage to my doorstep."

"Supervisor, you have to understand. This won't go away. Your blackmailer turned up dead."

"You must be out of your mind! To come here—"

"But I'm not running for mayor."

"What do you mean?"

"Someone wants you to lose the election, Supervisor."

"Yeah, a few hundred thousand people at least. Most of them Republicans."

"Supervisor, the best way to get rid of mosquitos is to drain the swamp."

"I've already been stung." She sat down, her fingers started drumming the ivory leather blotter. "Mother Maria." Her eyes focused on some faraway place, a moment of ecstasy with a high price tag.

"You have a mole somewhere, Supervisor. Look to your own organization. Who's your most recently employed staff? Who knew your schedule at the time of the photograph? Who are your advance people?"

"My aides?" Villanueva's eyes glinted at the ceiling, rang along the woodwork, figuring, thinking. "I hadn't declared my candidacy—"

"Check backgrounds. The same thing could happen again."

"The election will be over by then." Villanueva's voice was as chalky and flat as the ceiling she was looking at. What was revealed there?

"Supervisor, I'm trying to find a murderer. I need your help. Give me the names of your staff members, a place to start." The earnestness of my words was overcome by the brass whining from the party. The sentimental strains seemed to make Margo Villanueva's eyes open a little wider and the ceiling held no more interest for her.

"Excuse me," The Supervisor's face had gone white, her mouth was on automatic pilot. "I have a campaign to run." She stood up and turned her back on me, trying to put the Mark Hopkins behind her, but the Mark Hopkins had turned into murder. It must have been, must still be, quite a love affair. But would a love affair, no matter how illicit, sink the election? San Francisco was the city of love.

"Supervisor," I said to the stiffening red back. "First-degree murder has been committed on your doorstep. Nobody is going to take the fall for this; not me, not Willie." I sent a silent prayer to Diana for my job. "With all due respect, Supervisor, I'm sorry I looked up your skirt, but this is about murder."

"Miss Victor." Villanueva turned around and I saw the mask had been ripped off. Underneath, Villanueva's face seemed crumpled, defeated, all the preelection hype drained out of her. "I have four children, fifteen grandchildren, and twenty-two great-grandchildren."

"Mazel tov."

"There-is-nothing-I-can-do-now—" the words came from between gritting teeth.

"Supervisor." I kept my voice as low as possible and still be audible. "I'd let your friend know, whoever was on that bed with you."

"Never." Black eagle eyes spun pinwheels of fury my way. Villanueva's lower jaw jutted out, decision made. She walked to the door, twisted the golden handle. The door opened a crack, a black shadow stripe moved along the door, fled away. "Now, get out."

The living room was empty, the big black sheet of glass seemed hard, opaque. I could see the flaming colors of party goers in the garden. And then, behind me, quick as a cat and nearly as quiet, Dee Dee Hammerman was breathing down my neck, twisting my arm none too politely behind my back and showing me the door.

"Dee Dee, you can really hustle through the rug in high heels," I said, feeling a surprising strength in her grip.

"Let me know when it hurts." Dee Dee twisted harder. I barely caught a phrase of *"Guadalajara,"* as Dee Dee guided me through the kitchen, past the rest of the help. Cooks and caterers were wiping pans, caterers unbuttoning the tight vests of their uniforms.

They managed to ignore our strange dance as Dee Dee led me off to a small laundry porch. A solid door crowded up against my nose; Dee Dee's knee was in the small of my back, about where my kidney would be.

"It's sad, the things they teach press secretaries these days."

"Shut up." The collar of Rose's Chanel suit twisted around my neck.

"I don't want to think about what I would do to you if the stitches ripped. This is a loaner Chanel."

"I don't think you have much use for such a wardrobe in your profession."

"Yeah, and mink-lined gutters don't feel good to me either."

"You are a very tiresome woman, Ms. Victor."

"Then why do you find me so interesting? I think you're really interesting. Not to mention your buddy Bert. He's having a little trouble controlling his accent; maybe you could suggest a little self-tanning lotion while he naps in his coffin?"

"I work for Supervisor Villanueva. And she doesn't like you. She doesn't like you a lot."

"And here I thought we were buddies. After all, I do all the dirty work, you see. Nothing like killing the messenger."

"As long as you get the message, girlie."

"Well, since Villanueva's always voted against campaign reform, maybe you don't need to worry."

Dee Dee Hammerman's hands kept twisting around my collar and I started to feel faint. There was just a few inches between my feet and hers and I could have stomped her toes easily, but a higher principle stopped me.

"Here's the street, Ms. Victor. In case you don't recognize it." The sun hit my face as Dee Dee pushed me down the back stairs. I landed on the lawn, stumbled, and stood up and straightened out the suitcoat. "You know Dee Dee," I gasped, "you're giving democracy a bad name."

"Oh, yeah?" Dee Dee Hammerman laughed, a tight unpleasant sound. "So go vote Republican!"

The door slammed and I looked around me at all of Villanueva's carefully tended plants. The bright sunlight lit blazing bougainvillaea. Nothing like being thrown out of the house in broad daylight.

"Need a hand, lady?" The parking attendant was coming over to me. "Can I pull up your car perhaps?"

"Yeah." I waved his helping hand aside, limping off the lawn, an ungainly collection of long, sore limbs. I couldn't help regretting the whole preparation that had made me presentable. "I shaved my legs for this fucking party," I sighed.

"And you nicked your ankle too. I knew you was the help."

"The Chanel suit doesn't do the trick."

"No, the suit part is okay." He squinted down at my feet, staring at my plaid tennies. "It's the shoes."

CHAPTER TWENTY

TEAR
TRACKS

"We've got the prints!" Rose led me to a long console of re-cycled doors. Seven color screens showed black and white patterns, a pebbly pattern in swirls. Giant fingerprints. As she opened the door, guitars and a chorus leaked out. "Blake, turn that music down."

"This is the best part!" The whining protest came from in-side the computer room.

"Blake is downloading the information now." Rose put her hands on the back of an old office chair; Blake rode it like a horse. "We gotta work on your presentation skills, Blake." The air was heavy with spent hemp; the lime-green tube of the computer illuminated Blake's face, his features mischievous in green light. On one wing of an airplane ash-tray a marijuana bud, bluish, sticky, had been partially con-sumed. A thin pack of papers spilled delicate leaves over the area.

Today's newspaper lay open on the console. A picture of Calvin Smith took up most of the space above the fold. He smiled, a grin which conveyed a sense of delight, mutual de-light that you, as viewer, shared in. Calvin Smith always had that tricky, slick grin. I had never seen him without it. His valet had done a nice job. You could slice bread on the creases of Calvin Smith's pants. They said you could cut a lot of deals with Calvin Smith too. The air was suddenly full of the pungent smell of fine hemp bud.

"Do you *have to*, Blake?" Rose sighed.

"Mind candy for the faun of our technical times," I told Rose. "Blake works magic that brings us fingerprints from the FBI."

"And, Rose, I'm not a cybertheif," he protested. "Just a borrower who checks out information in the big cyberspace library. I take information, not money."

"You're a real moral animal," Rose said. "Too bad the National Security Council didn't see it that way."

"Man, some of the guys I met in Lompoc—"

"The prints, Blake." Rose was always trying to keep the lid on the young cyberthief. She'd met Blake when he was sixteen, when, on a tip from a social worker, she rescued the whiz kid from Juvenile Hall. He'd been caught hacking, and other than cyberspace he hadn't had a home for five years.

While in Juvie, without a keyboard, he was very well behaved but extremely depressed. A social worker who knew Rose tipped her off to the kid. When she first saw him he was dull-eyed and thin, mottled skin and the flat voice of despair. But Blake had no idea what was in store for him.

On his release from Juvenile Hall, Rose had taken him into her home and enrolled him in a pilot program for underachieveres. She gave him a teenage boy room and let him do whatever he wanted to it. A computer and a modem with a thousand cloaking devices were provided and the life came back into his voice. As Blake learned to break through each one of the cloaking devices Rose advised the company who sold the security software, eventually selling the information so they could upgrade their products. Thus Rose put Blake on the payroll, but all the money that was rolling in went straight into savings for his college education. The sizable amount meant that Blake could have been Ivy League or any League.

And then Blake broke into the military's NORAD defense computers in Colorado. There was a lot of media hype, and a piece in the *New York Times*, which didn't help his attitude. Blake was sent to Lompoc Minimum Security for fooling around in Pentagon cyberspace. I could see that his stint in Lompoc hadn't rehabilitated him. Blake's attitude was still a little stronger than his sense of self-protection. And he needed the security of Rose's love far more than he would ever admit.

"We'll have all the possibilities for your client within minutes, ladies." Blake punched in a code, bent over, and began picking up all the papers off the floor. He rolled what was left of the bud in one of them and put it all in his pocket. "Here's how it works: the system scans all available fingerprints and sends back five to twenty possibilities. We don't stay on the line too long; it would take too much computer time to analyze for the final identification; such is the glorious specificity of fingerprints, but—" he rifled a stack of papers— "I can download twenty possibilities in under two minutes. You can make the final ID pretty easily with your eyes." He pointed to the monitor where nicely organized boxes, fingerprints, names, and dates were whipping across the screen.

"Fucking hell," I breathed, "People-hunting made easy."

"Don't feed his ego, Emma."

"This is CLETS, California local data. We're going for the nine Bay Area counties, first. Nope, nope . . ."

"Two minutes, Blake." Rose's tones were the voice of doom.

"Hey, I'm routing it through Melbourne, it gives me an extra three seconds, Rose."

"Nineteen, eighteen—I'm not going for the extra three seconds Blake."

Fingerprints whizzing by on the screen; Blake's feet were doing a dance on the floor as he swiveled in his chair.

"Going through San Mateo Country," he said.

"Ten, nine . . ."

"San Francisco . . . almost through it . . . just a few more sec—"

"Three, two . . ." Rose's upper lip developed beads.

"Bang!" Blake hung up the phone. "Just got through with the City! Your boys aren't from around here, Emma. See, no problem, Rose. Next I'll do California Information statewide, CII, NCIC, the national system. You've got such nice, clear prints, Emma. We're really getting through the systems *fast*. Good work."

"That's what I love about computer nerds, they're such team players." I peered over his shoulder at the screen; the gray pixelated fingerprint hovered, big as a billboard in the darkened room.

"Totally awesome, isn't it?" Blake twisted in his chair, turned the music down. "Here's an example of the information we'll be getting." Blake clicked some gray buttons and a fingerprint with a case history popped onto the screen. "Fred Bruggeman. He's still in the joint. Homicide, one, I think. Robbed a convience store. So we know it ain't him."

To the right information was spelled out: Last Name, First Name, Social Security Number, Case Number, Record Number. Over that a row of boxes read: Search, Go, Stop, Select to Save.

"It's so user-friendly, I cannot believe!" Blake clicked on the Search button and the hard drive started humming. "Pretty soon we'll be in the New York State Welfare System, but we don't want to catch anyone from there," he said.

"Emma, Blake, you want a cuppa coffee?" Rose called out.

"Yes!"

"French roast, the good stuff," Blake hissed. "Otherwise she buys discount."

"Blake, can you look someone up by name?"

"Yeah, let me just switch phone lines." His fingers played with a large modem hookup. "Look up, Harlan Knapp." I spelled out the name. "Lives in San Diego."

Blake tapped the name in.

"Qwank! Qwank!"

"Sorry, Emma, nothing there for Harlan Knapp. "

"Who's that?" Rose asked, returning with brew.

"A deadbeat dentist." I took the cup and looked inside. Rose didn't make great coffee.

"Hurt that bad?" She handed a cup to Blake.

"The enemy of a client."

"How about—" I took the whiskey glass with the finger-prints of Bert Lubbers out of my jacket. I held it up to the light. The index finger was clearly visible.

"What's that?"

"Something that I picked up at a fund-raising party."

"Can't take you anywhere, Emma, you're always running off with the dinnerware."

"How about checking on this print for me, Rose? One last little favor."

"Yeah, Rose, I'm sure in a half hour—" Blake booted up his computer; the screen split into flying toasters. "Who's the dude, Emma?"

"Just some freaker I met at a party."

"No, Emma. No, Blake," Rose was firm. "We've done enough hacking for one night. I don't want you back in prison, Blake."

"Aw, Rose. It wasn't so bad."

"The next time, Blake, won't be so good."

"Hey, did I ever tell you how I kept my friend Daniel's sister from dating that serial killer?" Blake said proudly, putting three teaspoons of sugar in his coffee.

"What?"

"Seriously. I was in the joint and Daniel's sister, Geraldine, was going out with some freaker. I just tapped in the guy's name. Came up on a cross-index of aliases. Geraldine didn't think he was right, but she wasn't sure. It was kind of a joke, actually. So I punch in this guy, Frederico Tallman, and hell if a whole phone book didn't come up. Fifty-five aliases: Fred Talis, Frank Tallman, Teddy Francis. The guy had a record long as my arm and spooky stuff too. Liked to cut 'em up and eat 'em. Only certain parts—"

"*Blake*—" Rose sounded a warning.

"I remember that case. The Thanksgiving killer." I cut in. "Something about the holiday set him off."

"Something about the holidays sets a lot of people off."

"Blake, that was the one that ended with a high speed chase somewhere in Wyoming, right?"

"You got it, sister boss. I can tell you my friend Danny was sweating it out when we found out. Called his sister right away. Geraldine told the freaker that she had the flu and went to stay with her mother in Texas. That was one date that never happened. We called the fucking FBI from a pay phone in prison."

"How'd you get a line out from prison?" Even Rose looked impressed.

"Ever hear of cell phones?" Blake snorted. "It was so great; we watched the whole car chase, the arrest, all of it sitting in the rec room, watching TV, screaming like it was a Lakers' game. The FBI, they don't know what to say; said it was an anonymous tip. Wouldn't they just love to know we were just doing their work for them. And better."

"I'll never forget his eyes," I said, remembering the strange blank blue stare that the killer had aimed into the camera.

"Anyway, I saved his sister's head from being somebody's Thanksgiving dinner. The dude is seriously in my debt. He's a big cat in junk bonds. You need junk bonds, Rose?"

"Blake, I'm really glad you got a serial killer off the map. We're all glad. It's upped your karma enormously. Now, let's get back to Emma's fingerprints."

"Okay, let's go national now. And let's route it through, let's see, how about Toronto, via Hong Kong." He replaced the handset and the Star Wars sounds came through the wire. "Yes! We're *in*!" His fist popped into the air. "Okay, let'em roll." We sat back and watched while Rose crouched over a stopwatch.

"Three minutes minus two," she said.

"We'll have to go back in if—hey, wait—there's one, two, fuckin' hell, there's four possibilities coming up."

We watched the information roll up on the screen. "Okay! All right!"

"Forty-five, forty-four . . ." Rose counted.

"We're downloading now—"

"Forty . . ."

"Bang!" A grin nearly split Blake's face in half. "Downloading now. All safe!" Blake put out my photo enlargements; underneath them he made a row of the four 8½ by 11 pieces of bond paper all showing the familiar black and white pattern.

"Hey, look at this one. Number four. Could be your dude; look at that swirl, whorl, whatever you call it, right there."

"Tented arch," I whispered drawing closer. "Yeah, Blake." I scanned my photos against the print. "This is him."

"It's him." Rose had better eyes than any of us.

"So, who is this creep? Let's find out, shall we, ladies?" Blake found the accompanying rap sheet. "Philip A. Harmstead, burglary, first, burglary, first, extortion, forgery . . ." Rose read. "Pandering. He's a cutie."

"No person-to-person crimes. Good. Extortion, we like that," I said.

"Forty-three."

"It's the right neighborhood for the corpse. How tall is he?"

"He's five feet ten inches tall," Blake read off the rap sheet.

"In elevator heels he's six foot. The dead man is—was— Philip A. Harmstead. We found him," I said.

"Let's go to the market," Rose turned around. "Thanks, Blake." Rose wheeled over and gave him a big hug. Blake pulled Rose slightly out of her chair with the intensity of his embrace.

"Thanks, Blake," I said. "C'mon, Rose." Blake shut down the file, stretching his short legs, pointing his toes.

"Take a nap in the back, Blake. Take the day off. And take your goddamn drugs outta here," Rose said.

Born in Algonquin, Illinois, Philip A. Harmstead had a few short visits to Joliet Prison. Joliet, such a beautiful name, a romantic bird, a hell house in the middle of the prairie. Sweatboxes. Sleep deprivation. Where hardened criminals become concretized or turned to jelly.

And Philip A. Harmstead had put in more than a few semesters. His first conviction, at eighteen, was for selling stolen goods. A check kiting operation, a little mail fraud, and extortion netted him San Quentin. And now he was dead. A real American tragedy. Done and over. And an unknown on the loose. I told Rose about the glowing qualities of Philip Harmstead's corpse.

"Philip Harmstead had the money on him? You think he was going to double-cross his partner?"

"I would say so, just from the amount of fluorescent powder on him. And the little bullet that whizzed by my ear suggested someone wasn't too happy about it. And Philip glowed like a firefly."

"Piecing it together from the remaining partner's perspective, it doesn't look good." Rose looked at the bloody fingerprint on the index card. She squinted, her freckled face deep red from the glow of a pink computer screen.

"Yeah, he thinks I killed Philip and made off with the dough. That's what I'd think anyway. As for the double-cross, maybe that's why he came looking for him in the first place."

"What does he know about you?" Rose murmured.

"He probably has a make on my car."

"Follow you home?"

"Even if he wasn't shot dead or swept into the Pacific, he couldn't have followed me. Not unless he was a bird."

"Never say never. Be careful, Emma. Extortion. These guys in Federal prisons have a bad education. What do you know about him?"

"Short, five foot five, maybe. Built. A gym jockey. Steroids."

"A job this gross should be paying you well. What *is* Willie paying you?"

"Let me tell you about the dentist."

"I hope you're not working pro bono."

"Don't worry about me."

"Looking at your face, I worry. Those scratches still look hot."

"Great. I've got a matinee date with Mona Lee."

"The electrical inspector?"

"You know her?"

"Yeah. She inspected my building. Tough cookie. Gave

my contractor a sleepless night for rocking off a wall before she checked the outlet."

"Did she make you rip out the wall?"

"Naw. She just wanted to make sure he knew who was running the show. Go run a tango across Mona's palm, Emma. Just don't forget that she'll want to check all the wiring that's walled off."

"I'm not worried about Mona. I've got a dentist stalking me. He ran out on the kids and the wife sometime back; it's another story. But it's the corpse that bothers me, Rose. I was there too close to the time of death."

"You and homicide inspectors never did get along well. Gloves and treadless tennies, we hope?"

"We'll see if the corpse hits the papers."

"News blackout? I doubt it. It's just that Calvin Smith seems to be taking up all the print. The election is in the bag for Calvin. They say he's planning the inauguration already. It's going to be a three day block party. He's rented two of the piers. Bagels and pizza, chitlins and beer. He's bussing in the homeless and the whole of Hunter's Point. They're calling it a *coronation*, Emma. It could be Margo Villanueva's funeral."

"Unless *he's* somehow connected to the Sutro Heights corpse."

"Never see the light of day, my dear. Much less the newsprint."

I sighed. The bigger gig. It was time to go to the movies.

I left Rose's warehouse, feeling like a thousand eyes were watching me. The homicide inspectors of San Francisco, the homeless people living under the freeway, sneak and creep people from General Works up among the rooftops, and some ex cons running a traffic helicopter over our heads, all of them were watching. I knew all these things were the fantasies of fear; they only got in the way of the clear path to one unlucky criminal.

Who was he? "Roid rage, pecs and abs, crawling in closets. The one who did the dirty work. The one who jumped into the brig in the blink of my eye. The one who rolled over and played dead. He had crouched in the bottom of the pool and there was only one reason why he would do so. He wanted the video; he wanted the money; and I knew he would kill to get it.

CHAPTER TWENTY-ONE

MATINEE

Up above Castro, an early fog threatened the afternoon sun-light. A grey stripe of frog hovered behind Twin Peaks, and cast a shadow over the theatre. I cruised around in Romea looking for a parking spot. *Outlaw* had received rave re-views and good press had packed in the crowd. I circled and circled for parking; sometimes it seemed as if all fourteen hundred and fifty patrons tried to park within two blocks from the theatre itself. All the free spaces by the school along Sanchez were taken.

I settled for the only available spot: a two-hour meter, Sundays enforced, right outside of Cafe Flor. I would have to leave in the middle of the film to fill the meter, but the al-ternative was endless circling and late for the date with Mona. I checked my face in the mirror, added lipstick to it, and stroked my hair back off my forehead.

The fog was coming in; I hiked through the line of hun-dreds of mostly women, mostly shivering, waiting to get into Cafe San Marcos. I recognized no one. Yes, we are everywhere. We are strangers.

Turning the corner at Market and Castro, I saw the the-atre.

With nothing of the magic of the night, the Castro was a pale replica of its evening self. Its pink had faded away to a

chalky beige, and curls of paint added extra textures to the
flourishes and embellishments of swords and shields. The
doors opened and one house streamed out, clogging Castro
Street. Festival volunteers steered people from under the
marquee, but the crowds consistently clotted the way, making restaurant plans, exchanging the addresses of parties.

I stood in line to wait for my date, polishing the tops of
my shoes with my socks. A persistent buzz behind all the
noise caught my attention. A car cruised by with a bad muf-
fler and someone yelled.

"Yeah, that's the film. From trailer trash to auteur. Are we
going to check out this one?" A couple conferred, looking at
the posters advertising *Pale Refugee*. A big cutout of the
hulking Jason Jeeters, unshaven, grim grin, stood outside the
theatre. He had a wicked twinkle in his eyes, not unlike the
goat trapped between his legs. "I'd go just to see the hunk,"
one man said. "Finally," his partner conferred, "a gay
Fabio."

Everybody seemed to be cruising like crazy or meeting
five of their very best friends. They all seemed far too animated for my tastes, like a talk show crowd, making me feel
dizzy, alienated. I suddenly saw the source of the background buzz: the *O* in the Castro marquee was flickering
like an injured eye, nervous with neon gas.

"Emma!" Mona's face was something fresh in a world of
broken and spoiled things. Puffing slightly, she was pulling
a heavy brown woolen shirt over her shoulders, stretching
her long arms through the sleeves. There was sleep in her
eyes, and catlike she rubbed her face with the back of her
hand, her cheeks turning pink with the friction.

"You look like you had a Sunday nap," I said. Mona's
arm slipped through mine.

"Yes. Cleaned out a closet and napped a week's worth.
Been staying up late at meetings for Villanueva. She gave
such a great speech to us at headquarters last night. I just
wish she'd given the same kind of speech at Golden Gate
Park yesterday."

"The *Chronicle* said she was less than sparkling."

"It's the politics that count. She *will* win!" Her hand

clasped mine as the line moved forward. "Glad we got in line early. This looks like a sellout." Mona took her glasses off, wiped the fog from them and gave me a quick kiss on the cheek. The *O* above us buzzed and buzzed. "Pretty funky, the old tubing on these neon jobs.

"Hey, *Pale Refugee!* That's gotten great reviews."

"Want to go to the champagne reception? I have tickets." I immediately regretted my words. I didn't want to bring Mona into the shadier side of my business. But Mona was asking me more questions, like, how did I get tickets? Did I know Jason Jeeters?

"What exactly *do* you do, anyway? You work for Willie Rossini, right?"

We pulled up to the marquee and I slid my festival tickets under the glass.

"I saw your car," Mona confirmed, once we'd settled on the old red velvet seats. She was helping me off with my coat, her fingers managing to move across my neck. "Stuck at one of those shitty two-hour spots. I'll move it if the movie goes over—"

"That's okay," I said, as much because Romea's clutch needed a personal touch as I didn't want her to take the trouble. But Mona's hand was moving into my pocket. She found the enameled shield ring that held the Romea key and neatly detached it.

"Original key ring," she purred. *"Cool."* The key was quickly in her pants. "Don't worry. I'm sure I won't have any trouble with Romea's clutch." her fingers drifted over my knee. "I'll borrow your car, put a boom box in the trunk and troll the Castro, the Cafe, the Box, Red Dora's for every available woman around."

Just then Kimilar Jones came into the theatre, her brother Jason Jeeters laughing at her side like a nervous hyena. They passed in front of us and went to the front of the theatre; Overalls was directly behind them, carrying Kimilar's purse like a sherpa. Jason waving his big paw at a lot of cute guys. I followed their progess as they settled into their seats. I could see their heads together as they laughed. Overalls reaching across the armrest to find Kimilar's hand. Kimilar took her suitcase purse and put it on the floor. Her new lesbian life was just beginning.

Mona leaned over and gave me a small kiss on the nape of the neck. It should have been a wonderful moment, a tiny warm jewel of pleasure. However, I was not to enjoy such moments, or the Western-musical, *Outlaw.*

Suddenly Philip Harmstead's death mask slid up in front of my eyes. I could only see the jawless face, the sightless eyes. I tilted my head back and stared at the ceiling. The pineapple lamp of the theatre seemed coated with spikes. Mona smelled exactly like Christmas. Cinnamon and mistletoe. Some kind of aromatherapy? "Emma, hey! Are you okay?" she asked. "Your pulse is racing and your face is white as a—"

"I just need a good musical," I reassured her as the organ started and we settled down to the film.

"You need more than that," I thought I heard her say, but then the film started and she confidently took my hand in hers. The movie was not as expected. Every time I looked at the screen, Saturday night's death mask took over the technicolors. I imagined the grunts, the rage of the simian creature who seemed to disappear into the ocean.

There wasn't much that I remembered about the musical *Outlaw*. For years people talked about it, the choreography, the costumes, the narrative scope. All I knew was that a big spiked pineapple floated in front of my eyes and the Gibson girls were weeping on either side of the stage as Mona described a tango on my palm that made me wonder if she was watching the movie at all. I certainly couldn't make any sense out of anything.

That's why I hardly noticed when Mona got up and left her seat, pointing to her watch in the semi-darkness. I understood that she was going to move my car, as I saw the flash of my keys in her hands. Her face look purplish in the reflected glow of a dance scene from *Outlaw*. I turned my attention back to the film, but it was still impossible to focus. The musical faded and glowed in front of me, playing out a nightmare that only I was watching, a nightmare that was shot right within view of the Pacific Ocean.

"Bravo! Bravo!"

"Brava! Brava!"

The film was over and people were getting out of their chairs. The audience's applause receded, overcome by the crashing of the organ. I hardly noticed the house lights had blinked on, delivering me from one nightmare into another.

"Mona?" I looked around, checking my watch. Mona had been gone for forty-five minutes. That's when the thought occurred to me. The Simian One knew what Romea looked like. I pushed my way up the aisles.

"Excuse me." I pushed through the crowd.

"Sorry!" I called back, finding my way through the lobby beyond Spanish doors and into the street. The fog was coming in now, the crowd was boiling under the marquee; volunteers were trying to keep everyone moving along. I hurried down Market, telling myself that Mona had merely decided to wait for me at Cafe Flor, the movie not quite to her liking. Once I got past Noe I could see that Romea was gone. Disappeared, an Oldsmobile Cutlass in her place.

I went into Cafe Flor and cruised the tables, the patrons, asking if anyone had seen an antique Alfa Romeo pull away? No, said the cold stares of men involved in cool conversations. I went to the Record Collector's store, asking the personnel and worked my way up and down the street. No one had seen anything under the gray blanket of fog.

I called Mona's house and left a message for her. I called my number and listened to see if Mona had left a message for me. My pager was working. What had she said? *I'll borrow your car, put a boom box in the trunk and troll the Castro, the Cafe, the Box, Red Dora's for every available woman.*

Her words were twisted by my own sudden doubt. Willie out of town. Dee Dee Hammerman had me in her hammerlock. Whose gig was this anyway? Kill the messenger was a distinct probability. The complete video would undoubtedly hold the answer, if it was still in San Francisco. Mona was, after all, a foot soldier in Margo Villanueva's organization. I looked at the poster with the goat on it. Mona wanted the Supervisor to win so badly. We all did. The stripe down the goat's face made it look like it was split down the middle. I shook my head and the image receded.

Hiking back up to Market I inspected the place where Romea had stood. Nothing. The Oldsmobile Cutlass stood its ground, an obscene construction of rubber and metal that had nothing to do with Romea. I bent over and saw leaking oil and not much else under the car. I hiked up to the Castro, looking for Mona's spunky step, the yellow hood of Romea cruising around looking for me or every available woman in the Castro. I dove into the crowds. The fog had wrapped the big letters in mist. But there was still no Mona, no Romea, no valves ticking quietly at the curb, waiting for me. I cruised the crowds and ended up hiking back to Cafe Flor again to think. Maybe, just maybe, there was a benign explanation for Mona's disappearance. Maybe, but I didn't think so.

CHAPTER TWENTY-TWO

NO
SUITCASE

Could Mona have borrowed my car in a revengeful prank? That was out of character for a career electrical inspector. Had the palm tango sounded like a marriage proposal to her? Mixed messages can make people crazy. And how well did I know Mona?

She said she wrote poetry on her off hours. A quiet hobby, one which enabled her to disconnect her phone with impunity. Was there something going on in city government, something only Mona and her high-powered aunt knew about? Something that made it imperative that Margo Villanueva, not Calvin Smith, get reelected?

Or perhaps Mona had stalled the old sports car. She was an electrician. She wouldn't know anything about cars. She would be afraid to try and resuscitate the old vehicle, which would then be towed to somewhere, a heinously time consuming and expensive event.

A small accident. A big accident. Any accident, just so long as everyone was okay, just so long as it wasn't what I most feared. The empty horizon of the ocean stretched before me, stretched tight, just like the simian creature who had crouched at the bottom of an empty concrete pit, waiting, faking me out. Only he got Mona instead.

There was no way to call it in as a stolen vehicle. Not with

my car key in Mona's possession. Besides, as Laura had
pointed out, the cops were already calling Calvin Smith *boss*
down at the Hall of Justice. And I had a Margo Villanueva
bumper sticker on my car. Too many loose threads and I had
to talk to Willie.

I was all ready to drop the dimes when Kimilar Jones
came into the Flor, all alone, not even a suitcase to keep her
company. She made her way around the tables, glancing at
faces and quickly away, her manner wound up, agitated.
Kimilar was going to ignore me. I could tell from the way
she restricted her peripheral vision, the self-conscious flip of
her hair as she walked by me.

Her flaxen hair had been brushed to a shine for the
evening, a coral shade of lipstick, nearly the color of her tan,
had been drawn across her lips. Her shoulders twitched as
she walk past, the suede fringe on her leather jacket whipped
me. I stuck my arm out, forcing her to stop.

"Emma!" Her turned face was surprised, almost white
under her rugged tan.

"Kimilar, could we have a minute?"

"I'm looking for Jason, I have to find him." Her eyes scat-
tershot over the cafe, looking for Jason, or maybe Overalls.

"I have a report to make to you."

"Have you seen Jason Jeeters? Have you been up at the
Castro?"

"Nope."

"Oh, God," Kimilar was trembling. "He's disappeared."

"Funny, that's happening to a number of people."

"What? What are you talking about?" Kimilar looked at
me and I seemed to come into focus.

"John Osbourne? I was the person who was going to
give you back the farm, remember? The quitclaim? I went
to his letter drop. I showed the guy who works there the
picture. Sounded to me like someone is impersonating
your ex-partner. Someone who has a plane ticket to Brazil."

"Oh, that, hahahahaha," Big teeth flashed. "I thought you
was gonna say that my brutha had disappeared." She caught
her breath and got back some composure. "I am so sorry,
Emma. It turns out I sent you on a wild goose chase after all.

I just found out, really. It turns out a friend of my ex-husband's—"

"I thought you said he was just an ex-boyfriend—"

"Well, the marriage wasn't annulled, but that isn't the point." Her eyes kept darting to the window, to the garden gate where Jason Jeeters—or someone else might enter.

"It makes quite a legal point in regard to property."

"The point is," she sighed and started again, "the point is that it's all settled. A friend of Jack's was picking up the mail for him. I remembered his number, we got in touch. I went to Woolworth's and got a quitclaim just like you said. He signed it. And that's that. I meant to call you. Honest."

"But you were too busy tasting the lesbian limo life."

"I really do appreciate what you've done. Don't forget to give me your address. I'd like to send you something special from the farm. Of course I want you to keep the retainer, okay?"

"That's fair."

"So now that my *legal* problem is over with, can I buy you a beer? "

"Thanks, but no thanks. I'm looking for my friend, Mona."

"The Chinese girl?"

"Yeah. Seen her?"

"No. I'm too busy lookin' for my brother to notice. If I see her, what should I say?"

"That I'm going to keep looking for her until I find her. And to leave a message on my machine."

"Sounds serious."

"Maybe, maybe not. What's with you?"

"It's just that Jason Jeeters took my bag." Her arms flapped helplessly at her sides. "And it had the quitclaim in it. You haven't seen him, have you?"

"Your brother into purse snatching?"

"No. At least not at the moment. But he used to steal from Mom all the time."

"Really? Life of crime began that early?"

"In our house, an' that's a generous description, all we did was worry about money. Landlords chasing us down for the rent, splitting town before the grocer chased us down. It was that bad."

"But not everyone turns crooked."

"No, it's usually the menfolk, isn't it? Mom kept us going, all right."

"And while Jason was stealing from your mother's purse, what did you do?"

"Me? I used to *eat* money. Nickels and dimes and my grandmommy's wedding ring. Anyway, it was nice meetin' you Emma. Look me up if you ever get to Texas." She handed me a card.

"I just might do that."

"We could take the dogs out to watch the dawn, have a little fire and make some cowboy coffee. I wouldn't say the limo life suits me, much as the Castro has been a very interesting place." Kimilar brushed a few flossy hairs off my coat. "Bye now, Emma! Keep takin' care of business!" Kimilar made her way through the tables and out the garden gate, stopping once to wave. I watched her fade like the end to a future feature film in the festival: *She Came to the Castro*.

I walked by the Oldsmobile again as if, like a trick pumpkin, it would reveal itself to be my car, with Mona in it. But no amount of magical thinking was going to make things okay.

I made my way up Market Street, through the crowds, past the hustlers and out of tune street musicians, past the women from the suburbs looking for their first lesbo thrill and the pretty boys for whom thrills were a daily diet.

The Castro Theatre was still alive. The neon *O* on the sign was still buzzing around the corner and it was hard to miss the peculiar diamond-patterned bell-bottoms of Jason Jeeters. He was with a small, trim-looking man, Oxford shirt, burmudas, loafers with socks. It was Martel. Jason was carrying a backpack too small to carry Kimilar's luggage.

I watched them round the corner past Ben and Jerry's ice cream into the parking lot behind the theatre. I counted to thirty and when I didn't hear a car start I made my way along the wall and stopped. Baking waffle smells and silence. No car doors, automobile sounds, sudden flood of headlights. I crouched down and started moving, creeping along the bumpers of cars. The wind blowing through the trees gave me audio cover and in no time I could just see Jason Jeeters and Martel. There was the jumping flame of a lighter turned up high. And I could just see the utensils laid out before them and the eager, anxious smiles upon their faces.

Then I knew my hunch was correct. Even without seeing the movie I knew what he was doing. It was 4 P.M. and Jason Jeeters Jones was cooking an early dinner.

CHAPTER TWENTY-THREE

MAIN
COURSE

Jason had taken a dark, zippered bag out of his pack and took out several traveling toiletry bottles and a white handkerchief. He put the handkerchief down on his pack and unrolled its contents: a syringe, a spoon.

"It's hot shit, man," Jason's Bic had been set on high; it leaped into the air, dancing off the end of the green plastic rectangle. He laughed. Martel looked nervous. "Crack lighter. Let's get started." He took a balloon out of his hip pocket and unknotted its neck. He flicked the bottom of it with his fingers, the weight in the bottom making it swing almost organically.

"Honey, maybe you can just put it off for until after the film tonight," Martel was anxious, licking his rosebud lips, stroking the brown leather of his watchband. He looked more like he should be fishing with the Boy Scouts than doing drugs. With a sleight of hand, he helped wrap the scarf around the crook of Jason's arms.

Powder from the balloon had fallen into the bowl of the spoon now. Jason took one of the toiletry bottles and squeezed a drop of water into the spoon. Under the flame it came to furious boil. The scarf was still hanging, unknotted, from his elbow. I turned my head. I had enough bad images in my brain for the week, but just like car wrecks, I was doomed by human nature to watch.

"This stuff is too strong for you, Junior." Jason laughed as he had a slipknot in the end of the fine silk. He pulled the fabric until it stretched at the corner, and then made a deep indentation into his arm.

"Where'd you get money for this shit, Jason? What kinda laws you breakin', federal or state? Give me a clue."

"One hundred and fifty alpaca sweaters."

"What?"

"Aw, forget it."

"I wanna know! You stealin' from your own sister?" An anxious note from Martel. "I want to go back to the farm. You gotta get clean, honey."

"That there bottle is bleach, hand it to me, wouldja?" He pointed the needle, veins popped up, on the threshold a particular kind of ecstasy. Martel was looking at Jason's arm like it was a road map to something awful.

"You know, kid," Jason explained patiently, preparing his medicine, "sometimes I'm still in the hole. That place of forever darkness. You can stretch out your hands and feel the walls, all right. And there's a thin blanket on the ground. But other than that you don't see nothin' and you don't feel nothin' but hard cold fear. And somewhere you bring something up to fight that fear down. But you know, I don't think nobody is supposed to feel that fear. Because once you feel it you cain't never escape it. Somewheres its always there, and it'll git ya, in the dead of night and the heat of the day, Martel. Part of me is always inside a maze of concrete walls. And this here is the only remedy, man. It's like the big pain I've always had just melts away." The needle went in and he plunged; Jason found the relief he needed. His head flopped on his shoulder, and within a minute the huge man was felled, lying on his side in the parking lot. Martel just stood there looking at him. A tapping and clicking announced another visitor on the scene.

Kimilar was striding over the asphalt, her heels tapped out an anxious, strident rhythm that matched her voice. "Get up, Jason Jeeters!" A pointed toe prodded him tentatively, then kicked him hard, metal edges flashing. The man hardly registered a response. Where Jason was vacationing everything was pink and sunny, there were no rough edges or metal toe tips. Jason was a made man, made into mush.

"Hey, you goddamn fuck, you wake up and lissen to me!" The blows came harder as Kimilar realized how anesthetized her brother was. License to torture, the metal toes found their way into the hard flesh of his buttocks.

"Hey!" Jason responded out of his heroin haze.

"You gonna bleat like some kinda sheep, brotha, after I git through with you!"

"Nawwwww—" Jason was crawling across the pavement, the metal toe of her boot lingering in his face. "I didn't mean to steal them!"

"Steal *what*?" Kimilar's boots stopped their pummeling.

"Alpaca sweaters," Martel's voice came through the shadows. He was leaning heavily against a tree.

"What's he talkin' about, Jason?"

"Sorry, little sis, I sold," Jason was laughing, holding his sides like they might just fall apart, "I sold a whole buncha your fleece, honey!"

And with that Kimilar gave him a swift kick on the side of the head which threw the big man onto the pavement. She grabbed the top of his ear and twisted hard, pulling him along the pavement into the middle of the parking lot.

"And where's my bag?" Kimilar increased the pressure on his ear. The slightest amount of pain registered in his face. He lifted his hand, but a drug reverie interrupted his intention. He drifted back down onto the pavement with a smile, instantly in the land of happy dreams.

"Where the fuck is my bag, Jason?" Kimilar bent down and shouted as if he were deaf.

"Your what?"

"My bag, my *purse*, you idiot!"

"Ask your friend Overalls. Hey, lil'sister, you sure can sing in the sack. Even Uncle Jimmy couldn't make you howl like that."

Kimilar's silver toe found Jason's face and he took a direct hit in the nose; the toe-cap must have split his nostril.

Jason screamed, his hand flew to his face; blood gushed freely between his fingers; he staggered to his feet.

"My opening is tonight!" he whined.

"Now, big brother, where is my *purse*?"

"At the hotel," Jason panted. "They found it at the table and they put it in the safe."

"Well, wake up. Here, put this on your nose," she handed him a bandanna handkerchief.

"He wuz gonna look so cute for the opening," Martel whined in a sluggish voice.

"Everybody's looking at his dick, Martel, not his face. Jason. Martel. Listen. Concentrate, dudes. I gotta warn you. I hired a sort of private detective—"

"What?" That woke Jason stand up a degree, at least his eyes opened.

"Well, you haven't exactly been a lot of help. I had to try and find him, get clear title —"

"God, you didn't mention *my* name?"

"Of course not, walnut brain. Anyway, keep an eye out for our investigative moth, you guys. She's a tall babe, salt and pepper hair, walks fast. She doesn't say a lot but kinda lurks around in the shadows."

"You want I should I do somethin' with her?" Jason asked.

"You touch a hair on her head you're gonna be *real* sorry. Just keep out of her way. She's as snoopy as she is cute. And she doesn't need to know about any of our business. I've got clear title to the farm, so it doesn't matter now, does it? You hear what I'm sayin'?"

Jason wiped off his face with a handkerchief. "Lil' sister-love, you don't have to worry about the girl *or* the farm. I'll keep out of her way. And the farm is all yours now, ain't it? And you'll always let brother come visit, won't you?" He slung a big arm around her tiny shoulders. She pushed it off. "Don't be like that! Hey! I brought you here to the Castro! Paid for you way and all! It's been good for your business too, honey. I'm helpin' to put you on the map."

"And out of a hundred and fifty alpaca sweaters. No won-

der Blue acted so oddly when I asked her about that ship-
ment. You been at her?"

"Not a chance in hell. Just consider it a loan."

"Don't come back while you're on smack, brutha dear. I
got enough goats to take care of. You better take care of that
nose." Her tone was suddenly that of a practical nurse. How
many menfolk had Kimilar beaten up, and then nursed back
to health, in her time?

Jason was obediently packing up his works. He folded
the syringe into a piece of leather, and capped the bottle of
bleach. "My films gonna take care of alluv us. We got a hit
on our hands. Everybody in fuckin' America gonna see my
film and know what's goin' on in the joint. And just how it
feels."

"You're just high on yourself, big brother. I suggest you
attend to Martel. He's not having the same self-righteous
time as you are."

Jason Jeeter's companion, Martel, was sitting at the base
of a tree, his head on his chest. "C'mon, Martel, wake up."
Jason put a hand on his shoulder. "Martel, Martel, c'mon,
honey! I got a nice hotel room honey with a flocked bedspread. Martel! Hey, you there Martel?"

The young man didn't move.

"What the hell?" Jason bent down and a look of fear
passed over his face.

"He used your works, Jason Jeeters!"

"Oh, shit!"

"He doan look so good. Quick, we gotta get him on his
feet!" Kimilar's voice rose a note. "Jason! Jason!"

"Hey! Martel! Boy!" Jason was slapping the young man.

Kimilar hoisted the little man into her arms, where they
appeared to do an awkward dance. "We gotta walk him.
C'mon, Jason, help me! Jason, you useless piece of shit!"

Martel opened one eye. "Wha?" he said.

"This is *your* fault, Jason Jeeters. You better get clean; I
ain't pickin' up any more of your messes. Look at him! Martel, honey! You can't do this shit! You ain't used to it! Jason,
why don't you keep better track of your works; keep guns
outta the hands of children," Kimilar admonished. I watched

them walk Martel up and down the parking lot. "Martel, honey, you gotta walk. That's right, walk, step, walk, step," she crooned. The buzzing of the Castro crowd came into focus. Patrons were beginning to leave the theatre. "Someone's coming for their car," she hissed.

"Martel!" Jason hollered and Martel opened his eyes. The young man was coming alive. His rolling head becoming more firmly established on his neck.

"Holy Mother of Jesus," Kimilar let out a long sigh of relief.

"Hi Jason! Hi Kimilar!" He took his arms from around their necks and tried to stand on his feet. A helping hand from Kimilar steadied him.

"Let's get you some coffee," she said.

"Where we going?"

"The Clinton Arms. We're goin' to the Clinton Arms, honey!" Jason crooned.

"Arms?" Martel managed to mumble.

"All I know, Jason, we've had the entire farm riding on your fucking film even before we got clear title. So you better *show* up and not *fuck* up, big brother. Tonight is supposed to get us out of hock, so watch your step. Or you're gonna end up in Bridgeways Center. I read all about it in a newspaper article. They say you come out of there some kind of obedient Labrador."

"I'd like to see that," Martel was fully awake now.

"And, Martel, I'm counting on you to keep him outta trouble, and not get him into it by giving yourself an overdose."

"Man, I saw colors like I've never seen before. And things were floating up at me." Martel's voice held wonder. "Really, really cool things."

"Martel," Kimilar turned, "You were almost *dead.*" She walked right past the bush where I'd been standing. I could even make out the delicate pattern etched onto the silver tips of her boots. It made me feel warm and fuzzy all over to think that she owned the farm and didn't have to eat money anymore. She would replay the nights with Overalls as she sheared sheep and waited for spring. Maybe another mountain woman would walk into her life. Kimilar had a lesbian future waiting for her just over the next state line.

All the loose ends were going to come together, I thought. I went to a phone booth to call home. Mona had surely left a message on my answering machine. Mona, sweet Mona who fought with her feet for progressive politics. I reassured myself as I heard the message machine squeal backward on rewind.

The dry cleaner called; my linen suit was pressed, ready for winter storage. Someone who might or might not have been the dentist breathed into my phone. Nobody I wanted to hear from called me except Rose.

"Emma, Blake thinks he's found the partner of your blackmailer. You'd better get over here."

Blake's voice chimed over the line; news important enough to snatch the phone from his boss: "Turns out he's bad news," Blake said. "Haam Harmstead, alias Howard Harms, Happy Henley, has been convicted on assault, battery, rape, and second-degree murder. Served in the army, launched grenades. The guy's a freaker, Emma. He decapitated prisoners of war, there was a court-martial. Mayhem. He got out of the state pen five years ago and never reported to his parole officer. Charged with homicide in '79; a bar brawl in '89, illegally seized evidence got him off. He likes to break into buildings with skylights and stalk women in parking lots. He knifed people in bars when he got riled and allegedly once threw a child off a bridge. Sentenced to fifteen-to-life in Joliet he got off by snitching on another prisoner after a riot. And mayhem. Every time, there's been a charge of mayhem."

Mayhem. A reptile from the shallow end of the gene pool.

I hiked for the last time back down to Cafe Flor, anticipating the best but expecting the absolute worst as I approached the spot from where Romea had disappeared. The aromatherapy displays, crystals and vitamins and positive affirmations were deadly. The big, oil leaking Oldsmobile was gone. A Volkswagen Golf barely filled up the space now. Coming closer, I crouched down to the pavement.

There, just under where Romea's door had been, formerly obscured by the huge tire of the Oldsmobile Cutlass, was a toothpick. Orange and triangle-tipped, it was the kind that you ripped off the pack. The kind that you chewed, anxious on steroids, right before you, a mayhem kind of guy, carjacked a vehicle with Mona in it.

CHAPTER TWENTY-FOUR

MAYHEM

Mayhem is the willful disfigurement or dismemberment of another human being, depriving them of the use of a bodily part. It is a charge that belongs distinctly to sociopaths, people who are unable to empathize with another's pain, people who could burn you with cigarettes, people who could hear your screams and would laugh. People who could slit your throat and eat your lunch. It would all look like some kind of video to them, before, during, and afterward. You, if you survived, would never be the same.

Haam Harmstead had snatched the wrong person. He not only thought I had the thirty-five thousand dollars, he thought I had killed his brother. Philip Harmstead was dead. And he had been quite prepared to cross his brother. Somewhere there was an intersection of two points, between a violent sociopath and the Margo Villanueva campaign.

'Roid rage. Was someone else in control of him now? Or was he a loose canon? Or both. 'Roid rage. Back under the brightly lit marquee of the Castro, all was still and I was telling myself that I was just paranoid. Lots of people chewed toothpicks, people who ate the organic granola at Cafe Hairdo and picked the blueberries out from between their teeth. People who drove Oldsmobile Cutlasses and little Rabbits and rushed in to catch the latest Film Festival feature.

I punched my neighbor's number into the cell phone. Laura Deleuse answered and said I could borrow her car for the evening.

"Why do you need it?" she asked.

"A friend had to borrow mine."

Pause.

"Okay. By the way," she said. "I went to a Calvin Smith campaign party last night! A roller-skating doorman named Ronald greeted us, and a glitter mermaid, a live one in costume, lounged on a seafood table. It's going to be in all the columns tomorrow."

"What about Margo Villanueva? You're a lesbian, Laura. What about the Marriage Act? Calvin Smith signed it."

"I'm a cop, Emma. And Smith will appoint a DA who will convict criminals. That's more important to me than getting married, at the moment."

"I hope to pass a deadbeat dentist onto the DA any day now."

"Go for it, " I could hear her chuckling, a not particularly nice sound. And then I remembered something someone had said. Someone who wore a chamois shirt and dark glasses. *Too bad about the Pacific Ocean. You can't even wade in it.*

I called Blake.

"Blake, can you get into the file servers for the Villanueva campaign?"

"Cinch, Emma."

"See if you can check out Villanueva's press secretary, her name is Dee Dee Hammerman. And check out whoever is running the Bridgeways catering setup. Can you do it?"

"I can get through via file servers. For example, I think I'll try getting into Villanueva's files via the Registrar of Voters and Permit Department. They must have to take out any number of permits. Via two different sources I can track down the intersection that will reveal the source I want and I may get free entrée. It's like triangulation. You can use two points to find a third, if you can determine the connection."

"Triangulation?" I murmured, looking at the crooked intersection of Noe, 16th, and Market streets. "I gotta go, Blake."

"Where you goin'?"

"To find a bad little man who hides inside walls."

"Hey, Emma, Rose will want to—"

Blake's voice trailed off behind me as I hailed a taxi and headed home. I visualized the yellow Romea standing at the curb, a sweet lemon in the light of a lonely streetlamp. But with each light in the Mission I knew that all my worst projections were coming true. A sociopath wouldn't see any reason to spare Mona any pain, just because she was the wrong person. The taxi driver let me off at home. The place never looked sweeter, Victorian cut-outs, a sparkling clean kitchen and cats I might never see again.

I flew out of the taxi, my fingers mentally twisting the dial to my safe, I couldn't get to the stairs fast enough, I had no time to lose, until the snub nose of a revolver in my back stopped me.

"What's your hurry?" growled a voice. It turned out I had a lot of time to lose. As much time as the voice behind the revolver said I had.

CHAPTER TWENTY-FIVE

TRIANGULATION

"Move over there, off the street," said the voice. I moved slowly into the shadows between two houses. A woman stood directly behind me; a small woman, her voice low, smothered. For someone my height she'd be easy to take, but the gun would complicate things. She moved close into me, pressing me up against the siding of a neighbor's house.

"This is really bad for real estate values," I said.

"Quit clowning. Where's the video?" Her voice was muffled by something around her mouth, a scarf perhaps, her intonation a roller coaster of anxiety.

"What video?"

"Don't get funny." A hand grabbed my wrist, twisted; the gun muzzle prodded me.

"I'm not joking. I tried to buy it but the sale never went through."

"Yeah? This gun says that you know a lot more than you're telling."

"Don't listen to your gun. Listen to me. I don't know where the videotape is, or the thirty five thousand dollars that's floating around somewhere. I just know the salesman was hit. Most of his right jaw was missing. Maybe you know something about it?"

"If I did, I wouldn't be here, would I?"

185

"Well, I don't have the merchandise. It grew legs and walked away."

"If you do get the videotape, I could be a customer."

"What? And spare the rod?"

"Look, this wasn't a business I planned to go into." The gun pushed deeper, around my eighth lumbar. "You better be telling me the truth."

"I really hope you have a safety on. I'll let you know if, for some reason, I get the videotape. But right now I have no clues, no hunches and someone stole my car. How do I get ahold of you, if I get a lead?" I asked.

"Just remember your business is our business. We'll find you, don't worry."

"Who's 'we'?" I turned around. The butt of the revolver came crashing against my forehead, but not fast enough. I had seen a shadow, a thin thing. It was disappearing under a row of bottlebrush trees.

That's when my own little street in the Mission melted away in front of my eyes, the nighttime sky, a few constellations that made it through the neon lights, a lot of wooden Victorian fronts with geegaws, and the hard concrete which I felt against the side of my face. It all melted into a big mélange, a rainbow mess of boards and neon lighting. A split second later the entire street became one color: dark.

You are waiting in line. No ride without a ticket! Everybody has to have a ticket, that's the rule.

You, of course, are obedient. You follow all the rules which they made up in the not-so-fun house, Bridgeways. People stretch out in front of you. People stretch out behind you. Children are screaming and mothers have guns. Only mothers should have guns.

And then you realize where you are: Playland by the Sea! On the biggest and best ride of all. You had heard about it all summer. The speed of your descent was so fast, they say that the sun darkened. They called it the Eclipse.

As bodies push you from behind, you look up and see the infinitely high tower, disappearing into the clouds. How will you ever make it up the ladder? The crowd presses against you. In lockstep you go forward, hoping at the last minute that it will turn out to be a bad dream. You are carrying a lot of cash, and you worry about losing it.

Important questions fill your mind. Are we really going to go up the ladder? How many rungs are there? How long will it take? How high does it go? How high is the sky? How fast is the fall? You have a lot of questions, but nobody has any faces, much less mouths. They have been dodged away by an amateur photographer.

There is only one way to find out who has sent you here. You start to climb up, up, up.

You are at the top now. The world spreads around you like a big picnic on a blanket. You see the Tinkertoy town, and the sugar coated condominiums lining Baker Beach. The waves of the mighty Pacific are ruffles on the shore.

Just above the beach, something huge looms. A gigantic camera, five stories high, is perched. Its lens is bigger than the sun. It winks at you. It's taking your picture, watching everything you do, just like God!

After that you just look at your knuckles, skin white over the bone, stretching with every rung of the ladder. And, as it always is in dreams and diving boards, you must go forward. You have to reach the top.

Finally you are there. And doesn't everybody know it! The big camera has swung around, and is aiming its horrible cyclops lens at you. You can feel it thinking, that camera. It is not thinking happy thoughts.

You grasp the rounded top of the rails. At the top, now! Not too secure about your swan dive, you crawl onto the board; the prickly gray surface scratches your knees, the tender balls of your hands. The board bounces with every inch of progress you make, inching forward on your hands and knees.

You can feel the people behind you on the ladder. You can feel them thinking. Hurry up! Hurry up!

The camera lens turns, and records your journey. The end of the board is coming closer. You crawl forward, into the sky, inch, by inch. There it is. It's arrived. You swallow and your arms stretch out, and your fingers curl around the edge of the diving board. The people on the ladder are jeering. You pull yourself forward. But you don't look down. Not yet.

First, you listen to the faceless crowd. The little specks are

encouraging you: Don't worry! Jump! Jump! they cry. You
want to believe them, but you have the feeling that what lies all
those miles beneath you, after the clouds, and the air, and the
water, and the concrete, is the hard and final earth.

Now you think you are ready. You look past your knuckles,
and through the clouds. But when you see what waits below
you don't know what to think.

It's water all right. There a rectangular pool which looks,
from the height of the diving board, as big as a postage stamp.
But there's nothing safe about it. The pool glimmers, but not
with the coolness of water.

Kimilar Jones, white cloven hoofs on her feet, glows with a
lavender phosphorescence. She is saying something. Triangu-
lation. Cliffs and ways of seeing things. The omnipresence of
cameras, telescopes and binoculars. It's time to dive now,
Emma. To slice the air in front of you; to find out at last, what
lies below, and to fly.

I woke up on the pavement. I held on to my head, most of
which seemed to be there. I imagined the lone blackmailer in
his lair. He must have a vantage point that would include both
the parapet at Sutro Gardens and the Camera Obscura. And
that would be a very specific point.

I could see it all now; a man would look out the window and
follow me down from the parking lot to the camera. He would
see the way the two stone lions froze in their lounging position
at Sutro Gardens, the way the fog lay thick upon the lawn.
Diana would look grouchy in the mist, the green side of her
face grim and heavy.

Upstairs I opened the safe and loaded my gun. Laura's car
keys were in my mailbox. I threw open the car door, cranked
the engine, and tore away from the curb. It was said that if
Diana was on your side you died a quick and painless death,
which wouldn't include mayhem. I stepped on the gas.

Triangulation. How fast could I find that apartment? I was
none the worse for my respite on the sidewalk, and, checking
my watch, I had only lost ten minutes. But ten minutes could
mean a lot. Mayhem was experienced in nanoseconds, I told
myself, and lived with you for the rest of your life.

•   •   •

I sped along the ocean. The sunset had left a reddish smudge on the horizon. Laura's car had front-wheel drive; slightly out of alignment, it kept veering to the right, toward the waves which crashed upon the darkened shore.

The minutes stretched, no matter how hard I pushed the gas pedal to the floor. When the jaunty pointed top of the Giant Camera appeared it looked like a child's toy. The Cliff House, outlined in neon green, its gray and beige concrete coat looking as ugly as a tourist T-shirt. Seagulls wandered on the tarred roof, slick as a seal skin. They bobbed for crumbs amongst the exhaust pipes and tourist restroom ventilators. Even in the dark I could see the black waters churning around Seal Rock.

I stretched my eyes down the coast to where what was left of the Coast range slouched into the sea. The University Hospital looked like a black shoe box below the blinking towers of Twin Peaks.

There could only be a few points from which both the Sutro Heights parapet and the Camera Obscura were visible. And that intersection must be the condos at Playland. Playland by the Sea, anonymous apartments, perfect for mayhem.

The perfect place to monitor the blackmail scheme, condominiums cast blind windows at the ocean where once the tilt a whirl made everybody scream. The 38 Geary bus was crawling up the street just between me and rows of pastel housing. There were scores of windows at the Playland Condos. I searched the streets carefully. No Romea anywhere. Nevertheless, out of all those windows only a select few would be visible from both the parapet and the phone booth at the Camera Obscura. I walked quickly across the highway to where I had made the first phone call.

The little building looked so benign. I plugged another quarter in the telescope and aimed it at the hill. Two pastel towers of Playland, six flats, the top two turned six windows toward the Camera Obscura. And, I thought as I turned the scope toward Sutro Heights, they would probably provide a vantage point for the Sutro Heights parapet.

CHAPTER TWENTY-SIX

PLAYLAND
BY THE SEA

Playland Condos, a row of gray buildings, had a small utility alley behind the rows of apartments. Across the street a page link fence cordoned off what looked like a gravel pit, but the smell was more like a butcher shop.

A dusty construction crew looked angry as they worked overtime. A red and yellow crane languidly swung its hundred foot arm back and forth over the hill. A whistle blew. The crane stopped and the workers gathered their tools and left the site. A man opened and closed the gate to let them leave.

The entrance to the condo development began with a small library of notices. A large hand painted sign in red began:

PRIVATE PROPERTY. UNAUTHORIZED VEHICLES WILL BE TOWED AWAY AT OWNERS EXPENSE UNDER SEC. 22658 CVC FOR TOWED VEHICLES PHONE BILL WREN'S TOWING 341-3542.

Then in case you didn't get the point a small sign in sanserif letters restated:

PERMIT PARKING FOR RESIDENTS ONLY. VEHICLES WITHOUT VALID PARKING PERMIT WILL BE TOWED AT VEHICLE OWNERS' EXPENSE.

Nobody said anything about walking. Nobody ever did in California. A VACANCY sign was posted under the warning signs. PROTECTED BY KING SECURITY SERVICES. There were no kings or king's men around, so I drew closer. Two mid-night surfers pulled their van over to the curb, pulling out surfboards and wet suits. Slipping behind them, I drifted down the alley, behind the two northwest towers. A man came out in jockeys and picked up his afternoon paper. I wandered over to a series of metal mailboxes set into the wall. Names were written in ballpoint pen: Joseph P. Gunderson, Nisa Donnelly, Ho Tran.

Clank! A rumbling and groaning, tightening of slackening chains, and a garage door opened letting me see into a big cavern full of cars. A kelly green Jeep roared out and an electric eye closed the door quickly behind the Jeep, but not before I looked inside. Ten seconds to scan rows and rows of cars, any one of which could be Romea. I crouched in the bushes and listened to the sounds of condo inhabitants settling down for a Sunday night. Someone would work the graveyard shift, someone would be opening the garage door any second. I counted the bars on the iron gates that guarded the backs of the two northwest towers. I'd just gotten to forty when I heard the rumble and clanking and the heaving of the garage door. A white Chevy Corsica nosed its way carefully out of its den, the blue-rinsed inhabitant squinting and leaning forward over the dashboard anxiously. I stood up, drew closer, walked in front of the Corsica, putting the fear of liability into her and took a long look into the garage. Romea. Third row from the back. Way in the corner. In the shadow of a Volkswagen bus. The garage door closed five seconds after the Corsica's trunk cleared the electric eye. Drifting by me, its power brakes flashing nervously every several yards as it pulled out of the alley and onto Balboa Street. Romea. She was there or she was a figment of my imagination. I walked around to the front of the building.

Up close to the vestibule entry I slid a credit card into the single latch and opened it. Cheery tiled floors and rubber trees were a sharp departure from the faux Victorian facades as well as a fire door with GARAGE silk-screened onto the metal surface. The credit card bent nearly backward getting the plastic to the latch on the thick door, but a swift swipe at the right angle loosened the catch and gave me entry to the cool underground crypt.

Jeep Cherokees, Ford Broncos, Geos, and Festivas, no Town Cars or Cadillacs, just the everyday cars of people who worked everyday jobs and found the most affordable payoff was to live at the ocean. The kind of people who bought neon kiddie cars when they were forty. The kind of people who would never make a lot of money, who just liked to look at the ocean.

Clickety-clack, the no nonsense sound of high heels on their way to work sounded behind me. I started walking purposefully through the rows of shiny car hoods. Shoulder-length black hair as straight as a pencil and hips about as wide slid into a Honda Civic, gunned the engine, checked the lipstick, and backed out slowly. The headlights turned on automatically, small circles against the concrete wall. Taillights lit up a stream of exhaust fumes and just beyond the red glow I saw the faded lemon color of Romea, backed into a stall just beyond the Civic.

Lipstick was still sliding over lips as the Civic backed out of its stall in front of me and left me in a cloud of fumes racing toward the car. Romea. It was Romea. Stall No. 1B. One. Tower block one? B, the second-story apartment?

But Romea wasn't alone. There was another stall for No. 1B and next to Romea was a gray Chrysler, with a license plate from Illinois, not quite in keeping with the rest. But wedged in between Romea and her new, unlikely partner was an older vehicle that would never fill the garage with exhaust. A ten-speed bicycle, heavy treads of mountain bike tires, perfect for chasing your quarry, picking up thirty-five thousand dollars, or a few hundred if it came down to that.

Innocuous and silent, except for the sound of the chain slipping onto the sprockets and the panting of its rider who had stalked me on that evening. The man who had Mona, alive and well—I hoped—in apartment 1B. I walked around to the passenger side and peeked inside.

The history of a struggle: short, muted, failed but not final, in the darkened garage. Evidence of Mona's determination was all over the front seat. My extra pair of sunglasses lay broken on the floor, the tiny visor pulled at a raking angle across the windshield. The window on the driver's side showed a translucent stripe of blood, and it wasn't a windshield insect. There was a human fingerprint at the top, and then a clean stripe in the middle of the dried blood where Mona's fingernail had clawed at the window. And at something else.

A piece of horsehair stuffing from the front seat was caught between the front door and the running board. And a kinky strand was under my shoe on the asphalt. And, further down the blackened asphalt, I thought I saw another strand or two, spelling Mona's name, her hope, her message. Hansel and Gretal, except it wasn't a fairy tale and anyway there *were* ovens and the type of people who put other people in them. With each strand my heart pounded faster, feet picking up, running after threads, through the garage and toward another fire door. Behind it the utility stairway wove upwards. A series of large recycling containers were big enough to hold a few bodies. Heads of a sprinkler system dotted the ceiling. Concrete, metal railings, there would be fire doors on each floor. I slipped a matchbook into the doorjamb as I closed it; the door didn't quite make it closed; there was only silence, no click of the latch.

The horsehair threads like a promise, like a link in a happy chain that would lead me to Mona, continued up the stairway. As I went up I noticed scraping and skid marks. Continuing past the first floor, onto the second, the horsehairs stopped. I imagined him knocking her out with a gun, dragging her, a compliant deadweight, into his apartment with the window that overlooked the Camera Obscura and Sutro Gardens promenade.

I put my hand on the grip of the gun in my shoulder holster. Slowly, I opened the door onto the second floor hallway. Blue striped wallpaper with the regulation California poppy silk screens. Three doors with the letters A, B, C. A front stairwell with a chrome balustrade and a casement window on the landing between B and C.

To my left the northwest tower showed blank windows; a two-foot shelf with three spindles tacked onto the siding pretended to be a terrace in front of a sliding window. A showy white telescope perched behind vertical blinds in apartment 1B. I cranked the casement window open, took in a breath of deep sea air and a perfect view of both the Camera Obscura and the parapet of Sutro Heights. There was audio too. I could hear a slow, low, methodical voice, going over and over the same territory, with a limited patience that demanded cooperation, suggested punishment. His interrogation went on and on, like a mother, like a district attorney, like a man completely in control, until I heard the smashing of glass and a cry muffled by a hard and nasty sound that could have been flesh on flesh.

All was quiet in 1B now. The sky was a flat navy blue melting into a velvet Pacific Ocean. I was climbing out of a casement window, perching on a piece of molding from the windowsill below. There was only the churning of the ocean and the reckless surfers who rode in on one of her nighttime waves.

My toes bent at an impossible angle. Only my fingers, clasping the windowsill, kept me on the face of the building. From out of nowhere, a noise exploded behind my left shoulder. A casual cough. Once, and then it was over. More silence and then a muffled sound, like talking, explaining.

The little balcony was four feet to my left. My fingers crawled along the sill, and I extended my left foot until I found the spindles. I inserted my foot between the spindles, and wedged it as tightly as I dared. I would either make it, or break my foot. Toes grew longer, and a few ribs probably separated, and stretched. My hands gripped the banister and I looked inside the window.

At first I saw only darkness, as dark as a moonless night over the Pacific Ocean. In fact, it *was* a moonless night over the Pacific. Or at least the reflection of it in a full-length mirror in a condo. Other than that, the room was completely empty.

I crawled inside. The living room, a generous twelve by eighteen feet, had a great view of both the Giant Camera and the parapet at Sutro Heights. There were drapes which matched the carpets and the low end of a suite of rental furniture.

Tiptoeing across the nylon carpeting, I pushed myself up against the wall and listened for five minutes. I heard every creak and plumbing valve in the complex. Moving slowly toward the bedroom door, I opened it.

It was bad. Signs of struggle were everywhere. Clothes were strewn across a double bed. A heavy glass ashtray lay broken in the corner. Toothpicks spilled over a host of magazines and books: *Rifleman* and *Homemade Guns* and *Homemade Ammo* and *The Hayduke Silencer Book, Quick and Dirty Homemade Silencers, Hustler, Playboy,* and *The San Francisco Lesbian and Gay Film Festival Catalogue.*

A lamp had been tipped over. The closet door was open and someone had torn some, but not all of the clothes out of it. A good number of cardboard boxes were on the floor. Several drinks had spilled and a small white dot of ice was still frozen in the middle of three dark pools on the green carpet. And a knife. A clean, curved edge, hunting knife.

There was no blood and, except for the knife, no visible weapon. The blade was clean. The drapes were drawn. I swallowed hard. Mona had been in this room. Perhaps just moments before I came in.

I put my hand on the depression in the bed. It was warm. I had missed them by moments. I collapsed on the bed on the very spot, hoping, somehow, to receive an impression of Mona, of where they had gone. Only the shudder of a deep, dark tear came over me. I opened my eyes and looked over the horizon of the chenille bedspread onto the carpet where all the magazines lay.

Rifleman and *Homemade Guns* and *Homemade Ammo* and *The Hayduke Silencer Book, Quick and Dirty Homemade Silencers, Hustler* and *Playboy*.

I picked up the Film Festival catalogue and somehow, in some displacement of logic, I was not at all surprised to find my own notations in the catalogue. There *Outlaw*, 3:30 Sunday, circled in yellow highlighter, and that first film with Mona, *Demented Desire*, the late show I'd double-starred. And tonight, the film everyone wanted to see, the film I had

never marked, the film to which I had tickets to the closing
night reception. Chocolate-dipped strawberries and champagne.

It was only then that I realized that it was *my* Film Festival catalogue that was in the apartment of Haam Harmstead.
And that there must have been others who were coming to
the same conclusion as Haam had, as I was. The people I really wanted to meet might be converging at the closing night
reception at the Castro Theatre.

It was a hunch, but it was my only hunch. I gunned the
engine and sped over Twin Peaks towards the Castro. I sent
up another prayer to Diana. If my hunch was correct there
would be three hunters at the Castro Theatre, and one very
visible quarry.

CHAPTER TWENTY-SEVEN

RECEIVED

Closing night of the Film Festival and the Castro Theatre was jammed. The line stretched across the block and around the corner. I put Laura's car where it was sure to get a ticket and walked past the line. At the door I elbowed my way past Festival security. They were too busy keeping the crowd at bay to run after me. The long plate glass mirror in the landing showed me a strange scarecrow.

Scratched face, hands torn up, fingernails bleeding from hanging on a ledge over the ocean, but those elements were still familiar, still mine. There was something new in her eyes, a terror of the totally unimaginable, now imagined.

I looked up at the pink building and rehearsed the layout in my mind. The Castro had fewer hiding spots than one would think. My eyes scanned the building. The bathrooms, manager's office, and storage were all tucked under the balcony. The reception area would be filled to the brim. If you were going into a theatre and wanted to hide somewhere you could observe the scene, somewhere you could control a hostage with ease, where would you go? I looked up. The marquee. It would be the ideal place to hide and wait. Once the film had started they could come inside. In the meantime, the roof would offer a perfect vantage point to see all who came into the theatre. They had climbed out onto the

roof of the marquee from the mezzanine windows, I was
sure of it.

I jimmied my way through the crowd and into the lobby.
The mezzanine could be approached by one of two stairways. I went to the right and sprinted into the Castro's party
area. The room was so densely packed, people had started
filling up the ramped vomitories leading into the theatre.
There were maybe a hundred and fifty people. Velvet and
denim, a jungle of dropped and forgotten names, people on
their way up, people on their way down and all the other
people who made them that way. They jostled the food table
while the green backed Bridgeways caterers scurried around
with trays. I started through the crowd towards the windows
which would lead out onto the marquee. I saw people I knew
and ignored them, slithering through the press of bodies.

I was coming to the end of the room. Two vomitoriums,
the ramped walkways to the balcony were lined with red
curtains. Downstairs the popcorn machine sounded like a
kiddy shooting range. I jumped; the wafting smell of melting butter turned my stomach and I felt a horrible disap-
pointment settle into my bones. This was how parents felt
three days after their kids were kidnapped. Disposable family in the hands of sociopaths. I knew now what he wanted;
I knew how to buy him off, but there was no way I could
bargain over Mona's dead body.

"Emma!" Carla Ribera in a flame-colored silk bodysuit
that floated around her ample figure. "You look a sight—"

I ducked behind a caterer carrying a silver tray of champagne glasses. "Champagne?" Carla galloped after me.
"What's the big hurry? What are you up to?"

"Sorry, Carla, busy—" I dove into the crowd. "Later!"

A tray of champagne floated in front of me and hands
reached quickly for them. The film would be starting soon
and Mona was nowhere around. It was easy to pick out
Jason Jeeters. At six foot four, he towered above the crowd
in a white tuxedo jacket over shredded jeans and a T shirt
that must have been clean once. A bandage was plastered on
his nose where Kimilar had kicked him. Martel hung on his
arm and his every word.

I had almost made it to the other end of the room, past the groaning board where bodies jockeyed for position. Three deep, dipping their strawberries in the chocolate soup that was ladled out lazily by a Bridgeways inmate, they blocked the window.

The lights blinked; the film would begin soon. There were only a few more precious moments to think, to look around, to hope. Soon I would check out the roof of the marquee.

I could hear the house doors opening, the long line beginning at concessions; the murmur of expectation sounded like doom. The crowd would be coming up to the balcony soon, once the lower floor was filled. Behind me the reception crowd was moving into the theatre leaving a battleground of strawberry tops, chocolate drippings, and champagne corks on the linen.

Jason Jeeters had a big, big laugh for a balding white man who accompanied him and Martel and Kimilar down the stairs to the main floor. Kimilar was being followed closely by a big woman in a black leather jacket who was decidedly not Overalls. Then they all disappeared from view and the room was empty. The criss-cross pattern on the carpet looked like nothing more than little knife marks, little rounded knife marks on a giant field of flesh.

All four casement windows looked as if they would open. I chose the one on the farthest left, turned the latch and slowly looked outside, into the fog. The huge letters, three feet high, blinked just above my head and tinted the fog pink and blue. Spread out before me, the roof of the marquee was about thirty feet wide with a three foot wall around it.

The light changed and headlights coming over the hill shot into my eyes, causing temporary blindness. When my eyes readjusted I saw a shrunken shape moving around the edge of the marquee. It was them.

The first thing I saw was his face, an evil, crooked moon. Haam Harmstead had Mona's head in his brutal arm. Her body was twisted, doubled-over, as he dragged her closer to the edge of the marquee. Above them the six big letters blinked in pink and blue, three stories high. Mona's face was white and slick with sweat; the long nose of a silencer was held against her chin. She blinked twice. She was alive. The traffic below moved slowly, impatient horns honked and pedestrians mouthed off to drivers.

"Are you okay, Mona?" I addressed her as calmly as I could.

"Yes—"

"Shut the fuck—" I winced as Haam Harmstead took Mona's glasses off her face and let them fall to the tarred surface of the roof. He put his foot on the lenses and crushed them slowly and deliberately.

"Get out here," he commanded. I recognized his deep voice, the words that came halting and hoarse, as the voice on the phone. "Hurry up—or your friend becomes mince-meat on the sidewalk."

I climbed out the window. I leaned against the wall as instructed, feeling the leaden lump of the gun under my arm. On the tarred floor an orange toothpick was bitten clear in half next to the broken glass and twisted frame of Mona's glasses. A hostage situation in a crowded theatre. I took a deep breath. "I'm ready to do business, Mr. Harmstead. We're taking thirty-five grand, right?"

"Ok?" The man on the bike, the man who pretended to disappear into the ocean hovered under Mona. One thick arm, ballooned with muscle, twisted around Mona's torso like a boa constrictor. A gun pushed harder into the delicate flesh under her chin. Mona swallowed, which made the nose of the silencer move on her neck. A tight little smile on a face that could have been any white man in a crowd. Small blue eyes, thin lips, high forehead, and legs which were too short for the trunk of his body. His black turtleneck and slacks made him look nearly invisible against the night sky. A sprinkling of acne spotted the skin emerging out of his turtleneck. A peculiar pink-tinged hue clung to his cheeks, and his tiny lips were wet. He was as short and as strong as I thought he would be. He was a bad animal. 'Roid rage.

"She—scared—ain't she?" An orange toothpick, stuck to his lip, then flipped over and disappeared inside his mouth. "But you—" The sound of air coming through bronchial tubes that were chronically infected, or shrunk, the effects of steroids. "You gonna give me what I want?"

"Yes," I said, watching the shining nose come closer to Mona's jugular. "Why don't you let go of her and take me instead? She doesn't have anything to do with this."

"Em—" Mona croaked.

"Yew shuddup," Haam growled and stared suddenly at me. For the first time we made eye contact and the cold blue of his little eyes was so flat and final I had to take a deep breath to stay standing. Nothing to lose and nowhere to go. We had to strike a bargain. "I want my thirty-five thousand bucks."

"Sure, sure. I just want to make sure you get what you want so we can all get out of here okay," I said.

"Yeah, that's what I want. A little service around here!" A strangled sound fell from his lips and he pushed the gun deeper. "She scared—ain't she?" he asked me again. Her little red glasses gone, Mona's looked around her blindly.

"Let's go somewhere we can talk," I suggested. There had to be a good position to bargain from and I didn't have my bird in the hand. I only had my quarry in the theatre and I had to lead him to it. "I know a good place."

"Where?" he demanded.

I jerked my head toward the balcony. "Top of the balcony, the projection booth, it'll be pretty quiet. We can talk there."

"Yeah, that's—" wheeze, wheeze— "good." He moved his bulging arm and Mona's head came with it. I made out the nose of the silencer hidden in a deep pocket of his baggy pants. They emerged from the shadows. Pressing the silencer into her back, he pushed Mona forward toward the highly raked stairs of the projection booth. Mona wouldn't freak or bolt; she walked proudly, a Joan of Arc I hoped he would trade for thirty-five thousand dollars.

"You—you go first." The little lips drew tightly over his teeth, then slackened.

"Sure," I said, turning and beginning the steep ascent up the balcony. I walked slowly, staring at each glimmer of aisle lighting, the black spots of trampled gum on the carpet. Keep walking, each foot finding a stair, playing for time, trying to sort out all the possibilities of the projection booth and my final hunch. With Haam holding the gun and taking up the rear, we all climbed in the window and into the mezzanine. "The balcony's up here." I pointed behind the red velvet curtain. There must be a way, I thought, a way to resolve this, a way to make the sociopath rich and happy and keep all the bullets in his gun.

CHAPTER TWENTY-EIGHT

PROJECTION

The projection booth hung above us, its cutout windows dim while the houselights were up. The landing arrived, it was darker now. I put my hand on the iron railing which ran along the close, wooden stairway which led to the booth. And then I made my first mistake. I turned around to look; to look at Mona's face, to look at our captor, and to look and see if the balcony was filling up and if there was a way I could signal someone, get their attention and get us out of this mess.

"Turn around, you fucking—" His face twisted and he pushed Mona into my back; she cried out, her fingernails on my shoulder as I climbed through the window. I tripped on the stair, an iron rod hitting my ankle. A sickening sharp crack, a slap and a garbled cry of pain come from behind me.

The shabby little room was guarded by a thick, metal fire door with a small double paned glass window cut into it. Inside I could see the two aqua metal boxes that were the film projectors, lenses aiming through the rectangular holes in the wall, across the balcony and orchestra pit and onto the silver screen. Scores of film canisters piled up on the floor, along with their cardboard transport boxes with heavy straps. A series of rheostat switches would govern the houselights and a row of portable spotlights perched on the sill of one of the windows facing the theatre.

A fire extinguisher was prominently placed, along with a coil of rope. A middle aged man, five foot nine, skinny and bookish, squinted into the interior of a projector, threading a film, probably *Pale Refugee*. Behind him a long formica countertop held a splicing machine, various rolls of tape, and the remains of a take-out Chinese dinner. He had no idea there would be visitors soon. He was cleaning the lens as I opened the door.

"Hey! You can't—" He stood up, startled, then stopped when he saw Mona's pinched face and Haam's gun with the long ugly silencer. We entered the room. Mona tripped into a wall and leaned on it. She had a green face and her arm was dangling unnaturally at her side. Her eyes looked vague, unfocused. I found myself sucking in a breath, trying to make eye contact, but Mona was checking out fast. I blinked twice, slowly. Don't faint, Mona, don't fucking faint. I saw Mona's eyes respond, the lids rising and falling in response. I let my breath out slowly. Her color seemed to improve. Mona would learn to hold up a wall with a broken arm. I looked up to see Haam locking the door behind us, sliding a dead bolt into the woodwork of the door. His jaws tightened and the muscles moved in his neck.

"You—you—get over there." The gun directed the projectionist and myself over to the wall next to Mona. "Turn around!" he barked.

"But—but—the fil—" the projectionist seemed unwilling to shuffle to the wall until Haam walked behind him and kicked him onto the floor, with a forceful kick from his short barrel legs. The projectionist, sprawled on the floor was conscious but quiet.

"Now—crawl—over—to the wall." The man obediently crawled over to the wall as Haam reached behind him for a roll of duct tape on the splicing table. "Now, stand up, all-ayas."

We all stood up. Haam went to each of us and bound our hands with duct tape. Mona didn't make a sound when he took the wrist of her broken arm, but it must have hurt like hell. He pushed me up against the wall. He continued to make the point with his foot which hit the small of my back right above my kidney. A white wave of pain spilled over me. I caught my breath I looked over at Mona.

"Are you okay?"

"Yeah, yeah. I'm just sorry this isn't an on-the-job accident."

"Glad to see you've still got that civil service sense of humor," I was starting to catch my breath. Haam was engaged in scanning the audience. "What happened, Mona?"

"I got to your car and suddenly here was this guy. Looked like one of the body builders from the Market Street Gym. You know the type. He looked sort of familiar, and he came closer. I thought he was going to ask me directions only he stuck a gun in my side. The drive was sort of a blur. I kept thinking of all the ways I could drive into a ditch or whatever. Signal a cop. Never even saw a meter maid on the way over. And he had that gun." She shuddered. "I'm afraid of guns."

"But you weren't afraid of him?"

"Actually, no. It sounds crazy, but I just did the girl thing. I *pretended* to empathize. He knew he'd snatched the wrong person. He wanted to find you—"

"And you had the tickets to the reception?"

"Sure, I told him you'd be in attendance. Sorry about that."

"One good turn deserves another, Mona."

"We just walked in like anybody else. But then he got ugly. Once we were here he changed. I was suddenly this hostage and he didn't trust me. He trusted me enough earlier to believe that we should go to a party in a packed theatre with fifteen hundred people. When we arrived he was overwhelmed. Out of control, he had to frighten me. When he pulled me onto the marquee he started threatening me, worried you wouldn't arrive. I made a real effort not to listen to him. I didn't feel like living with that audio for the rest of my life. I started writing a poem, in my head. I just knew you'd find me. I just knew it."

"Mona, do you know anything about the switch setups in

the booth?" I whispered, pointing to a series of switched along the side of the wall.

"Let me see. I checked them all at least twice. The toggle for the house monitor is there—by your right hand—yes—the blue one."

"Shaddup! Face a wall!" The projectionist shuffled around. "Move!" Haam's boot found my kidney and my nose cracked against the wall. A shooting pain seemed to go straight to my feet and disappear. Then his hands were over my body and he found the holster. I felt him pull my gun from it, the gun slid from under my arm with difficulty, the duct tape pulled on wrists. "You, you—you—" I heard him wheeze behind me, an incantation of fury. I turned my head slightly and saw him raise the butt of the gun over my head, the heavy handle, the Packmeyer grips picking up light. He opened the chamber, held the gun horizontally, and five bullets fell out onto the floor. They rolled away, toward the front of the room, the floor was that uneven. "You, you—you!" his lower lip slackened, I saw a row of tiny teeth crowded under his tongue.

"I didn't kill your brother." My voice, unfamiliar, rang out into the room. "But I know who did."

The gun paused. "Where's the money?"

"Someone took the money off your brother. When I found your brother he was already dead. Somebody got there right before I did. And the thirty-five grand was gone."

"My brother, my own fuckin' brother double-crossed me."

"Think about it, you have no idea what really went on, what Philip was up to. I don't think your brother was crossing you. I don't think he was going to split with that money. Not really. You know what family is like."

Haam thought about it. He brought a cardboard folder out of his pocket and pried a wooden stick from the end. He pointed the sharp end at his mouth and laid it on his tongue. In a moment it was making somersaults over his lips. If Haam could believe that his brother wasn't intending to double-cross him then he might calm down. See a kind of future for himself, one that didn't feature the concrete walls in my plan.

"But I can show you where the money is."

"San Francisco, Open Your Golden Gates . . ." The Wurlitzer had arisen out of its pit. Haam stared at it.

"Mona?" Using the cover of the organ, I got her attention. "Is there a black light?"

"Funny you should—yes—the green one."

"Hey! Whaddaya? Shut the fuck up!" But Haam had been distracted by all the movement in the theatre. I could just imagine the scene: people marching up and down the red carpeted aisles, finding friends, balancing boxes of popcorn, and settling finally into their seats. Just as I'd hoped, we'd cornered him. There are two ways to deal with a cornered animal. The smart way was to give him an easy way out. And something to satisfy him for his trouble. Something a black light could pick out of an audience of fourteen hundred and fifty. "If I showed you who had the thirty-five thousand dollars you could make a good getaway. Make a clean break."

"Okay, lady-you-got-this all   " whcczc,whccze, "—figured-out." He reached behind him and my gun was in his pocket. "You-get-me-my-thirty-five-grand-and-out-of-this-theatre-we'll," wheeze, "all be friends." The man stomped over to Mona and grabbed her hair and held back her head. Mona's face went slack, the expression in her eyes was gone. "You?" wheeze, "—get—" wheeze, "me-my-fucking—" wheeze,— "money-or-your-friend-ends-up-in-a-body-bag."

"Don't worry. It's right here in the theatre. But first of all, you'd better let the projectionist run the film or this little booth will be the concern of fourteen hundred and fifty people," I said.

"Why-don't-you-just-tell-me-now?" Haam was getting nervous; there were too many elements, too many people.

"San Francisco, Open Your Pearly Gates . . ." The audience was clapping now, a thunderous sound.

"Hear that organ? That means the curtains are going to open any second. If the film doesn't start the audience will howl and the manager will be up here in a hot second that will lose you your thirty-five thousand dollars forever. So let the show go on. Otherwise we're going to have a lot of angry company. See, the film is already loaded. All you have to do is let him flip the switch at the right moment. Then we'll have ninety minutes for me to tell you all about the money and how to get it."

"Better-not-take-that-long. You!" He waved the gun at the projectionist, whose mouth permanently hung open. "Get over to-the-the-machine. You run that freakin' film, brother—" wheeze- "—or I'm gonna hang your balls from the ceiling. Don't try any funny stuff." He leered at all of us. "Now, let's all watch a fuckin' movie."

The projectionist walked over to the big machine and nodded toward the switch. "That's the switch," he explained. "The film is already cued up. All you have to do is flip this toggle bolt as soon as the curtains start to part. There's an automatic pull operated from downstairs. It's timed so that the image comes on when the curtains are about four feet apart."

"Okay, buddy. That's fine. You get in position there to flip the switch. Now you just stand like that and wait for the curtains." The skinny man turned so that a free finger rested on the switch. "And-don't you try nothin' funny. In the meantime, I'm gonna talk to my friend here who's going to tell me where my money is—"

"I didn't say I could get the money. I said I could show you where it is."

"Whaddayu-mean-you-can't-get-the-money?" Haam was breathing hard. The clicking of the film sprockets filled the room with a tense background sound. "Some kinda trick? I have tricks too. Maybe I could wait for a good moment in the film and torch this whole place. I could cut up your girlfriend here, limb from limb right in front of your eyes." Haam's little teeth were perfectly aligned.

The little bolt rattled on the door. We all turned around and looked at it. Haam stood up, gun trained on us, head twisting back and forth between the door and Mona, the projectionist and me. The bolt was rattling harder now, the screws that were keeping it in place were loosening.

I wanted to warn the person coming into this death trap, cry out to turn around and get help. But in the end there was no help. There was only a lot more trouble behind that door. More trouble and another gun.

CHAPTER TWENTY-NINE

THE MESSENGER DIES

Another gun and Dee Dee Hammerman was attached to it. She came into the room quickly, shutting the door behind her. She was a different kind of woman with a gun in her hand, even more businesslike than she'd been at Villanueva's buffet table. If she was scary then, she was terrifying now. Tall leather boots hugged her legs, and black kid gloves covered her hands. Her weapon was a small semiautomatic, like nothing I'd seen before. I saw a crillic letter on the edge of the handle. Russian manufacture? Who was she? A kamikaze missionary in a trench coat and a scowl that Villanueva had never seen.

Her gun was in Haam's stomach before he had a chance to react. A wobbly smile crossed his lips as he raised his short stubby arms. His weapon swung idly around his finger and dangled by the trigger guard. He was smiling as if he'd been chosen for pin the tail on the donkey. He didn't take Dee Dee Hammerman seriously, but his eyes flickered across all the surfaces in the room just the same. Then Dee Dee Hammerman plucked the gun away from him, patted him down, and found my empty weapon in his pocket. His expression changed.

"Drop it!" Haam dropped his weapon, the gun heavy with his silencer, fell onto the floor. Dee Dee picked it up, put it in the pocket of her trench coat, keeping her weapon trained on Haam. "What the hell did you think you were doing?" She poked the gun hard into his belly. Haam's lips pressed tightly together and I watched the history of a strange business deal gone awry. "Turn around!" Dee Dee picked up the duct tape and bound his hands; there were four of us facing the wall. "Double-crossing son of a bitch," she said as if he were a truant. Something in the trained tones of Dee Dee Hammerman rang bells in my head. Future Homemakers of America gone amok. But not quite.

Dee Dee Hammerman handled her weapon with ease. The long silencer was well made, unlike Haam's homemade model. She tilted her hand with ease, as if the long hunk of metal wasn't leveraging her wrist every time she waved it at us.

"You double-crossed us. Right? Just answer me!" Again, new, businesslike tone, the gun was nestling into Haam's back, running up and down the individual vertebrae on his spine.

"Hey, hey-I didn't-know." His voice was a whisper, his mouth chewing on the toothpick frantically.

"What? You shot the tape and watched your brother sell it to the highest bidder. You're going to find out who you're dealing with now."

"Like I said, how-how-was I—" He turned his head and I saw the tip of the orange toothpick in his mouth. I was watching all this and Dee Dee Hammerman's pocket where Haam's gun with the long silencer poked out like a broken leg. It rattled next to my revolver in the folds of her trench coat. "Look, lady, I-just-worked-for-my-brother."

"Your brother made a bad judgment call. Very bad. You trying to tell me you didn't know anything about it?"

Haam grumbled, and I saw in his face a little boy and heard a tinge of whine. "Hey, you-you-go-spend-the-weekend in-a-hotel-wall," he said.

"I've spent weekends in places worse than that." Dee Dee Hammerman's face twisted into something a press secretary never looked like. "I worked long hard hours at buffet tables, miles of telephone cable carried my voice in service of a politician who would turn our world into a—a *socialist democracy*. And I sat at her table and listened to all the propaganda and watched all the deals being made. All for one moment. The moment you crawled into a wall and took a picture. You would never have been there without me. And now I'm going to make sure that you spend a few years in hell, my boy." The metal seemed to circle around one spot in his back. "I think they call this the c-2 vertebra. If I take it out—," I saw the gun sink further into the black knitted material of Haam's shirt—, "you won't be able to ride around on your ten-speed bicycle." The room was beginning to smell very badly of frightened humanity. "But if I move the gun up higher," her hand came up, bump, bump, bump went the silencer over Haam's vertebrae. "You won't ever be able to take any pictures anymore. Because you won't have any hands. Or arms, for that matter." A sickening smell came over the room as Dee Dee's voice went even colder. "Hand it over, Haam. Hand over the merchandise."

"I don't have it!" Haam held up both his hands, thick, pink palms in the air. Down in the theatre I could just see a tiny little figure crawling onto the stage. The thank you's, the applause taking far too long. The projectionist was still waiting by the film; Mona was holding her broken arm together, leaning on a wall, biting her lower lip hard.

Dee Dee shook her head sadly. "You should know better than that. We don't kill people unless we have to. But we can't be double-crossed. After all, we have a reputation, I guess you could call it, a *tradition* to uphold. Now, about that videotape." She moved closer and I saw her put her gun on Haam Harmstead's temple, execution style. "You think I'm too much of a lady to do this?"

"NO! NO!" Haam's eyes slid to the side and sweat broke out across his temple like a pearl necklace. The toothpick floated like a tiny raft out of his mouth and landed on his chin. A small clicking meant that Dee Dee Hammerman had popped off the safety catch in a quick, tiny pulse of a fingertip.

"No, I—" he swallowed, a thick lump moved up and down the brawny neck.

"Give, Haam," she purred.

"I don't have it, I swear I don't—"

"That's too bad," Dee Dee sighed, a strange sound, as if she were watching a béarnaise sauce congeal before it's time. "When someone gives you a commission you don't run off with the work. It's a bad business practice. Very, very bad."

And just like that she crooked the index finger of her left hand, squeezed the trigger, and sent a bullet through the chamber and into the left temple of Haam Harmstead.

CHAPTER THIRTY

THE KIND OF
THEATRE IT WAS

A bullet to the head causes instant death; it is the preferred execution style of professionals. Dee Dee Hammerman executed the man with alarming ease and without a second glance. He landed with a thud on the floor, a black hole in the side of his temple and a surprised look which never left his eyes.

Watching someone die instantly is an experience that most people are fortunately spared. Haam Harmstead was now a deadweight, from perfect steroid pumped health to inanimate flesh, eyes gone blank, and all body functions coming to an instant end. There was a black tattooing of gunpowder on the skin above his right eye, a burn ring around the entrance wound to Haam Harmstead's head. His eyes, unfortunately, were open and the orange toothpick struck his chin like the exclamation point to a bad joke.

How we all took it: Mona and the projectionist stared at the dead body, unable to take their eyes away from the spot where the bullet had exited Haam's skull.

Dee Dee Hammerman was the consummate professional, checking out what were now *her* hostages, our hands still skillfully bound with duct tape. She was taking the area under control, monitoring the doors, ceilings. There was work to do and I thought I would help her do it.

"I think I can help you find what you're looking for." I said.

"What?" Dee Dee said, her gun pointing toward me.

"I think we'd better let the projectionist run the film."

"Oh, Jesus," Dee Dee Hammerman said and I had the feeling that she wasn't swearing.

"It tends to keep the audience happy."

"You're right," Dee Dee said, as if told the dessert tray had a squeaky wheel.

"Here come the curtains," the projectionist said.

"And then I can tell you everything I know."

"Okay," Dee Dee sighed, looked at the projectionist who couldn't meet her gaze. "You ready to run the film? You can do it with your hands tied?" She looked him over carefully, assessing his condition.

"Yes." The projectionist's voice squeaked. The silver bolo tie shimmered at his neck. His shirt was soaked with sweat at the collar, under the arms. He turned slightly and wiggled his fingers at a toggle bolt. The applause swelled in the auditorium. The filmmaker and his sister were dismounting the podium.

"I just got the signal from the house manager. The curtains are parting."

"Just do your job and everyone will be all right," Dee Dee said.

"Not to worry." The projectionist swallowed, looked for a brief second at the body of Haam Harmstead on the floor. The butt of Dee Dee Hammerman's silencer was in the small of his back, somewhere around his kidneys.

"Do it. " The two words hung heavy in the room.

"Yes, yes, I'm flipping the switch." The projectionist put his faltering finger under the toggle bolt. He flipped it upwards and we all heard the sharp *click*. The slack film shuddered, tightened through the machine; the reels started turning in tandem. Outside the windows I could see the lettering: PALE REFUGEE.

The film reel was moving, the images flashing on the screen, far, far in front of us. Goats grazed across the screen and a lonely electric guitar solo seemed to undulate on the

wind. Reaching behind me I flipped the switch that said
"house monitor" and the applause filled the tiny booth.
"And now we present *Pale Refugee*!"

Dee Dee spun around, looked over at me, at Mona, at the
projectionist whose eyes kept traveling to the whirring of
the film.

"How did that happen?" She looked again at all of us.

I felt the weight of the room, of Mona's life, of the projectionist's life, of the future of the Castro Theatre all hanging in the balance.

"I think it's just automatic," I said, and the projectionist
bobbed his head like a puppet. The whine of a guitar solo, a
lonesome thread of a melody, with gamboling riffs in between. It was the music of Jason Jeeter's Jones. His twentieth-
century shepherd's pipe charmed us all and for a moment
there was no dead body on the floor in front of us and the
tape on our wrists didn't bind any longer. Something in our
human souls made us follow the soaring melody for strange
precious moments, a magic no one expected to feel as our
eyes were drawn toward the screen. The magic was de-
stroyed by silence. A still, black-and-white photo of something that looked like a large black rubber cross.

*"The 'protection and restraint twenty-four' is a two foot
long club."* said Jason Jeeters's voice. *"It weighs twenty-
seven ounces. Manufactured of molded polycarbon, it has a
perpendicular handle for locking onto a man and dragging
him by his wrists back to his cell."*

A green hillside stretched before us. A close-up of the soft
grasses revealed two figures, two young men, in excellent
physical condition, one bending behind the other. Superimposed over the couple, a large white triangular shadow appeared. Nearly blocking out the entire screen, the shape was
translucent enough to allow a glimpse of the extraordinary
length of the penis of Jason Jeeters splitting the creamy buttocks of Martel. The shadow superimposed over the couple
became clearer and a pair of eyes appeared. Split pupils and
little horns atop the domed forehead indicated the head of a
goat. All this happened in seconds and it seemed that just as
Jason's final riff was over and done we remembered the gun

in Dee Dee Hammerman's hand. She was staring at the huge head of the animal. She was transfixed.

"The false prophet," she was murmuring.

I was a statue. The tape bit at my hands, the projectionist was bathed in sweat, Mona's arm was still limply dangling be her side like a broken toy and Haam's body was so freshly dead on the floor that I couldn't believe he wasn't still breathing. As Jason's wistful lingering melody wafted over us, I heard the further words of Dee Dee Hammerman.

"Tool," I heard the words come from between her lips, the war-cry of a right-wing banshee: *Tool of Satan!*

LET THERE
BE LIGHT II

Dee Dee Hammerman was asking me something, but it was hard to concentrate on the answer. She had once again removed the safety from her gun and was pointing it at my head. "What?" Her voice was a chilling hiss in the room. "What kind of theatre is this anyway?" The question echoed in my brain and it seemed like an eternity before I could imagine an answer that just might satisfy her.

Watching the film, I heard the labored breathing of Mona Marie and tried to think. The muzzle of the gun was still warm from the previous shot Dee Dee had fired. The fuzzy white goats and the boys in Calvin Klein underwear were frolicking to Jason Jeeter's amazing guitar riffs. The editing table behind the projector featured a fine set of blades. "Surely you've heard of the Castro Theatre," I said calmly. "The Castro Theatre is the finest extant example of a 1920's neighborhood movie house in San Francisco."

"Huh?"

"Dee Dee, I think I can help you out. Put the gun down and let's do business."

A plaintive goat bleat whinnied through the monitor. I looked at Mona and the projectionist. They looked at me. We all looked at Dee Dee. She made up her mind and re-engaged the safety on her gun. "Talk," she said.

"Let's get you that piece of missing merchandise. Haam didn't have it. And neither do I. The party you're after the other person who was up on Sutro Heights, the only person left who could have what we're all looking for, is right here in the Castro Theatre."

"How do you know?" Hammerman asked.

"Because I was up there on Sutro Heights, right after you were. I was Haam and Philip's latest customer. Hey, I had no idea we were horning in on someone else's deal. I simply expected to make a payment. How did *I* know it was a paid commission?" I watched Hammerman listening and I took a deep breath. We were all relaxing now. I let my voice fill up the space of the room. Even Mona was listening attentively.

"Ready with the cash, I waited for the signal. But there was nothing. No light. Nobody home. I went down to investigate. I found Philip Harmstead and he'd already been picked over. First by you. Then by his former wife."

"His former wife! I hate these jobs." Hammerman stamped her foot. "Divorce? I told Gunter it wouldn't work." She shook her head. I told him! "We never should have gotten involved with those clowns."

I continued, "The thirty-five grand that I had originally thrown over the cliff had been marked with a phosphorescent powder. When I flashed a light on the corpse it lit up like a neon sign, indicating that he had been carrying the cash quite recently. Unfortunately, the cash was gone. Along with, presumably, the merchandise."

"How do you know?"

"I found Philip Harmstead and he'd already been picked over—twice. First by you, and then by his former wife. She knew his secret hiding place. And you didn't."

"I didn't take anything—"

"You didn't take the thirty-five grand, that's true. But that wasn't what you wanted. You missed the video, Dee Dee; it was in a hollowed out compartment in the sole of his shoe. When I came upon his body someone had already opened the heel of his shoe. The tape was a miniature job. Easy to hide and hard to locate. But I know where it is. And I can prove it to you. I believe we can locate our thief right here in the Castro Theatre. Want me to try?" I pointed to the toggle switch.

"Oh sure, what the hell," Dee Dee shrugged her shoulders, but kept a grip on her weapon.

I turned on a switch that was a roving blacklight. A pale purple glow moved over the audience, adding a lavendar hue to thousands of heads of hair. The purple glow was nearly invisible until it came in contact with a certain seat, which took on an eerie, green glow.

The effect was shocking. Kimilar Jones was Queen of the Light, on a throne of fireflies, a marvelous matinee effect. Her flaxen hair was a silver helmet, and sparkles seemed to spray off of the fringe of her leather jacket. The glowing Kimilar Jones was clearly visible to the entire theatre. The crowd hushed, their heads turned away from the scenes of frolicking goats and Texas landscape to the strange vision in the theatre itself.

Kimilar rose, looking like a pale and beautiful Ophelia rising from the grave. She turned around to face the crowd; her teeth were a row of headlights. She squinted, following the source of the light back into the projection booth where Dee Dee Hammerman couldn't wait to get off the finish line.

"The burning seat!" I could hear someone yell over the monitor. The audience began to call out to each other.

"What?"

"The seat that catches on fire!"

"Fire!"

"Burning seat! Burning seat!" echoed through the hall.

The crowd was on its feet racing to the exits. *"Fire! Fire! Burning! Don't panic!"* The horrible sounds of a panicked crowd were broadcast into the booth. Mona managed to stifle a scream; the projectionist had fainted dead away; Dee Dee Hammerman was stepping over him. Kimilar, out of the black light, was making her way toward the stage right exit. The crowd stampeding, making progress difficult. I already had my back to the splicing table, working a standing razor device up and down over the tape on my wrists until I was free.

"False alarm! False alarm!" A new cry was sweeping

the audience as a new scene appeared on the screen. Someone called for people to sit down and watch the film. My eyes kept track of Kimilar Jones as she pushed forward towards the exit. A lot of men in leather blocked her escape; Jason Jeeters was deep-throating Martel in CinemaScope.

The crowd began to return to the theatre. Drawn by the promise of steamier scenes and the overriding insistent melodies of Jason Jeeter's guitar, they pushed the little woman back farther up the aisle. My hands were finally free; Dee Dee Hammerman would probably be in the mezzanine already.

I turned my fingers to the glass bar in the red metal box behind me. In seconds the entire Castro rang out with real fire alarms, bells clanging through the auditorium, up and down the halls and over the popping of popcorn. The relentless metal sound rekindled the panic of the crowd, drowned out any cries of "false alarm" and gave me a shot at finding Kimilar Jones.

I gathered a Stanley knife and freed Mona. "Are you okay?" The blade was sharp and sliced through her bonds cleanly. Her right hand moved quickly, but her entire left arm was limp and she moved it carefully.

"Yes, I'm fine. I'll get him loose—you go get her "

"Okay—but count to a thousand before you call the cops, okay?" I took a backward glance as I left the booth. Mona was having trouble loosening the bonds of the projectionist with her one good arm. It would probably take a thousand counts before he would be free.

The balcony had emptied and I knew that Dee Dee Hammerman would be stuck in the crowds below. My feet flew down the steep stairs to the front of the balcony where two very large women leaned over the railing. They looked at the crowd like birds of prey staring at fish in a shallow pond.

"False alarm!" one shouted to me over the bells.

"Right," I said too quietly to be heard. I leaned over the railing with them. Kimilar Jones was still stuck at the doorway, battling a flank of leathermen who insisted on seeing the film unfold. A few hundred people pressed together at the front of the stage, and I saw on the edge of the crowd a shiny black pageboy. It was Dee Dee Hammerman. She was making her way through a lot of horny leather with her silenced gun and at least three bullets left. I looked over the territory. The huge pineapple chandelier hanging in front of me, glowed over the crowd. Dee Dee Hammerman was pushing and shoving her way through the crowd, coming closer to her quarry. At my feet a long orange extension cord snaked under the railing. It was lightly taped and tucked under the carpet. A swift pull and it came loose from the socket. Fifty feet of unbroken outdoor insulated extension cord was mine. A heavy metal outlet box with four outlets had been clamped and screwed onto the end of the cord.

I turned to the women next to me. She was six foot four, at least two hundred pounds and not all flab either. The Giantess sported a thin scar striping her brown neck and biceps like Popeye the Sailor Man. I checked out her arms and her attitude, made my assessment and popped the question.

"Excuse me. I have a problem. I have to get down to the orchestra pit. Fast."

"Huh?"

"There's a crazy dude who's after my girlfriend. I gotta get to her first; last time he carved up her face."

"Where is she?" The face wrinkled immediately in protective response.

"See her? There? That woman who's pushing through the crowd. She's trying to get away from him." We looked down at Dee Dee who battled black leather.

"Man, she's really moving!" The Giantess nodded with concern.

"There's no way I can make it through the crowd, unless—" I looked at her biceps one more time. "—unless I can jump down there without killing myself. Now these extension cords are made of triple coiled . . ." We discussed the situation.

"That chandelier looks farther away than I think it is," she squinted. "I think I kin do it. I reckon I can try," she took the cord out of my hands and gathered a few coils next to her on the ground. Lifting the outlet box over her head, she began a twirling motion, the heavy box gaining in speed. Faster and faster she spun the weight until it was a black blur against the golden ceiling of the theatre. When she let go the box flew like an angel toward the pineapple chandelier and return again, traveling around the metal rod and landing with a thunk in the pan of the light fixture.

"Fuckin' hell," the woman exclaimed.

"You did it!" I cried.

"We dunno yet, honey. We gotta test it."

I picked up the end of the cord and gave it a hard jerk. The chandelier didn't move.

"You really gonna ride that thing, sistah?"

I looked down at the hundreds of people beneath me, at the black pageboy which had entered the fray, pushing aside the brawny bodies, Kimilar Jones trapped again closer to the exit. I gave the cord another jerk, pulling with all my weight. The pineapple light fixture swayed, but only a few inches. "I think I'm gonna try," I said.

"I believe you are," my comrade said as I climbed up on the railing and took in all the slack from the line. Whatever I had for fingernails dug into the rubber insulation. As I pushed off I saw the Giantess waving. The last thing I saw was the back of her shirt and that most familiar green-and-white logo: *Bridgeways.*

CHAPTER THIRTY-TWO

AERIALIST

The air part was easy. There was no resistance as I swung through space. I gave a thousand thanks to those who manufactured extension cords and the inspectors who approved them. I flew quickly, and with the greatest of ease. My flight described an arc of forty-five feet that no one witnessed or remembered with accuracy. There were a few leathermen who would never forget me landing on them from out of nowhere, but they would have to rationalize it later. Perhaps it was the hypnotic tunes of Jason Jeeters, they would think, discussing it with friends. It had been so disorienting, the fear, the crowd the tilting landscape on the screen. They would always remember the steamy sex scenes stretched sixty feet across the silver screen but they never really knew what hit them at forty miles an hour. A hundred and thirty pound armed woman dropping out of the balcony landing in their midst? I had my feet forward, which was too bad for a particular bald head, but I landed immediately behind the flaxen haired farmer, Kimilar Jones. My hands fit perfectly on either side of her waist. But where to dance with her? The floor was a chaos of maleness, the smell of leather, perspiration, panic and pre-ejaculate, filled the air. The organ had arisen and started again to play, *San Francisco, Open Your Golden Gates!*

The sea of men pressed toward the exit. The one fish who swam against the stream was Dee Dee Hammerman. She was headed right toward us.

I ducked and pulled Kimilar down through the crowd.

"Where are we going?"

"Somewhere safe," I lied. I just wanted to put distance between Dee Dee Hammerman, myself and Kimilar Jones. "We gotta hide. There's a trained assassin who's about twenty feet and forty bodies behind us. So keep moving." Pushing hard, I pulled us through the crowd. People were yelling as I shoved and stepped on toes.

"Rude bitch!"

"So sue me!" I fled past the field of leather.

"I will! I'm a lawyer!"

I looked behind me and saw Dee Dee's helmet hair coming closer. The crowd was thinning out. Where could we hide?

I could see Dee Dee's hand in her pocket and it wasn't a banana she was holding. The crowd was thinning; she and her Russian semi automatic moved through the crowd like a knife through hot butter.

"Fuckin' bitch!"

Dee Dee had bumped into a misogynist in black leather who was hassling her admirably. I pulled Kimilar up the wooden stairs to the stage.

"Keep moving!"

"Yeah—nobody saw *that*—" Kimilar said "You need a few huntin' lessons—"

"Shh!" I put my hand gently over her mouth. Taking Kimilar's elbow, I waltzed her back through the thick velvet curtains.

"Where we gonna hide *here?*" she said quietly. There was no exit from the stage to the street. No exit at all. The stage was a big dead end, and I had waltzed us into it.

The big silver screen stretched before us. Off to one side I could see the concrete wall close behind it. The Castro had always been a movie theatre; there were no green rooms or fly towers in the building. Just a lot of seats and a stage big enough to hold the silver screen.

Then I remembered what Mona had told me about the original Castro Theatre.

How had the old movie house been constructed? I looked up to the ceiling to see how the screen was hung.

"What are we gonna do?" Kimilar.

"Shut up, please," I whispered, squeezing her hand.

I ran my fingers along the edge of a screen, where a wooden frame about three feet thick, held it taught. I pried along the edges of the screen, my fingernails digging into the wooden frame. The expanse of silver shuddered. My fingers felt air, and then the complicated curlicues of another proscenium. I peeled the screen aside. There it was: the secret castle of the Castro Theatre.

Minarets of gold were topped with sapphires, rubies, and diamonds. Columns twisted and twined, emerging after years of darkness. And in the middle, a modest, nearly square piece of canvas, the original silent film screen of the Castro.

"What the—" Kimilar's eyes had lit up with the discovery of treasure.

"Careful, the whole thing is only about three feet wide-probably made of cardboard—"

Step, step, step. I heard footsteps on the boards; someone had just come on stage. The house was emptying quickly.

"Come on!" I pulled Kimilar through the narrow split. We edged along the front of the gilded frame. The miniature wrought iron railings, woven with moons and stars, pulled at our clothes. Past more golden spires we reached the silent screen. I held my hand up in a motion to stop. Then I returned to where I had pulled the big screen away. A lightweight glue on the edge was still tacky.

Step, step. A hesitant step was coming closer.

I squeezed the edge of the big screen back onto the frame. Except for a space about as big as an eyeball, I had resealed the screen to the frame. I slipped back along the front of the proscenium, the big screen moving enough to let me pass. I hoped the surface was not noticeably billowing.

Step, step. Stop. Quiet.

Had she seen my silhouette move across the surface of the

big screen? The theatre had emptied, quiet and empty before the next audience would be allowed to enter.

I could see Kimilar's flaxen hair in the darkness; the pastewax gems glittered in ambient light which came through the leftover slit in the screen. Kimilar took my hand and moved closer. I held her tightly to me. The mountain smell of her, campfires, pine needles and wildflowers rose from her hair, her buckskin jacket. I felt her breath on my neck and the small, strong hands circled my waist.

Step, step.

"Are you in there, Emma Victor?" Dee Dee Hammerman's voice was tentative, a good sign. She walked around the screen. I could hear Kimilar's heart beating as Dee Dee paced off the fifty feet of screen facing the audience.

Step, step. "Emma Victor, Emma Victor," her sing-song voice sought me out. "You don't have a chance, you know. I saw you come back here with blondie. It's so sad to think of you both. Unarmed, trapped behind one of these velvet curtains. I can pump you both full of holes before you even knew what hit you. Sort of like being blindfolded before the execution. They say that's the best way, you know. Or do you think that's just projection? Sorry for the bad pun. It's just easier on the executioner that way. Guess we'll never know, *will we?*"

"Coma! Coma! Coma!" Marriage Apartheid

A commotion on the street filled the empty theatre,

"Completely Over Marriage Apartheid!"

"Marriage Act Passes, Marriage Act Passes!"

"The Marriage Act!" Dee Dee breathed.

"President signs Marriage Act! Come and Get It! After-noon Examiner, Special Edition!" shouted a roving news-boy.

"Fascism!"

"Riot! Riot!"

The calls to arms came from the street. Somewhere in the distance glass broke and a siren wailed in response.

All was quiet, now, in front of the screen.

Then I heard a laugh. A sound so joyless, so full of righteous hatred, that I shuddered. That laugh was branded in my memory, along with Dee Dee's final words.

"Hahahahah!" Tap, tap tap. Dee Dee might have done a little dance on the stage. " Your liberal president will sell you all down the gutter for a second term." I thought I heard her holster the weapon. "Gay marriage? Not in *your* lifetime Emma Victor. Which has just, due to the joyous occasion, been extended. Lucky, lucky, Emma Victor."

"We're here! We're queer! Get over *it!*" The chants swelled in volume, in anger.

"Hahahahahaha!" I thought I heard Dee Dee Hammerman laugh. The metal fire door closed with a *clang,* and I thought I heard the eerie chuckles continuing outside.

Kimilar and I clung to each other, in fear, in relief, and finally, in pleasure. Kimilar started to move, but I stopped her with a kiss. Her lips told me a mountainwoman's tale; her tongue hunted my desire and found it. What a way to keep her quiet and stay behind the screen.

I didn't want to think of Dee Dee Hammerman ambushing us. And I didn't want to stop kissing Kimilar. We continued until the next crowd began to arrive, filling up the theatre. We left our secret castle reluctantly. Dee Dee Hammerman was nowhere to be seen.

"President signs Marriage Act! Come and Get It! Afternoon Examiner, Special Edition!" Angry, expectant, the voices of my people filled the huge space. Kimilar and I emerged, weak-kneed and wet, into the Castro Theatre, and the angry community.

CHAPTER THIRTY-THREE

PALE
REFUGEE

"I didn't kill Philip," she said.

Kimilar and I were having a sit-down in the parking lot behind the Castro Theatre.. The mob on the street was finding a focus; people were talking about demonstrating at the Federal Building. We watched the crowd become a march and start filing down Market Street. Soon the neighborhood was quiet. I looked at the woman next to me. Her flaxen hair tangled with the leather fringe on her jacket and her fingers made small circles on my knee. She still smelled good and the plot value of her kiss had been considerable. But it was time to tell the truth. The whole truth, and nothing but.

"I didn't kill Philip," she repeated.

"I know. Hammerman got to him first. But I wouldn't play the innocent if I were you. It's time to tell the whole story, Kimilar."

"Ain't no judge or jury gonna believe it, Emma. I been in prison before. Check kiting. Way before I got the farm. But I don't have no money, Emma. I cain't hire a lawyer. And I cain't go back to prison, Emma. Oh, God, I cain't—"

"Don't worry," I took her hand off my knee gently. "I work for one of the best criminal defense attorneys in San Francisco, Kimilar."

"You really think she'll help me?"

"Sure," I said. "Why not?" For one reason, I didn't know where my employer had been for the last forty-eight hours, but I was certain that was a detail which would be cleared up.

"You deserve the whole story, Emma. I really wasn't scammin' you. You know that?"

"Lose the disclaimer. Just start from the beginning," I said. "It's always the best place. How did you meet Philip Harmstead?"

"I met him just like I told you. Philip was in at the community college, but he wasn't exactly the ivory-tower type. He wasn't any good, but what the hell did I know at twenty-three? When my mother died, I sold the motel and bought this little farm. Philip was history, except when he needed somewhere to hang out in between gigs."

"What kind of gigs?"

"Listen, pretty lady, I might be called accessory after the fact."

"Attorney-client privilege. And we're alone here. Besides, I know all about Philip's record. I just didn't know the downtime was spent on the farm."

"Downtime! He fucking held me prisoner, man. I was supposed to cook and do all the ironing. The bastard had to sleep on,"she ground her teeth— "he had to sleep on ironed sheets. And he said he had to sleep with me. Fucking bastard. But that was before I had me these silver toe'd boots. Ain't nobody messin' with me *now.*"

"And then what?"

"Well, Jason Jeeters put me onto what was up with Philip. Prison telephone, you know. Gigs get around. Jason, well, he met up with Haam in the weight room in Joliet. They did a lotta steroids together," She shivered. "You know, prison. It's just one big fraternity of bullies and shitheads. And if they weren't bullies and shitheads when they go in they is when they get out."

"So Jason told you what Haam was up to?"

"Jason got out of prison this last time and came straight to the farm with Martel. He and Martel had this plan to make this film and damned if they didn't do it. Jason had been clean for six months and on his best behavior. At least I thought so at the time."

"And Martel?"

"Martel is a sweetheart. I probably wouldna done it if it weren't for Martel. But he's too young. Watching Martel with Jason is like watching someone walk into a concrete wall day after day. Anyway, Philip never came around when Jason was on the place. And Haam, that freaker, he ain't allowed on my land. He knows I'm plenty armed these days. But there wasn't too much anyone could do about Philip.

"Jason made *Pale Refugee* and entered it in the festival. That's when he told me about Philip and this big all important gig that was going to set up my ex for life. Some blackmail scam, big money in San Francisco. I didn't know and I didn't care. But I just had to get the farm in my name, Emma, I just had to."

"So you hired me?"

"Yeah. I thought it was going to be a clean deal."

"Yeah, you were just going to sic me on a rough customer."

"You look like you can take of yourself. I thought maybe he was onto some money and he wouldn't care anymore about the farm anyway. Jason had said Philip was going to leave the country. Said he had to get out of the United States. Brazil, that's what Jason said. So I figured what the hell, I would try and get the farm thing cleared up before he left. How was I to know you were involved in the whole thing?"

"You heard Haam's voice on my cell phone, at Cafe Flor, right?"

"Hard to mistake that voice, comin' from under a rock, as it does. Man, that threw me for a loop. You were talkin' to Haam on the phone! That's when I had to change my story. Quick. I had no idea what to do. After all, how was I to know you were on the level? Haam's never up to any good and you were part of whatever that was. Meanwhile, you were talkin' to the brother of the guy I was lookin' for, and where Haam is Philip is never far behind. The only thing I could do was pull back, send you on a wild goosechase with a picture I just happened to have in my wallet. I figured I'd follow you until you led me to one or the other of them. I never thought you'd lead me to a dead Philip with thirty-five thousand—"

"—in marked bills—"

"Yes, in *very* marked bills, it has turned out. I took the money and split. But, I swear, Emma, I swear to you, that I didn't kill him. The minute you headed onto that coast, I cut my headlights and parked. It didn't take me long to see you head for the phone booth. I knew they'd have you hikin' somewheres. I watched. I timed the whole thing and then I saw you leave. It was all over and I never even got to see Philip or Haam. But I was lucky. I kept you under surveillance and pretty soon you went out a second time to that park. This time I was clever. While you was parking your car I was already on the grounds lookin' for my man. I had my moccasins on. I reckon that park was pretty busy that night. But I was the quietest of all o' you.

"I heard a scuffle and when it was over I crept forward and found Philip. Somebody got to him before I did. Fucker didn't have a face left. I couldn't have done it better myself. Probably running out on someone. He was wearin' his travelin' shoes."

"You helped yourself, didn't you?"

"He was already dead."

"You scared the murderer away, Kimilar."

"Her?"

"The lady in the trench coat murdered him. She's a pro."

"*That* lady?"

"That's who did Philip."

"I should thank her."

"Except she almost did you too. So continue. You found Philip . . ."

"It looked like whoever had been there went through his pockets already."

"But they stopped short, didn't they?"

"Yeah, you could say that. They left thirty-five thousand dollars."

"Which you picked up, right?"

"Yeah. Thirty-five thousand dollars that turned me into a freakin' stop sign in the middle of my brother's film."

"Nobody has to know about the money, especially if you give it back. Now, about the thirty-five thousand dollars . . ."

"Course I'm gonna give it back. Like a ninny I left it in the hotel restaurant. Guilt, I guess. Never was any good at crime. Just at goats. When I do something wrong I just give myself right away. Good honest hard work, just like my mother. Leave it to the menfolk to be criminals. But I went back and got the money at the hotel. It's all here."

"Good, because I need to return it to my client. Now, the money, please?"

"Here." She handed me a wad of cash. The thirty-five grand was quickly in my pocket. "And one more thing, Kimilar. A last detail about the Sutro Heights night."

"What?"

"You said Philip was wearing his traveling shoes?"

"Yeah?"

"Give, Kimilar."

"That little piece of black plastic?" Her grin was almost mischievous and for a moment I was frightened at the thought of the images that might be let loose on the world.

"I really hope you're not going to be coy."

"Okay, Emma."

We were interrupted by the sound of sirens. They weren't fire trucks or paramedic squads, brought on by a false alarm in a major movie theatre. It wasn't the TAC squad either, coming to put down a riot. I watched the fleet of vehicles move up Castro, into the parking lot and in front of the theatre. We were surrounded.

Kimilar shuddered and hauled herself onto her feet. As we stood up, she put her fingers briefly in my pocket, lingered a moment and withdrew. As we walked down the street I found myself smiling. The small, hard rectangle of a miniaturized video was in my pocket, something that would never make the festival.

It was hard not to smile. Mission accomplished and I would live to tell about it. My cut of the thirty-five grand would cover mortgage for a year and a month in Baja. I would need a vacation. As we walked out of the bushes, we saw enough late model sedans to comprise the entire FBI fleet. Fortunately, it was not the FBI.

It was the Secret Service. The backup that was supposed to have been there on Saturday was only a few days late.

CHAPTER THIRTY-FOUR

HAUNTING OF
THE CASTRO

She was the one who was obviously in charge. She leaned over the hood of the car, talking into a receiver whose long curly cord extended back inside the vehicle. She was giving orders with one side of her mouth and talking into the mike with the other. Her eyes were scouring the roof, the sidewalk, and the thinning crowds coming out of the theatre.

Under her direction the theatre was being emptied and yellow plastic caution tape was being strung in front of the doors. A group approached us. We looked like two leftover lesbos from the film, although I had sprouted a mustache of dried blood under my nose. Kimilar would have lit up a small restaurant if you trained a black light on her.

I pulled Kimilar closer, to comfort her and to make sure she didn't escape. We watched the tide of jackbooted flak-vested men fill the street. They jumped the cyclone fence which separated the parking lot from the theatre. Before I knew it we were watching the Secret Service crawling along the roof of the Castro Theatre.

On the street I watched the woman in charge and listened to her yell in fury, "Who the hell called an ambulance?" Whining, an ambulance came down the hill off Divisidero onto Market and Castro.

I moved us closer to the yellow plastic tape that had now surrounded the theatre.

"Move along, move along," said the voice of authority.

"I know who called the ambulance," I said to the man guarding the perimeter.

"Move along, there's nothing to see here."

"There's a dead man in the projection booth. He was executed with a silenced automatic in the left temple. The projectionist is okay, but the woman who made the call may have broken her arm. Other than that there isn't a lot of interest inside the Castro Theatre. But you may want to debrief me."

"Hey, Agent Pranzini—" he called to the woman leaning over the sedan.

"What?"

"We got somebody with some information."

Two steely gray eyes turned my way and a forty-something woman, long brown hair, five foot seven, put the microphone back into the car and jerked her head at a colleague who was right behind her. The woman had recognized me, I was sure of it. Together they came toward us in lockstep.

"Kimilar," I turned to see her eyes full of fear. I put a finger under her chin and tilted it upwards and tasted her salty lips. They trembled. "Why don't you go and wait for me. I don't think this will take all that long."

"But—but—"

"Just go, honey. You've got the key," I passed a key to her with a whispered address and propelled her into the crowd. Waving, I watched her disappear and waited for the law to find me. It didn't take long. Special Agent Suzanna Pranzini tromped over on some heavy high heels, demanding, "Where is she?"

"Dee Dee Hammerman?" I took a chance and won.

"Yes. *Yes!*"

"Sorry." I felt a terrible certainty, the mission was accomplished, but I'd let the bad guy get away. "Dee Dee Hammerman, or whoever she is—" I raised my hand toward Twin Peaks— "she went that a way."

"Fuck!" Special Agent Prazini slammed the door to her

sedan hard enough to rock the entire suspension system. I didn't say anything. It seemed like just the right thing to say. I watched as Prazini folded her arms on the car and put her head in them. At least I had kept Kimilar Jones out of the mess, a loose strand that didn't need to be there to make the pattern complete.

Pranzini's shoulders slumped and a long breath came out. "Okay, okay," she said to herself and picked up the microphone and said something that translated into all the people coming off the roof of the Castro. Soon the caution tape which had decorated the streets and kept the crowds at bay was gone too.

"Okay, c'mon," her eyes were duller than old pennies and she seemed tired. She escorted me to her car and put her hand on the top of my head as I slid into the seat. "Don't bump your head," she said, taking good care of me, just like I was a prisoner. Her partner slid into the driver's seat and started the car. Suzanna got into the car.

"Emma Victor?" she asked me.

"Yeah."

"Willie thought you might be at the movies."

"You guys showed up a little late. You kinda missed the best part."

"Don't worry, I think I have heard enough stories to last a lifetime. Besides," she said as we whisked down Market Street to the Federal Building, "I've seen a lot of movies and read a lot of books. And truth is stranger than fiction."

That was fine. Just so long as I didn't have to go to prison and nobody picked my pockets.

The sedan stopped and started with the flow of traffic, but speeded up as we came closer to the Federal Building. Then we swooped down the concrete driveway into the basement of the building. Pranzini gave me a security badge and with a look she lost her chauffeur and we were alone in an elevator with one unmarked button. The car started down and we slowly fell for seventy seconds before we reached a spot far into the soil of San Francisco.

A long linoleum lined hallway led us to a room with a table and two chairs. There was a rug on the floor underneath

the desk. A cushion on the seat had a brown and green splat-
tered leaf print. I sat on it. Pranzini took her seat behind the
desk and turned on a lamp. She brought out a pad of paper
from the desk and a pencil. Then she checked the rest of the
drawers without trying to be too obvious about it.

"I'm going to fill you in on something, Emma. And I want
to know that I can trust you not to go to the press, to keep it
out of all your conversation."

"That's the kind of business I'm in," I reassured her.

"Even pillowtalk," Pranzini demonstrated a mobile eye-
brow.

"That's *especially* not the kind of business I'm in."

"That's not what I'm asking you."

"I can keep a secret."

Again we listened to the silence. It irritated me. The whole
drama irritated me.

"Good."

"Look, Agent Pranzini, I understand this is your job and
it's heavy for you. But I have a friend with a broken arm back
at the Castro Theatre. And an employer who disappeared. By
the way, where were you when someone tried to pick me off
on Sutro Heights, anyway?"

"I'm sorry, Emma. Willie Rossini only got your message
late this afternoon. We would have been ready to follow up
on Saturday when the final drop was made. But, as she never
called us, we couldn't help you out. But I want you to know
that the Service thanks you heartily for your contribution to
national security."

"What is this national security issue, anyway?"

"Listen, Emma and listen good. Democracy has never coexisted with a huge class difference."

"Okay," I said, "So Democracy has never coexisted with a
huge class difference."

"There are plans, Emma, *big* plans to make sure that we
have a huge class difference in this country. And those plans
are in effect."

"Some call it twelve years of Republican administration."

"Emma, a particular right-wing coalition is trying to desta-
bilize the administration. And you helped foil them."

"Anything I can do to help. The President just signed the Marriage Act."

"So I understand."

"No, you don't understand," I said. "I don't mind being your errand girl, that's my job. And there's a whole lot worse things to ask for. But don't pretend I'm a part of your system. I don't have any civil rights in the United States of America. And I'm not feeling so good about that these days."

"Change is a slow process. Besides, the Lesbian and Gay Civil Rights bill lost by only three votes. It will keep coming up on the agenda—"

"It's just the wedding cakes and the kisses that bother you guys, right?"

"Lose the attitude, Emma and focus on the enemy. These people would make J. Edgar Hoover look like a Boy Scout. We are talking about *fundamentalists,* Emma. Global fundamentalists and their training and their funding is global."

"Sort of a bad YMCA?"

"You don't get it, do you, Emma? We're talking German industrialists manipulating Shiite Muslims. Japanese pharmaceutical giants trading with Middle Eastern gunrunners. A Latin American dictator, recently deposed, but highly influential and wealthy who has three assassins hired to kill the President. There are certain elements who have taken hold in the Vatican. These are sophisticated businessmen. These are the forces of fascism."

"Fascism," I murmured. The word seemed to echo off the walls, in the streets.

"The Third Reich was carefully, meticulously orchestrated from above. It is happening again. But with a different kind of global twist.

"We need to know more about their operations, how they are communicating, training their recruits. It would be wonderful if we could turn one of them, or at least, debrief them. They know how to manipulate huge elements of the population. Skinheads. Evangelists. Everyone who's frightened of losing their job, of being homeless. They want to return the world to an über klasse and an ünter klasse. All the economic indicators are favorable. They just need to manipulate a few

politicians who have democracy on the brain. J. Edgar
Hoover had it right. Don't get your enemies. Get the goods
on them. I knew Ulrike Ariens was in the country. I could
smell her workings, I found her partner, Gunter at Yale law
school. There appears to have been some connection to Tim
McVeigh, the kid who blew up the Federal Building in Okla-
homa—" she twirled a pencil in her fingers.

"The Federal Building? I thought that was—"

"I wish. I wish it was some country music loving sur-
vivalist, but the tune is bigger than that and a whole lot of
people are dancing to it. Without even knowing it. Remember the third unidentified suspect? The plan was to make it
look like Shiite Muslims, but it was a botched. McVeigh is
low on the rung of bottom feeders. We need to go high up on
the chain. Where Dee Dee Hammerman lives. And the people who run her, the whole cadre of provocateurs, arms spe-
cialists, and media moguls. It's going to take a long, long
time to unmask them." The tip of the pencil found the edge
of her pointed tongue and landed back on the paper. "It may
be far too late. But Dee Dee Hammerman was my big hope.
I was convinced with a few weeks, just a week—"

"Of gentle therapeutic techniques, no doubt."

"Nobody said sensory deprivation was fun. But mass murder wasn't a picnic for those it happened to. And you *had*
her!"

"She almost had *me* for dinner."

"One woman, one woman could have given us a view into
the workings—" the agent snapped a pencil in half.

"There was something mechanical, spooky, about her.
Like my home economics teacher run amok," I mused.

"To think we were that close," Pranzini murmured. "Dee
Dee Hammerman, Ulrike Ariens, Hannah Moore. A professional killer for Christ."

"What's her biography?"

"She started out in Chile, just an arm decoration of General Pinochet, drinking champagne to the tune of the firing
squad. She never had a problem with cruelty. She lived in
France where they taught her how to place subway bombs

and effectively blame it on the left wing. And now she's been stalking buffet tables in San Francisco," Prazini sighed.

"I can give you all the details on her attire and dialogue."

"Yeah, well, I guess we'd better get down to it." Suzanna picked up a new pencil, wet the tip with her lips.

"What, no tape recorder?"

"I'll ask the questions," she said.

Many hours later, just as Monday morning was dawning, she thanked me for my cooperation. It was a light I wanted to forget, a light I would never see. I would lose that Monday to a deep sleep. And emerge just in time for the election.

"Now I've got to talk to that projectionist," Pranzini signaled to her driver who pulled up a car. She said if I had any information I should get in touch with her immediately. She gave me her card.

"If you aren't available who should I speak—"

"If I'm not available you'll have to let it keep."

"And what if—"

"If I'm no longer with the Secret Service—if I were you—I would just forget you ever met me."

"Where should I take you?" asked the driver. I was looking at Agent's Pranzini"'s back.

"Take me to the Castro," I said. "Eighteenth, just off Market." We cruised back up Market Street and everything looked so familiar and strange at the same time. The demonstration had come and gone and the street was full of the ephemera of last night's anger. Banners were wilted on the street. Signs piled up at the entrance to the Harvey Milk Muni station where people were emerging for work. There were new Victorians for sale in the window of Herth Realty, and a woman on a ladder was changing the letters on the marquee of the Castro Theatre.

I got off in front of Walgreens. Crowds were herding themselves across the intersection. I and stepped over a sign in the gutter. AN ARMY OF LOVERS CANNOT FAIL, COMA—COMPLETELY OVER MARRIAGE APARTHEID. A long row of newspaper vending boxes stood ready with the latest editions. DEFENSE OF MARRIAGE ACT ENDORSED BY VATICAN, read one

headline. PHYSICIAN CONVICTED OF PERFORMING THIRD
TRIMESTER ABORTION, read another.

Never had the Castro felt more like a ghetto.

A table in front of the Bank of America was staffed by volunteers for Calvin Smith. "Vote tomorrow! Don't forget!"
they cried.

Honk! Honk! Rose's van pulled up to the curb. "Hey girlfriend, I owe *you* an apology," the passenger window came
down with a hum. "Come on in." She popped the button on
the passenger side. "I just picked your boss up at the airport."

"What?"

"I had Blake start checking the airlines. He found Willie at
Gate 37, just coming in from Detroit."

"Detroit?" My heart sank. Willie had said that she would
be in New Orleans. At a certain hotel. Willie had said a lot of
things. "You picked up Wille," I stated. "Why?"

"It seemed like the right thing to do."

"It was the snoopy thing to do."

"Willie's not stupid. She said she'd missed your message.
When she did get the information, seemed like it was too
late, or something. Who was the intended backup anyway?"

"You don't want to know."

"I'm starting to get used to that phrase. By the way, you
look like shit."

"Nothing that a bath and twenty hours of sleep can't cure.
What was Willie's story, Rose?"

"Like I said, Emma, she was concerned about you. And it
seems I was wrong about Willie. I said I'd be seeing you later
and that I'd give you the scoop."

"Okay, why did she disappear? What could be the reason
for leaving me out on a limb?"

"Seems Willie has a niece in Detroit—"

"Yeah. She goes there every Christmas. Stella. She must
be about eighteen by now."

"Well, Stella, it seems, needed a third trimester abortion."

"Third trimester abortion. The kind Congress just out-
lawed?"

"That's right. I guess she'd been in India, started a relationship, and she got sick, and then she got in denial. When

she came home she was in trouble, as they say. It wasn't easy to arrange. It wasn't easy to get through.

"It wasn't a coat hanger job. There were complications. Willie had to extend her visit and stay an extra day. The surgeon was an old friend of the family's. Nevertheless they couldn't perform the procedure in the hospital. And the surgeon was scared. And that made Willie scared."

The sound of laughter made me look up. On the other side of the glass a couple walked by holding hands. Two women, deeply in puppy love, their eyes warm and dewy, their leather jackets heavy with metal, their faces fierce with tattoos.

"Here's a copy of the B.A.R.," Rose said. "I thought you might be interested in seeing it."

Bay Area Reporter, San Francisco

HOMO HAVEN HAUNTED?

by A. Sapphire Poore

Sunday saw the strangest closing night of the San Francisco Lesbian and Gay Film Festival ever. *Pale Refugee,* the much acclaimed closing feature, was interrupted when a strange glow appeared in the audience.

Rumors about ghosts haunting the Castro have always circulated; none is more enigmatic than the "burning seat" in the third row. According to legend the steamy seat comes to life when the heat on the screen is too much to take. A supernatural censor? Or a ghostly being getting off on the highly charged sexual energy of *Refugee's* star, Jason Jeeters Jones? Or a matter of mass suggestion, especially when a film as disturbing and hot as *Pale Refugee* is shown?

Whatever the explanation, the strange luminescence seen by hundreds on Sunday evening was never explained. Nor was the flying shadow a few claimed to have seen soaring over the crowd from the balcony.

While several filmgoers swore they were attacked and one man had a bruise on his forehead, others saw nothing and were disinclined to believe witnesses.

"I know what I saw," Joseph Capriani insisted. "A young man dropped off the balcony and landed in the crowd. I looked around but I never saw him again. I've got a bruise on my brand new tattoo to prove it." An extension cord later was said to have fallen off of the balcony and someone said a large spark was visible. A spokesperson for the San Francisco Building Inspections said that the Castro recently passed an electrical inspection and that the one extension cord had been approved in a variance hearing. The mystery, clearly, will never be explained. Yet another colorful chapter will be added to the lore of San Francisco's one hundredth historical landmark, no matter how many disclaimers like that of projectionist Dodd O' Malley.

"There have always been rumors of ghosts in the Castro. But look at it this way. There was a lot of sexual energy followed by panic. People were beyond confused," said projectionist Dodd O' Malley. "I could see everything from the projection booth. The fire alarm and the ensuing movement of the crowd made it unclear what was going on. It would be easy to imagine anything under the circumstances. And don't forget, the Castro Theatre is a building designed for illusion."

What's clear now is that film buffs and fans of the tender brawny style of Jason Jeeters Jones will get another chance to see *Pale Refugee*—and Jason—in their entirety. The acclaimed feature will be reshown next Saturday night, bumping a new print of Judy Garland's *Easter Parade* from the Castro calendar.

The body of Haam Harmstead had completely disappeared from the story.

"Take me home, Rose," I said. "And drive gently, will you?

CHAPTER THIRTY-FIVE

BORN
THAT WAY

Tuesday was election day. I drove over to Glen Park to visit Mona, determined to talk to her before she cast her vote. The little houses on Mona's street looked like Penny Lane. White stucco, green stucco, pink stucco, all with the same picture window facing Mount Davidson. There were sirens in the distance. It seemed that there were always sirens in the distance.

"Mona, I'm really sorry about your arm." I caught up with her as she was leaving her house. Mona's arm rested in an improvised sling.

"I know you are Emma." She shifted her arm uncomfortably. "Walk with me; I'm going down the street to vote." She nodded toward the little garage where the League of Women Voters had hung up their flag. "I've been thinking a lot," she said. "I can't believe I got mixed up with you!" Mona Marie Lee drew back and looked me up and down as if she were really seeing me for the first time, shaking her head, bangs lying over a new pair of glasses. Mona was laughing to herself. "And I think you'd probably be a lot of fun in between risking our lives. Sorry to tell you this, but it's the end of the road for us, Emma. You're an exciting woman, but a little *too* exciting."

"No hard feelings?"

"No hard feelings," she reassured me. Shell pink lips came towards mine for a good-bye kiss. Mona sighed, a sound which, in my better fantasies, was redolent of regret. And then Mona Marie Lee walked out of my life. Until the next softball game, barbecue or *Lesbian and Gay Film Festival.*

I drove back to my own neighborhood where the flag drooped low over a garage down the street. I punched the pin for Supervisor Villanueva, Independent candidate for mayor, and went home.

The kitchen was clean and the cats had been fed. The office door was firmly locked. The bedroom door was open.

Inside, lying on my bed, Kimilar Jones was taking a nap. On her stomach, she seemed to sink into the down coverlet, only her head twisted to its side for air. Her jeans were tight. A long ribbon of spine wove between her downy shoulder blades. One arm was slung over her head, shading her eyes. I could just see her mouth, a perfect *O*. Her white teeth were bright against her brown skin. She was breathing regularly. Her black cashmere sweater laid next to her on the bed, a small puddle of fleece.

I went over to the dresser; there was loose change jingling in my pocket. Kimilar's backside was nicely framed in the big round mirror on the bed. Asleep, Kimilar looked like a child, face released from all past, a slight bloom to her cheeks. Dreaming, she smiled, a woman whose slate was made clean by the mystery of sleep

I emptied my pockets onto the dresser. An electrical clip. A pile of pennies, loose change in a life without a lot of neat endings. A folded brochure from the Camera Obscura, a complicated origami from living in my pocket for a weekend. I parted the paper. Kimilar shifted in her sleep. *"Light filtered through a series of lenses,"* the brochure read.

I watched Kimilar dreaming, feeling somehow less voyeuristic with a mirror between us. My eyes followed the ripple of vertebrae, the small, iron-hard muscles. The face that saw all the weather in all the seasons, fixing fences and going out with the dogs.

"Oh, yes, Emma." She smiled as she awoke. "And the Castro." She looked at the sweater which had fallen on the floor. It was just out of reach. Kimilar's hips squirmed on the coverlet, fingers reached out for the sweater failed. She wasn't going to knock herself out trying to be modest.

"I was hot," Kimilar said as she turned over. The moons of her breasts rose off the coverlet as she stretched out on the pillows.

"You are a very beautiful woman, Kimilar Jones."

"Didn't work out with that Chinese girl, did it?"

"Didn't work out with Overalls, did it?"

"Come over here, Emma." She patted the bed next to her. I sat down; her small hands found their way to my neck, my shoulders. "Emma, you're so tight. Let me give you a massage." Kimilar turned me over on my stomach and put her hands under my shirt. As she leaned deeply into my muscles I felt her breasts fall gently onto my back.

"I have to keep the videocassette," I said.

"I don't even wanna know what kind of shit Philip and Haam were into," her tongue darted across the skin on my back, a butterfly kiss whose effect flew between my legs. Eventually, the hardness of her nipples traced a question across my skin. I turned over.

Our American heritages met then; Texas two-step, Pennsylvania polka and the San Francisco side-step. Kimilar Jones was hot. And she was grateful. But it wasn't gratitude that made her skin so soft, that made her want to curl around my hand. Kimilar Jones had come to the Castro, in more ways than one.

Afterward, she sat astride my waist. Her silken hair brushed my face like a golden curtain. She kissed me, stopped, looked me in the eye for awhile, and then kissed me again. "You sure are a firecracker," I thought I heard her say. "I have the feeling, Emma, that your life is a lot more exciting than you make it out to be."

"At this moment, yes." I enjoyed the soft skin on the sides of her breasts, my long fingers trailing across the front of her nipples which stiffened and made her bite her lip. I read the effect of my hands on her face until she was panting. Kim leaned across me and found the flashlight next to the bed.

"Is this that funky light?" she asked, "that makes things light up?"

"The black light."

"Hot shit," she reached over and turned off the lamp. In seconds she had the flashlight on, "You're gonna like this," Kimilar reached out for the lamp switch. As darkness flooded the room I heard Kim get off the bed. "Get this, Emma." She turned on the flashlight. Striking a pose, her arm raised and aiming the flashlight upon herself, the sinewy body of the outdoorswoman lit up. Moving towards the bed, never taking her eyes off me, she twisted and turned in the darkness. Kimilar was the statue of Diana come to life, glowing just a few feet in front of me. What followed was a fantastic dance which created a luminescence spreading to both our bodies, broken only by the ribbons of sweat that eventually streaked our shuddering flesh.

The next morning the dawn looked as it never had before; I had that very rare feeling that the world had significantly altered. I wondered who had won the election; and how hard it would be to say goodbye to Kimilar. Stretched out next to me, her body was now coated in the gold tones of morning. The rugged, heart shaped face that lived in all four seasons was again at peace. Slipping from between the sheets, I rummaged in the dresser drawer, found an envelope.

"Emma?" A voice caramel-thick with sleep, came from the bed. I looked into the mirror. Kimilar rolled over.

"Good morning."

"Yeah. Come here, you."

And then, it was even better.

Afterward, I made coffee, and found the envelope that had been lost in the sheets. "Kimilar, I think it's that time."

"I know."

"I look forward to seeing you again too."

"But not for a while, huh?"

"It's for the best."

"I know."

"So, here's a plane ticket." I handed her a thick envelope.

"Albuquerque—via Atlanta?" She thumbed through the carbon triplicates that I had filled in according to the shuttle schedule.

"All the better to confuse the trail. Leaves in three hours."

"Sylvia Hernandez," she read.

"I've got a really nerdy dress for you too. Doesn't do to be *La Fashionista* during a getaway." I watched her search the envelope. The driver's license for Sylvia Hernandez and the ticket for the shuttle planes had been prepared in advance. I kept handy a number of getaway items and sets of identification in my desk. It was a habit Rose's father, Fred, had taught me.

"Emma! There's two thousand dollars in here!"

"Stay put for the winter. Buy supplies."

"You don't have to do that."

"Have yourself a nice time. Stay put. Right now it would be best for you, and for everyone, if you were just history. Just because you didn't kill him doesn't mean you couldn't avoid a grand jury indictment and whole lot of heartbreak, hassle, expense and—"

"Two thousand dollars will make it a nice, soft winter. With a lotta books. Maybe I'll even order me an extra cord of wood, some good tobacco, herbs."

"That's the idea. Just let everybody forget you were even in San Francisco."

"Winter is thinking time, dreaming time."

"And here," I handed her a bottle of L'Oreal Hair Color, Ivory Black.

"This shit is gonna look like shoe polish on my hair."

"Wait until you see the clothes I have in store for you."

One of Frances's' banker uniforms hung loosely on Kimilar's small sinewy frame. "Here's a pair of spectacles, just clear glass. You must learn to look imminently gray, Kimilar, to fade into the background. And keep your lips clamped over those fabulous ivories."

I told her the plan. "The idea is to stash you away on the farm, fast. No one will recognize you on the plane if you're quiet and keep your head down."

"You know, I'm kinda sorry that the psycho killed Philip,"

Kimilar mused, looking at the bottle of hair rinse in her hand.
"I wouldn't have minded doing it myself; he sure was one
rotten bastard. By the way," she looked up from the instructions, "You ever kill anybody, Emma?"

"I never shot anybody," I said. "But I've tried."

"I hope I *never* want to again. I'm going to be real careful
who I'm gonna let into my life. I have the feeling, now that
I got the woman thing going for me, I ain't never gonna want
to kill nobody ever again."

"Don't count on it," I promised. She covered my mouth
with her hand and threw me down on the bed again.

Afterward her voice was quiet, serious. "Hey, Emma. Can
I ask you something?"

"Of course."

"Do you think I would make a good lesbian?"

"You're already a fantastic lesbian, Kimilar."

"I might just have to spend the winter thinkin' about this.
I'm gonna be a lesbian, Emma." Soft, deep kisses traveled up
my neck to my ear. "And to think," she whispered, "you
don't even have to *be born that way.*"

This time we slept a delicate, light napping, a luxury before Kimilar's transformation and departure. Dreaming, I
wandered through gentle mountains. A wind blew across the
plains and I looked up into the face of the moon. It was smiling. I awoke with a start.

"Time to check the fences, Kimilar."

"Oh!" Kim awoke with a start. "I was home already. The
time the Indians call the hunter's moon. It was the first frost
and I could see clear across the plains. It's time to go.
Thanks, Emma. Thanks for keeping me out of prison."

"I haven't kept you out of prison, yet." I watched her legs
disappear into her bluejeans.

"I'm gonna try to get back to the Castro someday, by hook
or by crook."

"Just hook will do."

Kimilar promised to send me a profit and loss statement
every year, and a black cashmere bathrobe for the winter sol-

stice. I picked up the phone and called a cab while Kimilar holed up in the bathroom to complete her transformation. She went in a country western lounge singer and she came out a Mormon, just as I'd planned.

Then there were light and airy kisses, nothing too dramatic, as we waited for the taxi to arrive. I put her inside gently, as if she were breakable, which was silly. The taillights of the taxi were refracted through two happy tears.

Back in the house Mink meowed and I fed her. Watching the cat eat I thought about spending the winter in a new way, sitting in front of a crackling fire with only the wind and the clouds—and Kimilar Jones—for company.

In the coming months I would think often about Kimilar and I would know that, as wonderful as her life looked from San Francisco, her life would never be for me. It was too quiet, too soothing in its patterns. I wasn't a farmer. Some where, somehow, I thought, I had become married to chaos.

I walked back up the stairs. Laura Deleuse was awake. I saw the curtain in her window move, and I wondered who had won the election and if the sergeant would be stuck in an office without a window for the next four years.

Mink herded me into the bedroom where I straightened up the dresser top. I hung up my clothes and felt carefully in the pocket of my leather coat. The tiny videocassette that Kimilar Jones had put there when we came out of the bushes to meet the Secret Service was still there. It would be my own personal closing night feature of the Lesbian and Gay Film Festival.

Back in the living room I flopped on the couch. Mink landed on top of me, a marvelous heart-warming, overly-fed love object. I looked at the tape in my hand. What had put the entire series of events, from social secretaries to hotel rooms, from San Francisco to Washington, in motion? But, of course, after meeting the Secret Service agent I had no doubts about the identity of the couple.

What had they shared in a dormitory, in a not-so-distant past? Trapped in the University of Iowa, far, far away from anything familiar. In those long wintery nights, when ice

covered the phone lines and the country roads became slick
as mirrors, had they huddled together in a narrow dormitory
bed, only to meet years later at the Mark Hopkins?

Or was it a constant, something they had never given up,
something that had found its way to the enemy, something
that had set a huge plan in motion. The inside of the Jacuzzi
Suite had never had a more important occupant.

The lens just waiting behind that wall had stolen the privacy of star-crossed lovers. And was I any different? Wasn't
I just another voyeur?

Yes.

I pushed the tape in the VCR and pushed play.

The First Lady's face looked marvelous in repose as she
smiled. Her fingertips rode up and down the mature thigh of
Margo Villanueva, spelling out a message that was obvious
from the way Villanueva squirmed and laughed. Moving up,
the First Lady turned her head away from the lens and found
the lips of the mayoral candidate. The two women kissed,
slowly and then with more hunger; their hands clasping, letting go, finding favorite spots.

When the tape was over I set a fire in the grate. Dried
lavender, pine cones, and eucalyptus made a fragrant bier for
the scene that no one would ever see. I threw the plastic box
into the flames where it twisted and melted. I would give the
remains to Willie to let her know the job had been done. The
sun was breaking through the fog and a new day had begun.
I looked down and saw the morning paper on my doorstep. It
may have news that would change everything. But certain
things were already indelibly different.

The memory of the face of the First Lady would remain.
It was my personally enthralling mystery, a narrative I could
form and reform at will. And so it would remain with me for
years. In fact, the happy looks on the faces of the First Lesbian Couple gave me great comfort on those difficult nights,
the nights when I would worry about democracy and never
get to sleep.